Kafka in Richmond

Also by Gilbert Wesley Purdy

POETRY

Mind Dance

NON-FICTION

Discovered: A New Shakespeare Sonnet (or three, actually)

Was Shakespeare Gay?
Straight Male Scholarly Angst and Shakespeare's Sonnets.

The Ties of the Railroad Tracks Home:
the Poetry of Jared Carter.

Henry David Thoreau and Two Other Autistic Lives:
before the diagnosis existed.

Edward De Vere was Shakespeare:
at long last, the proof.

Gilbert Wesley Purdy

Kafka in Richmond

V irtual

V anaprastha

Richmond, Virginia

ISBN-13: 978-0-69274-191-7
ISBN-10: 0-69274-191-7

to Mari-Lynn

Contents

Chapter 1

K woke with a start, which was quite common when he traveled. After the normal bleary confusion of first waking, he stretched. As he did so, his face slowly took on a puzzled look. He was lying flat, with his frock coat drawn about him, no longer seated in the carriage in which he had fallen asleep. He did not feel the motion of the train beneath him. The sun seemed to be out.

He did not seem even to be on the train. At these facts, he sat bolt upright savagely bumping his head against the metal frame of an upper bunk. Had he missed his station? He was supposed to arrive after nightfall, had fallen asleep as dusk descended.

He had not taken a sleeping car, K reflected, as he cradled his head and checked for blood. He did not remember rising from his seat in second class. A pair of legs swung over the side of the upper berth as he surveyed the space around him. It was filled, barracks-style, with metal-frame bunk beds. Most were filled with men struggling against waking, blankets half pulled over them, tall metal cabinets facing each bunk to form a narrow passage.

A voice, somewhere behind him, called out "Up'n'at'em, gents!" He craned around to see a man of about 40 years, in nothing but a yellow t-shirt and pair of blue workman's trousers. The trousers were somehow strange. The lack of a shirt was stranger still. The color of the t-shirt was surprisingly bright, thought K, as the man turned and walked up the passage, down which he had apparently arrived, going beyond his sight. He would have to ask the man where he had found such an undergarment once he had made arrangements to get back on the train.

The pair of legs that had been hanging from the upper bunk descended with a thud to the floor. The gentleman who belonged to them was entirely in underclothes of the sketchiest description. A testicle hung out of one side of tiny sky-blue undershorts. The man brusquely returned it to its presumed place and looked inquiringly at K who only then realized that he was the only person in the room properly dressed.

His suit jacket was wrinkled with traveling and he tried to press it with his hands. He adjusted his waistcoat, which had been twisted askew, apparently from tossing in his sleep, carefully settled his tie and looked around for his fedora. He was relieved to see the hat on top of his travel trunk situated behind the metal locker associated with the bunk in which he now sat. His valise was leaning against the side of the trunk.

Suddenly he reached inside the jacket, as if to verify that an article of value remained properly in its place in an inner pocket. He pulled out a white envelope. There was no need to check its contents yet again. He had done so, in his obsessive way, several times already during the trip. But these entirely unexpected circumstances made it seem imperative to do so again. Indeed the ticket was from Prague to Matliary, the date January 20th, and the service 'Direct'. Thankfully, all was in order.

Next he reached inside his jacket and assured himself that his pocket watch was in his waistcoat. In the opposite pocket, he found the key to his trunk also where he had left it. There was no telling who had moved him from his seat to this strange barracks. He would have to verify the contents of the trunk and valise when the opportunity came available.

"Yur new," bellowed his bunk-mate. "Juh get in last night?"

Still earnestly reviewing his surroundings for something that might make sense of the situation, he sought for an answer. What could he possibly reply? Had he "gotten in"? Where had he gotten in *to?* He managed with great effort to ask "Where am I?"

"You're at the Roach Motel," he bellowed. "You really *are* new." Laughter and muttered comments followed, all around, too many to make out any of what was said.

The man in the yellow t-shirt returned. "Breakfast is ready. C'mon, let's go." He walked around the barracks nudging those who had yet to rise. He gave K several lingering looks as he did so and passed on his way back out.

One and two at a time the barrack-mates wandered in the direction from which the yellow shirt had come and followed him out of sight. They were clearly not the passengers who had bustled by him as the train jostled them in a mildly entertaining fashion. Many were physically large. Nearly all walked with their shoulders thrown back. He suspected they might be stevedores. All wore t-shirts and trousers, once dressed, some even short-pants. Quite some number, astonishingly, were Negroes. He must have somehow stumbled in his sleep into the crew quarters.

For crew's quarters they were unusually spacious. Overhead were long straight lines of electrical lighting of a kind he had never seen before. This section of the railroad line must have been upgraded. It was surprising to see crew quarters so brightly lit with electric fixtures. He had heard no news of it and had never seen such a strange space or fixtures. He was sure that it must represent a modernization. The world was changing so rapidly these days that one could hardly keep up.

K was remarkably hungry. He followed the others, who seemed to know their way, toward what he assumed would prove to be the dining car. There he found several rows of rectangular metal tables with green linoleum-like surfaces and attached metal benches. On the far row sat plates, tableware of some metal material he did not immediately recognize (perhaps tin) and rectangular pans with steam rising from them.

He looked intently at the contents of each pan and accepted as much of beans and potatoes as the attendants behind the table put on the plate he held out. He timidly held his tray away from the tongs of the attendant who offered what appeared to be a meat patty of some sort and the one holding a large spoon of scrambled eggs.

For their part, the attendants seemed almost as confused to see him as he was to find himself in their presence. Behind them stood two young women, in light short-sleeved blouses and lightweight trousers, who spoke in whispers between themselves. When he noticed them, he stood staring in stunned silence. Where was he that women wore trousers? Not only that but trousers that clung tightly to the contours of their unmentionable parts. They were also wearing slippers of some sort instead of shoes. The way they peered at him, without the least reserve, he could only think that they must be prostitutes. After he issued a stern complaint with the manager of the line, for having been so badly inconvenienced, he would have to complain that modernization should have its limits. Providing such amenities to the crews went well beyond the pale.

K ate with more than usual appetite. Others were hungrier still and had returned quickly to the service table for second helpings. Noting this, he felt reasonably confident that he was allowed to do the same. Questions could wait until he'd had a proper meal. As he took his place at the end of the line the two women peeked through the tiny windows in a double-door, when it settled from swinging back and forth, as attendants passed to and from a room behind the table. Their expressions suggested confusion regarding something.

His own expression must also have been confused. He noticed that there were windows in the dining hall (such as it was). What he saw simply could not be. He left the line to take a closer look. There were leaves on the scattered trees outside. They were showing hints, here and there, of the pale green preceding a seasonal change. The sunlight had a slight autumnal pallor.

As K sat finishing his second plate, trying to puzzle out what was happening, a number of the men began gathering up the soiled tableware. One of them gathered up K's tray. At the same time he took K by the elbow and lifted him to his feet.

"C'mon, *Dude*," he cried out. The room erupted in laughter. "It's your day for kitchen duty." The man forcefully escorted K toward the double-doors. As he stumbled toward the back room, at a loss for how to react, one of the women stepped through the doors. K's escort stopped before her, K's elbow still firmly in his grasp.

"He has to go see Mrs. Smith," she announced. The man obediently transferred his elbow to her care. His expression made clear that she had ruined the fun. She led K down another passageway. He was so surprised at being taken by the elbow and directed one way and then another that he walked beside her speechless. He was guided past a series of small offices, their doors standing open, and then into another where she set him in a chair beside a desk. Both chair and desk were set against a wall and he craned around to see where he might be. Everywhere he looked were photographs, large and small, of the most vivid colors. Many strange items were scattered on the desk and filing cabinets. A white coffee mug displayed the words "God grant me the serenity to accept". A single, tall thin window of some sort extended the height of the far wall.

In the distance he could hear the breakfast implements being attended to with what must have been considerable clangor. This was irregularly punctuated with shouted comments. Somewhere nearby he could hear a curiously artificial voice. It recited a date and time. Following this a young woman's voice said "Hi, this is Kim" and recited a request of some sort. This done, she asked someone else to "Please call back. I'll be in between nine and eleven." The artificial voice recited the date and time once again. A nondescript male voice announced its name and addressed the listener.

As K strained to hear, a woman of perhaps 50 years entered the office and sat at the desk. She at least was wearing a dress of some sort. It reached no further than her knee, almost like the skirts of a young child, and he could not help staring with wonder at such a thing. She looked a long moment at K. and pulled a board of some sort toward herself. It displayed letters arranged after the fashion of a typewriter. He finally found his tongue and extended his hand with the words "Mrs. Smith, I presume."

She was busy typing and did not seem to hear. As she rapidly touched the letters, which appeared to be merely printed on the slender board, the corresponding letters appeared on a small projector screen of some sort before her. When she noticed that K was looking at the screen she turned it away so he could no longer see it. This typing did not go on for long before she adjusted her chair so she was seated partially toward him.

"The question," she said, "is what *your* name is?"

"Dr. Franz Kafka," he replied.

She twisted herself to type this onto the projector screen. She peered intently into the screen and typed a few more strokes. "Mr. Kafka, I don't find you in our system."

"*Doctor* Kafka," he replied.

"A medical doctor? I know all of the doctors associated with the shelter and you are certainly not one of them."

"A Doctor at Law," K replied.

"You were a lawyer, then, before you sought our help?"

"Your help?" K inquired.

One of the two young women K had seen earlier now stood in the doorway watching. "Ellen, you know that coffee cup is not appropriate here," said the presumptive Mrs. Smith quite firmly. K read the inscription: 'Sexy and I know it.' His confusion was growing by the minute. Did all coffee mugs have inscriptions here? Was Mrs. Smith the madam? If so, what objection did she have to this crude but topical assertion?

The young woman apologized for her lapse and said that she would replace the cup. She spoke the words with a broad smile.

Mrs. Smith returned to the business at hand with K. "Alcohol or drugs... or both?" she asked.

If the coffee cup had left K a little nonplused, this offer went altogether beyond comprehension. "Neither," he replied with obvious offense. "I do not indulge in either."

Mrs. Smith typed with a pronounced scowl. She was obviously not pleased with his answer. "May I see your I.D., please?"

The man in the wrinkled suit sat before her with an uncomprehending look.

"Your ID card. Your identification."

K was unsure what to do. Nevertheless, things were so impenetrable, the situation so inexplicable, that he decided he had no choice but to comply. He pulled the small packet from his jacket pocket and handed it to her. She unfolded the papers and stared at them intently.

"These are not in English."

"Of course not," he replied without thinking. "They are in German as are all such documents." This all was simply impossible to make heads or tails of.

"Where are you from?" asked Mrs. Smith.

"Prague, of course," came the answer.

"Prague in Indiana or something?"

"In-dee-anna?" K sounded the unfamiliar word out slowly. "Prague in Czechoslovakia. What is In-dee-anna?"

"And when did you arrive in the United States? Are these," she asked, pointing to K's papers, "some kind of passport?"

"Where exactly am I? What is 'the Roach Motel'?" K asked.

"We prefer you not use that name, please," interjected Mrs. Smith in obvious exasperation. She mentioned some sort of formal name that K did not catch. His head was swimming with new impressions.

"What is this place?" he fairly shouted. His remarkably pronounced Adam's apple bobbed when he spoke with force. His interrogator made an effort not to stare at it.

"It is a shelter for homeless alcoholics and drug addicts."

"And you offer drugs and alcohol as part of your service?" The question was out before K even realized he had asked it.

Mrs. Smith was now even more confused. She could not understand what might have given such an impression. After recovering from her shock, she simply went on as if the question had never been asked. "Where, may I ask, are you *supposed* to be?"

"On the train," replied K.

"The *train?* On the train to where? The train station is miles from here."

"The train to the spa at Matliary." K took the ticket from his jacket pocket and handed it to her.

"This would appear to be in German," she cried out. "I can't read German." But then she sat, her face gradually suggesting a furious anger. "This ticket is dated January the 20th of... *1920.*"

"Yes, and it would seem clearly to be early autumn here."

"It is also," Mrs. Smith said, after a distracted fashion, "2015."

"What is '2015'? The train number?" queried K, further confused.

"No. That is not what I'm saying. It is the *year* 2015. Mr. Kafka,..."

"*Doctor* Kafka."

"*Doctor* Kafka, what organization referred you here? Have you been receiving addiction or any other psychiatric treatment before your arrival here?"

"I am not an addict of any kind, madam. I'm traveling to Matliary for treatment for the tuberculosis."

Mrs. Smith reflexively moved her chair to a greater distance and sat pondering the man before her. Neither could think of a next word to say. She called Ellen back into the office. "Please take Mr. Kafka to the TV room."

"It's not a scheduled TV time," Ellen replied. "Should I leave it off?"

"So then," thought K to himself, having misunderstood the young woman's instructions, "they do treat TB cases." But it still seemed highly unlikely that he had reached the spa. He had seen photographs of it and nothing here looked in the least familiar.

Mrs. Smith was staring intently at her screen, occasionally tapping a few letters in rapid succession. "No, please turn it on. Mr. Kafka may be waiting a while."

"*Doctor* Kafka" K persisted. Mrs. Smith went on as if she hadn't heard.

The TB room was perhaps half the size of the dining room. There were no windows. Several lines of chairs were attached together, one to another, with metal clips. Ellen instructed K to sit wherever he wished. All of the chairs faced in a single direction. The young woman reached up beneath another miniature projector screen, high on the wall, where she extracted a black wand of some sort. She manipulated it in some way and an astonishing brightly colored picture appeared. She carried the wand to K. As a matter of course, he held out his hand and received it from her.

"Choose whatever channel you want." With that, she left the room.

On the screen, a moving picture showed a panel of three people talking: one man and two women. One of the women was Asian in appearance. Each was better dressed, it seemed to K, than people generally were. The man wore a suit of a strange style. Look as he might, K could not make out the material. The women wore tight dresses of a sort that ended well above their knees. They too seemed to be wearing slippers. All three displayed simple, precise manicures.

Astonishingly, the entire scene was in the most vivid colors. K could not detect even the slightest discontinuity in the movements of the figures. But, most astonishing of all, he could hear the figures talk. It was almost as if they were right there beside him.

In an instant the continuous smiles disappeared from the three faces. The patter they had been sharing came to a stop. The Asian woman seriously announced that the fighting had continued in such and such a place overnight. With that K found himself observing a desert landscape with a youngish man in the middle of the screen, as hatless as an explorer, talking rapidly. It seemed this was some kind of a talking newsreel.

Just as quickly, K was watching some dozens of men brandishing rifles of which he had never seen the like. Next (again so quickly that he could not help but flinch) the men, or others like them, were shooting from behind a wall. The rifles were repeaters and discharged more rapidly even than a Gatling gun. Next some sort of twisted wreckage of a vehicle was shown. The youngish man then reappeared and spoke with the three figures on the panel. Following all of this the three figures talked among themselves, the youngish man and his desert no longer in evidence. Nothing else in the world existed. K could not take his eyes off the screen.

The man on the panel announced that they would 'be back with the weather.' After several vignettes a Negro man in a sleek suit appeared on the screen, before a backdrop of little suns and clouds, like a wallpaper for a child's nursery, and stood smiling. Him they referred to as the 'weather man' and they greeted him by name and with considerable affection.

Just as abruptly as the scene had earlier changed to a desert, a little girl was pouting as she stared at a scrape on her knee. A woman, surely her mother or an aunt or the like, wiped it with a tiny napkin and the child smiled. Several more changes of scene occurred in succession, each the location of a short vignette, in which some problem was magically solved, or some item of food savored, and all the characters were left smiling after a most satisfied manner.

One vignette, in particular, attracted K as it was about insurance. But this was 'car insurance,' not worker's insurance such as was provided by his office. By 'car' they seemed to mean a motorized carriage, a motorcar. But these cars were a wonder to behold. They were like nothing he had ever seen or imagined.

This car insurance struck him as a most excellent idea, or, actually, pedestrian insurance. How many pedestrians had been injured by the impact of a passing motorcar that simply sped on its way without concern. The streets of Prague were filling up with those mechanical beasts. He had often observed that some amount of regulation was very much in order.

As he considered these scenes, the weather man reappeared waving a marker in his hand and calling out temperatures and what must have been place names (as evidenced by the map onto which the suns and clouds were impressed). He was especially pleased with his task and repeated the numbers that appeared behind him. He swept his hand over the map following the clouds, which magically changed their shape and began to move, and traced their progress over several seconds talking rapidly all the while as he did. This he called doing 'Dahp-lur Ray-dahr'.

Following the weather there were some half-dozen more vignettes. The audience must like them especially, reflected K, considering how many there are.

The panelists next appeared outside of a building, apparently in a city street. The building appeared to be constructed entirely from enormous panes of glass. Inside, people went about some sort of office business without concern for what was happening without. He could not imagine how a building could be constructed almost entirely of glass.

They were enclosed within a fence outside of which scores of people waived signs, called out greetings and applauded with regularity. The male panelist announced that something was about to appear and the applause grew sharper. Shouts of glee were interspersed.

Next, three young women jumped onto a nearby stage and the shouts grew louder. The three were all dressed in nothing but underclothing, and very little of that. On their legs were tightly laced, black boots that reached just short of their groins, leaving only enough room for white lace garters bordered above and below by bands of soft white flesh. One sat down behind an enormous set of sparkling drums. The other two took up some strange sort of stringed instrument, perhaps a kind of lyre. They smiled even more enormous smiles than the weatherman and waved, their breasts astonishingly high and flecked with pink glitter. This was followed by a clangor such as K had never so much as imagined before. The stringed instruments were clearly not lyres.

One moment they sang plaintively, with young girl voices that touched the heart to the quick. The next their facial expressions implored (presumably their words would have also had he been able to make them out). Next they raged as fiercely as Bacchantes. All the while, their movements suggested sexual intercourse, their legs spread apart as if they were wrestlers.

K had risen to his feet. He stood gaping, could not take his eyes from the screen. He had no other reaction, could not form thought. Instantly, the vignette with the little girl and her scraped knee reappeared. He let out a tiny little cry that he was not even aware he had uttered and collapsed back into his chair.

It might have been a good time to reflect on his dilemma but K barely took his eyes off the screen for the more than two hours he remained alone in the TB room. He thought of nothing else. After the panel discussion and weather reports came to an end, a 'doctor' of some sort appeared, in a flimsy suit jacket without a tie, and two young women who claimed both to have had physical relations with a third woman's boyfriend. The third woman claimed to have had a child by the reputed Don Juan.

There was a great deal of low, throaty shouting and occasional threatening poses. K sat breathless, awaiting the worst. Next the boyfriend appeared and was ushered to a chair between the women. The doctor continued to ask questions designed to keep the dispute alive while seeming to be sensitive to the plight of each of the young women. The discussion, such as it was, had an audience which interjected ooohs and aaaahs and sometimes delighted laughter.

After this went on for nearly a half of an hour, by the clock on the TB room wall, the doctor announced that they would soon be back with the 'dee-and-ay results'. K's favorite from among the little vignettes, in which a little lizard made amusing remarks, next appeared. He was shocked to realize that he was laughing — something he rarely did — as he watched. Several more, less engaging vignettes followed before the doctor reappeared and called upon the audience to vote on the issues at hand between the women and the man. Each seemed to vote somehow by tickling the arms of their chairs. A result was announced and more vignettes were immediately shown — so many, in fact, that K began to wonder whether the vote had been the conclusion to the affair.

Eventually, the doctor reappeared holding a number of small note cards. He waved the cards, and, announcing a number of confusing things K did not understand, declared that he was about to read the 'dee-and-ay results'. Ominous music began to play and the audience was perfectly silent. The third woman's child, he cried out, was *not* the child also of the man. A great deal of oh-ing and ah-ing followed. The doctor waited patiently for the reaction to subside.

After concluding observations, and a great many more vignettes, one of which promised comfortable 'feminine protection' of some sort, the doctor introduced a second topic. A woman had stolen her sister's husband. Again, the announcement was followed by a loud, lingering 'oh' from the audience. Again, the female principals entered from the side of the stage. The one presumably the wife was scowling. Again, after a great deal of low, throaty shouting and occasional threatening poses, and weeping on the part of the wife, as she described her plight to the doctor, an audience vote was taken.

After more vignettes, most of which he had seen numerous times by that point, K found himself peering into what appeared to be a hospital room in which a patient was unconscious and connected to many strange devices. He strained to try to make out whether this patient was either of the two men against which the audience's votes had gone so poorly.

Next, two nurses were behind a desk talking about a doctor for whose welfare they were concerned. The doctor's name was different but otherwise of no concern and he instantly forgot it. This doctor, it seemed, was especially compassionate and had joined some organization that took him to Africa where he fought the deadly 'Ee-bow-luh'. This had entailed heroic personal risk.

But, in another instant, K found himself whisked away to what appeared to be a private home. A man and a woman were talking most seriously. They were sure they knew who had shot Ted. Who Ted was, K could not yet guess. As he tried to piece together who Ted might be, Ellen launched through the doorway to the TB room so forcefully that K's legs buckled slightly with the violence of her entry. He was to follow her. The magic screen rambled on behind them as they returned in the direction of the offices.

K was once again left alone inside Mrs. Smith's office. He was delighted to discover his fedora lying on her desk and placed it on his lap. After this, he waited for some considerable period of time, obediently remaining in the chair beside the desk, and craning around to inspect the room. The photographs on the desk, and on a small shelf above it, were also remarkably vibrant with color. They seemed to be portraits of family members engaged in various activities. How they remained in such poses for long enough for the picture to be taken was something of a mystery. In some they positively looked like they were photographed while vigorously moving. But surely such photographs took less magic than did the remarkable moving pictures he'd witnessed in the TB room and they were no surprise given the fact.

The posters on the wall were also apparently photographs, quite large and with perfect focus nonetheless. They were overlaid with phrases like 'Workplace Safety' and 'Report it to your supervisor'. The technology that created them was much needed at the Workers Accident Insurance Company, he reflected. He would have to make a report once he arrived back from Matliary.

Also on the desk was the magical screen and typing board and a small counting device of a material he had never seen before. It displayed the amount in lights somehow shaped into numbers. The counting device incremented in such a way as to suggest that it might keep the time. Upon further consideration, he decided that it must indeed be a device of some sort to measure time. There was no other likely answer.

Even the floor of the office was new to him. It was covered by a dull light brown carpet somehow pulled tightly from wall to wall. The carpet had a faded geometrical pattern and many small, irregular darker brown spots he suspected were coffee stains. But anything was possible, given the present circumstances, and all of his surmises could be laughably wrong.

As K mused on the possible interpretations of the various objects in the office, Mrs. Smith finally arrived. As she settled in her chair, she noticed the fedora in his lap. "So the hat is yours," she said.

"Indeed it is," replied K.

"Well now, Mr. Kafka,..."

"Doctor Kafka," interjected K. His doctorate has cost his family considerable money and him considerable time and effort and it was inappropriate not to employ the proper form of address.

"MISTER Kafka,..." Mrs. Smith fairly screamed.

"You may rest assured that I will be filing a complaint with the railroad," K replied. He could not bring himself to raise his voice to match hers. Still, he felt he had made clear that he was indignant at the insult and the disrespectful tone of voice. Her behavior was outrageous.

The thought came unbidden that should the inhabitants of the Roach Motel be called upon to tickle the arms of their chairs, the presumptive Mrs. Smith would not likely fare well. K was not given to unbidden thoughts in offices and his head was aswim in respect of it. Panic, however, was never a good response. He steeled himself against any other such stray thought and presented a perfectly composed face.

Mrs. Smith, on the other hand, stared, smoldering, into her picture screen and typed rapidly as much to control her temper, it was obvious, as to do whatever it was, exactly, she did. "Mr. Kafka, we do not find you in the records of this or any other addiction program."

"Doctor Kafka," K calmly corrected, "and I should hope you wouldn't."

"None of the *doctors*, associated with this facility is available to evaluate your case until tomorrow."

"To evaluate my case?" asked K in a querying tone.

"As you do not seem to have any money," she went on as if he'd said nothing, "I've been authorized to provide you a bed here until then."

"To evaluate my case?" repeated K. "I have money in my trunk, madam, and more in my *brieftasche*, and have no intention of remaining beyond the hour for the next train to Matliary."

"We have taken the liberty of checking your trunk,..."

K pitched backwards in his chair as if he'd been struck a physical blow.

"…and the only money in it is German Marks issued before the Second World War. They were called-in on more than one occasion since then, I'm told. They are worthless. You are in Richmond, Virginia, from which there are no trains to European spas. To say more is to encourage you in your delusion."

K pitched back slightly again at the mention of a 'second world war'. What was a 'world war' much less a 'second' one? "This is bizarre. I wish to talk to your superior immediately."

Again, Mrs. Smith went on as if she hadn't heard. "Perhaps you will be pleased to know that you will have your own room until we determine whether you do have tuberculosis. I will have to ask you to follow our instructions strictly. You are not to mix with the general population. You will be shown to your room. Your meals will be brought to you. You will remain there."

"I can only suppose that I will be allowed in the TB room."

"The TB room?"

"Yes, the TB room with the magical moving picture screen in which I waited until you were ready to talk further."

"You have misunderstood," replied Mrs. Smith, unable to suppress a laugh. "That is the Tee-*Vee* room and you will most certainly not be allowed to leave your room to go there. We must take precautions. That is a public space available to all of the population here at prescribed times."

K surprised himself by another unexpected comment: "Will my room also have a magical moving picture screen?"

Mrs. Smith laughed louder still. "TV means 'television'. As you well know, it is not called a 'magical whatever' but a television. You will certainly need something to keep you company. If the doctors approve of it, I'm sure we can find a television for temporary relocation to your room."

"And my belongings?"

"Your trunk and other personal property are in your room as we speak. Ellen will come by to escort you there shortly."

"One more thing," queried K. "When will I be allowed to speak with the director?"

"I *am* the director. Now Mr. Kafka, please do try to cooperate."

K did not try to correct her failure to address him as 'doctor'.

Chapter 2

As Ellen escorted K to his room, he considered a question which had been growing more urgent while he sat in the office of Mrs. Smith. He now considered the request (for the question amounted to a request) uncomfortable for two reasons. The first, he did not know the young woman walking slightly ahead of him by any other than her Christian name. However much the ladies called each other by their Christian names, even in front of strangers, he had yet to be introduced much less to have known them for long enough to use the familiar form of address. Of course, he would not have considered for a moment asking Mrs. Smith.

He would refer to her as "Miss," he decided, but the next difficulty was not so easily overcome. The request was of a sensitive nature. It was not the kind of thing one asked a young lady. He had not been in the presence of any of the group of men among which he awoke in the morning for quite some time. When he had been in their company neither the need nor thought for the eventual certainty of the need had occurred to him. Now there was little time to wait on the off chance that one of the men would come to hand. It seemed there was no other option but to ask.

"Miss," said K in an inquiring tone almost a whisper. Ellen walked on not apparently having heard. Having screwed his courage up to the effort, there was no going back. "Miss," he repeated, this time almost loudly.

Ellen stopped and turned to face him. "Are you calling me?" she asked. "You can call me Ellen."

K stood sheepishly looking at his hands which he held folded before him. "Miss, is there a latrine available?"

A latrine," repeated Ellen, lingering over the word. After a moment her face lit up slightly with recognition. "You mean a restroom," she replied. "Yes, just up ahead. I'll show you where."

As they reached the door of the 'restroom,' Ellen turned and pointed. It seemed established that she was not to let him go far from her and that she would wait for him at the door. He hesitated, before he went inside, in case she might have something to say in that regard. She did not.

The door before him was perfectly flat with a rectangular metal plate in the midst of which was the cylinder of a miniature bolt lock. K stood before the door like a question. "Just push on it," Ellen commanded.

K reached out a tentative hand. The door opened slightly then forced itself closed once again. It took a surprising effort to open, on a second attempt, given its size. A small but noticeable gust of air rushed past him as he opened it. It closed gently behind him with a muffled thud.

Inside the door was a partition covered with ceramic tiles. Upon rounding the partition, K caught his breath slightly. To the right and to the left were counters inset each with three miniature white porcelain sinks. Over them were poised shining metal fixtures, flanked by what could only be handles, shaped almost like flowers, and over them mirrors their reflective surfaces lightly mottled with age. Everywhere he looked the walls were covered with ceramic tiles. Unlike the fixtures, the tiles were dull and displayed chips and cracks throughout. They were pea-green. The seams between them had once been white but were now also mottled with age.

Behind the rows of sinks were shallow porcelain boxes mounted vertically on the wall. Above them were more shining metal fixtures. K's need was not so urgent that he could resist looking closely at these boxes. What could they possibly be? Entirely at a loss, he walked up to a sink and fiddled hopelessly with a flower handle. In short order, he learned to turn it in order to initiate and alter the flow of water through the associated spout.

With all of the shocks of the morning, he had not thought once about his appearance. He saw, in the mirror, that his hair was impossibly disheveled. His jacket was askew and visibly wrinkled. He was distraught to think that he had cut such a poor figure all during the morning. Beyond the sinks and the porcelain boxes were rows of metal dividers. He peered into the spaces between and discovered the strangest looking latrines he had ever seen. They, too, were entirely of porcelain. They had no pull-chains or wooden covers and there were no water tanks on the wall above them.

There was now no time to linger. Directly, K sat on the strange white seat and relieved himself of his burden. As he was in the process of doing so, he manipulated the shiny metal lever mounted on the shiny metal pipe behind him attempting to ascertain its function. With great suddenness, a rush of water and air flew from the latrine. If he had not dreaded soiling his clothing, he would have leapt away.

Between his legs, in the latrine, he could see water racing furiously around the bowl. In an instant, his burden — or what he had deposited of it to that point — flew down into the floor not a speck of evidence remaining behind. K gave out a shout that sounded disconcertingly like an involuntary cheer. With that, the door to the 'restroom' opened and Ellen called out "Are you okay?" K replied that he had been surprised but was otherwise well enough. He emerged some time later, hair as perfectly combed as he could manage with his fingers (for he did not find his comb in its customary pocket) and his jacket settled, trying to look as if nothing of consequence had occurred.

For all of his effort, however, there was no hiding the fact that his hands were dripping wet. Ellen emitted a great sigh and entered the latrine. K stood outside confused and aghast until she called out, in a notably unladylike fashion, for him to enter as well. This he did, with trepidation. The situation promised no good as best he could tell.

Once inside, Ellen made him place his hands beneath a silver box. With that, she fairly punched a large silver button on the front of the box and hot air flowed over his hands. The implications not being immediately clear, he quickly withdrew them. His guide nodded for him to put them back under the air. She exited to wait for him outside where he joined her after his hands were dry.

A short distance further, Ellen opened a wooden door with a diamond-shaped handle and motioned for K to enter. He first peered cautiously in. There he saw his travel trunk and valise against the far wall, just beyond a bed that dominated the room. Beside them was a more or less normal window replete with sill and sash, both white.

Upon entering the room, the door closed behind him. He opened the door and craned his head around curious to see if his guide remained on the other side but she did not. Gently closing it once again he turned to survey his accommodations. The floor was covered by faded linoleum, vaguely green. There was but the one window. The bed was without a head board or any other amenity beyond a night table. Above the table was an electric lamp.

He stood peering out of the single window to the outside world for long minutes. He considered escaping. But to where? For all the world outside was vaguely familiar it was dauntingly strange. It seemed unlikely that there was any way he could manage to return to the train. Of course, he could not possibly be in America. But where was he?

The motorcars that passed did generally resemble those he had seen on the... television (he intended to learn the names of things here as quickly as possible). Men were manicuring the lawn between him and the street. He thought he recognized one of them from the morning's breakfast. They were probably inmates here. They did not have manicures, did not wear clothing as crisp and well-laundered as the actors in the little vignettes. He had a sense that they must have fallen in stature as the result of their addictions.

As Ellen had motioned him into the room, she somehow turned on the electric light, mounted on a small stanchion, beside the bed. This gave K a hint as to how to operate it and he turned it on and off several times from a switch beside the door. It did not have a chimney, only a bare bulb. He inspected it closely. The lamp itself was milky white and shaped like a curly-cue. He had never seen anything like it. A coated wire of some sort, the thickness perhaps of a thick piece of string, exited the base of the fixture and terminated at the wall. He knocked on the wall. It sounded remarkably light-weight and hollow behind.

Of course, he could not possibly be in America. But where was he? After every new discovery he asked himself the question. Suddenly it came to him. Perhaps he was still asleep. Perhaps he was dreaming. Of course it would have to be a particularly long and vivid dream — moreso than any he had ever dreamed before — but that did not change the fact that dreaming alone could explain the strangeness of this place.

For all of his insomnia, whenever he did sleep he had the most exotic dreams. These began, most particularly, with the first signs of the tuberculosis. After bouts of spitting blood, when he fell back in exhausted sleep from the effort, the dreams were particularly fabulous. He was quite certain this was the cause although he had not brought up blood in some time.

On the other hand, he could not remember ever realizing that he was in a dream while he was in a dream. Nevertheless, what other theory better explained what was going on? Even with the inconsistencies? If so, he remained in his seat, in the second-class section, on the train to Matliary. His situation in this 'Richmond' was a gift so long as it lasted. A gift of imagination which he could not have believed he could either give or receive.

As K looked out the window, a knock came at his door and an inmate (by all appearances) entered without waiting for a reply. The man looked around for somewhere to set down a tray he had carried in. Finding no convenient place, he held out the item, where he stood, just inside the doorway, and waited for K to cross the room to take it. As K crossed the room, the man held the tray further away from himself, and turned his head, as if anticipating an attack. K accepted the tray. The man launched precipitously out the door. Behind him was the young woman who had been companion to Ellen, peering out the little windows in the swinging doors, during breakfast. She held out a large drinking vessel. It was so much lighter than K had expected, for such a large vessel, that he almost threw the beverage into the air before realizing his mistake. She blanched slightly at his unexpected movement and quickly escaped as well. K pushed the door closed behind them.

He could find no suitable place to set the tray and arranged the lone metal chair in the room so that he could eat from the small table beside the bed. Being impossible without leaving the room, his earlier stop at the 'restroom' would have to do by way of washing before the meal.

As he was eating, a magical screen arrived. Another inmate carried it in. Yet another carried a small table behind and carelessly banged it against the wall, leaving a small pyramidal dent, before setting it down. The screen also had a coated wire. Ellen entered as they quickly left and pushed the end of the wire into the wall. This time when Ellen handed him the wand he enquired after its role. She informed him that it was called a 'remote'. She demonstrated how the tiny little buttons on it worked to turn it on and off and alter the volume. It turned out that there were a great many 'channels' and he 'changed' them repeatedly until he began to feel more or less the master of the device.

She next showed him the use of what turned out to be a telephone (though much different from any he had ever seen). This, too, was operated by pushing little buttons. She handed him a piece of paper with a number written on it. He was to press in the number if he needed to 'use the restroom' or experienced an emergency. Under no circumstance was he to leave the room without being accompanied by a member of the staff. With that she, too, left in a manner suggesting some degree of anxiety and concomitant haste.

Once alone, K inspected the damaged wall. It was of the flimsiest construction, made of heavy paper filled with some sort of whitish powder. The walls of the other rooms had seemed to be made of bare, painted cement. Perhaps he was now in some temporary structure, lightly built in order to minimize construction expense. He knocked again on the wall, again noted the curious hollow sound.

He next pulled the small table on which he was eating away from the wall and placed the chair behind it facing the screen. It was already active, as the result of Ellen's demonstration, and his experiments, and he saw no reason to further change the channel. He ate entranced, after which he took only enough time to place the tray and vessel outside of the door, on the floor, and returned to his seat. Soon he moved to the bed, which was much more comfortable than the chair.

Until supper arrived (together with another table to set inside of the door, obviating the need to hand the tray directly and at close quarters) nothing else existed for K except the magical screen. (It was proving difficult to think of it as a 'television' as 'magical screen' captured the essence of it so much better.) From time to time he changed the channels, going rapidly from one to another. This was somehow especially invigorating. There were a great many of these 'channels'. He was transported instantly from one scene to another. One minute he was absorbed in the love machinations of a young couple, the next watching as a murder was discussed, the next watching something called a 'paper towel' absorb more than all others.

So much that he saw was astonishing. There were vignettes about flying in giant aeroliners. They were unimaginably bigger than the aeroplanes he and Max Brod had watched fly at Brescia and had no propellers that he could make out. They had large halls filled with perhaps hundreds of passengers seated on rows of chairs. In others trees fell on motorcars and klaxons sounded. The owners frowned to learn that they were not 'covered'. There were a great many vignettes about medications in which the actors smiled in such a way as to suggest a state of the most complete bliss in spite of the most horrifying 'side effects' imaginable. They must be Dadaist plays. The Dadaists promised such mental chaos that he avoided their works, and he intended to 'change the channel,' henceforward, whenever he was presented with their vignettes.

Curiously, not all of the channels were shown in color. One showed a young boy in a world that looked quite different for all it remained foreign. His name was 'Beaver' and an invisible audience gently laughed at his adventures. While Beaver existed in a world without color, his adventures were interrupted, as always, by color filled vignettes, one showing a family of cartoon bears, each a different color. Their lives were absorbed in admiring a particularly soft toilet tissue. It seemed that no subject was considered indiscrete on the magical screen.

Beaver's mother and father were wonderfully kind and he always ate everything on his plate. Their house was remarkably spacious. Curiously, there were no shelves laden with family memorabilia that K could see. Somehow he was confident that Beaver never had nightmares. He was never terrified of failing at school. His father never told him that he was incapable of ever doing anything right.

Another channel showed someone called 'The Rifleman'. He inhabited a world without even the scientific advances widely known in K's Prague. There were no electric lights in evidence. All travel was still done by horse and wagon. Yet it all was on the magic screen. How, K wondered, was such a thing possible?

If he thought 'The Rifleman' was confusing, the program he watched intently as he ate supper (carefully leaving aside the meat portion yet again) was far more so. It was called 'Star Trek'. In it, people traveled through the entire universe. They wore the simplest clothing, almost as if they were dancers, and they traveled from star to star in minutes. They said the trips took days and they apparently made no moving-picture record of the time between. K's limited experience suggested this was common practice on the magical screen. He found this inconvenient as he was endlessly curious about the details of how they spent their days.

A number of the people, on the 'Starship Enterprise' (which looked nothing at all like a ship, which might, perhaps, be expected) were of the strangest imaginable type. Perhaps, K reflected, some were Esquimoes. But from just where 'Klingons' might come he was at a loss even to guess. Perhaps the Kamchatka peninsula. He'd heard stories about the strange appearance of the natives of that region. Or perhaps they came from somewhere in the stars.

As K watched the adventures of the starship, a different kind of vignette broke in from time to time. There were no more vignettes about car insurance or particularly absorbent paper towels. Instead vignettes about tiny little magical screens called 'phones' were quite common. Their operation somehow required contracts. They conversed with the holder in an attractive mechanical female voice.

In a particularly gripping vignette, a group of people even stranger than those on the starship, called 'The Avengers,' were battling a very evil-looking mechanical man called something-tron, as well. The Avengers were glum and smutched with soot and seemed to be faring particularly poorly. The sky was ominously dark. K wondered if they were here on earth or on another planet in some distant part of the universe. Everyone at the Roach Motel seemed to feel quite safe so he felt confident that the ravaged landscape The Avengers occupied must be at a considerable distance. Perhaps in the desert where the fighting he learned about in the morning was underway.

"Could it be possible," wondered K, "that there were other planets like earth?" Hadn't he already experienced so much that seemed impossible in just this one brief day? All but the blue trees, on the planet the crew of the starship were visiting, were very much like earth, but the inhabitants looked like giant speaking lizards that stood on their hind legs. And what of the mode of transportation by which people disappeared from one place and instantly appeared in another? Tomorrow, K intended to ask that he might be permitted to see these 'transporters,' maybe even be 'beamed up'.

But all of this was so utterly impossible. This could only be a dream. No other explanation sufficed. He would have to remember to write it all down immediately after he woke up, for dreams are quickly forgotten if one does not. A dream like this was a wonder and must be preserved and analyzed at length. He could imagine his life being worthy of having been lived just for the fact that he had dreamed this dream.

There was no watching the magic screen in the morning. A knock came on the door before K had woken. He rose to the sitting position and looked around him expecting to see that he was once again on the train to Matliary. He found himself in the same room in which he had fallen asleep. How, he wondered, was it possible to fall asleep in a dream? During the night he had had vivid dreams. How was it possible to dream within a dream?

Another knock came at the door. This time the person knocking did not wait for a reply. She entered wearing a white laboratory coat over black tights and a t-shirt, pushing a metal cart. The tights, in particular, left little to the imagination. For a moment, K stared. Behind her came two large men. One had been the man with the bright yellow shirt the day before.

This was simply too much, thought K. He fought to control a growing fury and managed to speak in a firm but civil tone of voice. "This is an outrage. One does not barge into the bedroom of another person without waiting for permission. I did not say you could enter."

The young woman was new to K. She handed him a soft roll of gauze and instructed him to squeeze it repeatedly. He accepted it, out of a habit of courteousness, then thought the better of it and opened his hand letting the roll of gauze fall on his blankets. He meant this as an act of protest.

"I am going to take blood and send it to the lab to see if you have tuberculosis," she said. "If you do not squeeze the roll I cannot guarantee that I will not have to give it several tries." She paused and looked at him in a vaguely unconcerned way.

"Take blood?"

K had asked his question more timidly than he would have liked. Perhaps, he was soon to reflect, it had not been understood. In any event, there was to be no further explanation of what this 'taking blood' might consist. The young woman grabbed K's arm and deftly wrapped a rubber tourniquet around his upper arm after which she began tapping just below it on the soft inner side of his elbow. As she did so, the two large men moved ominously forward. K thought it a matter of personal dignity — if not safety — to let the procedure pass without a struggle.

The implements of the procedure were small and sleek. K had never seen them before and wondered about this 'taking blood'. The young woman seemed to consider the entire operation a common matter, even the stroking and tapping of a strange man's arm. Seeing his blood enter the clear vial was distressing. His eyes grew enormously wide as he watched, especially when it became clear that a second vial would be 'taken'. But it did not seem wise to struggle or protest.

After the young woman removed the rubber tourniquet and applied a tiny brown bandage over the spot where the needle had entered, she took another smaller needle from the tray and quickly pricked his forearm. There having been no preliminaries — not even so few or mysterious as preceded the first operation — this had been entirely unexpected. In the state of mind he was in, he flinched so violently that the three visitors could not quite hold back a collective chortle. This done, she attached labels to the vials of blood, returned all implements to the rolling table, carefully situating them as she did so, and the three of them walked back out of the door. The last to leave pulled it shut behind him.

Beside the door, as they left, K noticed that a breakfast tray lay waiting on the little table that had been introduced, the previous day, for the purpose. Someone must have stepped in to leave it there while his attention was riveted to the 'taking blood'. K stared at the door half-expectantly until at last he felt confident that the two men were gone for the time being. He then rose and brought the tray to the bed. Carefully swinging his legs and covering them with the top blanket, in order to prevent being seen in such a state of dishabille, he balanced it on his lap and placed the glass of apple juice beside him on the table above which the curlicue lamp was poised.

As disconcerting as the invasion had been, K's thoughts almost immediately returned to the fact that he had dreamed within a dream. Or rather, to the question as to how such a thing was possible. He had never experienced such a thing before. In all his extensive reading he had never read of such an occurrence.

A great deal of time seemed to have passed in dream terms. The world in which he found himself was finely detailed far beyond any dream he could remember. He genuinely appeared to be stuck in this place — a material place if his senses could be trusted — and who knew for how long?

Was he, perhaps, in a coma? Such states were an absolute mystery to him. On those few occasions when he even reflected upon them, he could not help but wonder what the person in the coma might be experiencing.

No other answer seemed possible. A sudden attack of coughing up blood, on the train, must have depleted his animal spirits to such an extent that he had lapsed into a coma. His actual body must be lying in a hospital bed, his grieving family wretched to think of it. His parents might be on a train this moment to return that body to Prague. Even there, expert medical doctors were enormously expensive. He would yet again be a grave disappointment to his father.

What was there to be done, then? It was an impossible question. If he were struck by a motorcar, in this world, would he suffer injury? If he had chosen to struggle with the two large men would he have? He'd never heard of the body of a coma patient exhibiting mysterious wounds, but what of the body he had here? It felt too real not to be his own, not to be fully material, fully subject to injury.

After he finished breakfast, which, on this occasion, did not include a meat dish, and dressed, he began absently pacing the room touching each of the items and surfaces in it as he considered the possibilities. Some subconscious part of him called for this validation, as he was not even aware that he was doing it. He realized it only when he reached the window. It was another beautiful sunny day outside. He gently opened it. A cool breeze wafted past him. Motorcars passed along a road that ran along the edge of the property in the distance. He could hear their motors rumble.

After a few minutes, he returned absently to the bed, took up the wand and turned on the magic screen. Soon he was lost in what he was watching.

K was not sure exactly how much time he had been watching the magical screen when another knock came. He stared at the door intently, wondering whether the person on the other side intended to barge in uninvited. A second knock pleased him so much that he called out "Enter".

As a middle-aged man entered, K rose from his bed and stood waiting before him. "I am Doctor Stephenson," he said. His clothes appeared not to have been pressed in quite some time nor his hair combed. K had noticed that the breeze outside had increased considerably as he sat watching the magical screen. He guessed the doctor had just arrived and was neglectful of his personal appearance, perhaps due to haste.

The doctor did not offer his hand but went to the chair beside the bed and settled on it. "Hello, Mr....?" The man who asked was about K's size and a bit broader through the shoulders. (But who wasn't broader through the shoulders than K?) He carried no bag, bore no other badge of his profession.

The only chair in the room taken, K sat on the edge of the bed. "*Doctor* Kafka," he replied.

"A doctor," the doctor said with a repressed smile. "Impressive."

"And your first name?"

"Franz," said K.

"Franz Kafka, as in the novelist?"

At this question, K evidenced some confusion.

"I'm sorry, I didn't catch your reply."

"I have published stories, if that is what you mean."

"Have you published no novels?"

"None," replied K, with a quizzical look.

"Not *The Trial, Amerika, The Castle*?"

The question left K speechless. How did this 'doctor' know of novels he had not yet completed, suspected he might never publish? In his confusion, he simply looked vaguely away. How he could possibly gather his thoughts he did not know.

"What year is this, Mr. Kafka?"

"I'm told it is 2015."

"What do *you* think?" the doctor asked. "What year do you think it is?"

This all was quite impossible.

"Were you carrying these papers from 1920?" the doctor asked, pulling them from the inside pocket of his crumpled suit jacket. "They look quite legitimate to me. The embossed seals are an impressive touch. May I ask where you got them?"

K replied automatically, his mind overwhelmed by questions he knew from the first he could not answer. "From the State Bureau. I am not aware that one can acquire such papers anywhere else."

"Or perhaps they are available on the Internet, somewhere?" The doctor ran his hand over the surface of the papers. "Of course, the embossing you would have had to do yourself. Is that difficult? You have done a remarkable job of it."

"The 'inner net'?" The 'doctor' before him, he was growing certain, was a psychoanalyst, not an actual medical doctor. K was deeply ambivalent about the field. It seemed like everyone fancied themselves brilliant amateur practitioners, which only made matters worse.

"Do you own a computer?"

"What is a computer?" asked K. "Do you mean a calculating machine of some sort? We have calculating machines in the office but I see no need to own one myself."

The psychiatrist had removed a small magic screen from the inside pocket of his suit jacket and was tapping on it with his fingers as he asked his questions. "Well, of course a computer is a calculating machine if needs be. When were you born, may I ask?"

"I cannot agree to be interrogated. On what authority do you do so, *may I ask*?"

"I'm here to help you,… Franz. You must remember that."

"It is deeply troubling that you address me by my given name. It constitutes a blatant disregard of even the simplest courtesy. I am addressed by those who do not know me intimately as 'Doctor Kafka' and I must ask you to employ the proper form of address."

As K replied, the psychiatrist continued tapping on his small magic screen. "Well, you do know your Kafka. His novels were only published after his death. Do I understand you to say that you do not own a computer?"

"I can only suppose not. The term, however, is not familiar to me."

"Did you use the computer at the public library?"

"My novels were only published after my death? I seem alive enough. Nothing about you suggests that you read futures. It's impossible, in any case. I really must ask you to leave."

"I don't see anywhere that you knew how to speak English."

Again K was utterly aswim. Until that moment, he hadn't any thought that he had been speaking anything but German. His English was limited to a few functional phrases. Or at least it had been. But it could not be denied, now that he specifically considered the matter, that he was thinking and speaking English. And then to be referred to in the past tense… "I really must ask you to leave," he repeated, this time in perfectly formed German. He was unable to think of another thing to say.

"So you can speak German. Or at least it sounds like German. I really wouldn't know."

At that K felt near to fainting.

"Quite impressive. But, still, how can you speak English?" Noticing K's discomposure, the doctor clearly recognized his powerful advantage. "If you weren't napping on a train before you arrived here what do you think you might have been doing instead? I realize that you are clear that you were on a train, but just as a lark, what do you think you might have been doing if you were not on a train at all — at least not in 1920?"

So then, the good doctor had arrived long enough ago to have time to conference with the presumptive Mrs. Smith. He was to be ganged up on without conscience. "A 'lark'?" asked K, his brow furrowed.

"An amusing way to pass time."

"I assure you my papers are legitimate," said K. "I was on the train. I leaned back to take a nap. The next thing I knew I woke in the workers' quarters. I have asked to speak with a representative of the railroad and have been repeatedly refused. It is my right. I am sure that this matter can be put right once I have spoken with a representative."

"Tell me, Mr. Whoever-You-Are,…"

"Doctor Kafka."

"Yes. Tell me, do you have any money? Any bank accounts or other sources of funds?"

"I am carrying several hundred Marks," K replied, ignoring the impertinent questions as to his finances.

"German Marks. You have German Marks on your person."

"In my *brieftasche*."

"May I see one of the bills?" the psychiatrist asked. "I assure you, it will be immediately returned."

K saw no harm in the request. He pulled out a large billfold from an inside pocket of his suit jacket, removed a large colorful bill and handed it to the man.

The doctor scanned it closely and handed it back. "Do you have any American money, I mean? You are in America, after all."

"No. None."

"Do you have any family in the Richmond area? In the area in which you are presently located?"

"No. None of which I am aware."

"How do you expect to survive when you are discharged from here?"

"I will board the next train and continue on my way to Matliary."

"Matliary? Oh yes, the spa you claim was your original destination." Again, The doctor repeatedly tapped his miniature screen. "There is no longer a spa in Matliary. I suspect it closed many years ago. And there is certainly no train from Richmond to Matliary. A vast ocean lies between us and Europe."

Chapter 3

Arthur made it a habit to dress early on those rare occasions when he accepted an invitation to one place or another. If he did not, he was inevitably deep in some absolutely absorbing activity when his ride arrived and the kind source of transportation found him- or herself waiting while matters were wound up and he changed clothes.

His shoes were passably shined and his shirt only worn twice since he last laundered it a year or so before. His entire ensemble, such as it was, was (had anyone been present to see) quite out of place among the wires strewn every which way across the bookshelves that filled his modest apartment. He was more or less appropriately dressed, as he peered into one of the computer monitors in the front room, for a small get together at his brother's house. But not at all appropriately for tinkering, with screw drivers sticking out of his pocket, and an adjustable wrench in one of the hands with which he was typing an operating system query.

Jeremiah, his brother, would pick him up in a few minutes to go to his niece's birthday party. Arthur already vaguely regretted being taken away from his various projects, as always. Besides the wires and computer equipment, books and magazines were strewn on the plastic shelves at every hand: here a Wired Magazine, there a book of Spanish crossword puzzles that he rarely found the time to work on, on this side a study on Rabelais, on that side another on fractals. There was always too much that needed doing and too little time to do it.

Every niche and nook (and there were a great many) was occupied by something: in the front room mostly utility bills, grocery store fliers, boxes of printer paper and of envelopes of various sizes. In the bedroom the niches were filled with linens, candles, and other items of general use, neatly settled between rows of books. The clothes in the closet hung above tool chests, socket sets, soldering gear, and below a shelf loaded with cookware that didn't fit in the cabinets in the kitchenette. The one thing there wasn't was room for a bed.

As he was entering a troubleshooting command, the wrench dropped gently out of his hand and onto the keyboard. This was followed by a rapid stream of random characters and curses. Why did he never think to put down items in his hand before typing, he fumed? Well, if it weren't one thing it would be another. In a matter of a few seconds the wrench was sitting beside the keyboard and the spurious characters were deleted.

On the shelf below the computer monitor was a collection of books about Franz Kafka. Arthur had pulled them off the shelves weeks ago and had been looking back through them for a few minutes most evenings since. He hadn't read most of them for years.

Jeremiah and his wife, Lori, had taken in some guy from the Roach Motel (apparently the nickname of a rehab center in the South End). Jeremiah has been sober now for almost 20 years and attends an AA meeting there, once a week. He knows pretty much everyone in the program in the Richmond area.

Anyway, this guy fancies himself to be Franz Kafka... as in *the* Franz Kafka. He claims to be as confused as anyone about how he appeared out of thin air in the Roach Motel. Even though this Kafka refuses to so much as touch drugs or alcohol the staff psychiatrist was about to have him committed.

Jeremiah being Jeremiah he heard what was about to happen and loaded this Kafka on the back of his Harley, after a meeting, and drove the man to his house, out Mechanicsville way. Later he drove one of the family cars over and strapped the guy's gargantuan travel trunk onto the roof-top carrier. Kafka and accessories have been house guests for almost three weeks. From time to time Jeremiah stops by to pass a half-hour chatting with Arthur about life. Inevitably, of late, Franz becomes the topic of conversation. He is a bit of an eccentric. "But then what would one expect from someone whisked in an instant 95 years into the future?" Arthur reflected with a wry smile.

Franz, it turns out, is a vegetarian. Lori was so pleased to have another vegetarian in the house that she enjoyed preparing meals for the two of them for a while. This led to conversation. Lori is taking a hiatus from her accounting business. She and her girlfriends are enjoying the extra time to get together for regular lunches and coffee-klatching, generally in the sunroom filled with high-backed wicker chairs, dream catchers, scented candles and the like. Franz has been introduced to her circle during these visits. Slender and formal, and much more given to listening than speaking, he quickly became an admired new furnishing of the room.

He was surprisingly engaging at first but more than a little tedious as time went on. He spends most of the day intently watching the big screen television in the living room. If anyone else wishes to watch a particular program, no matter the type, he watches along with them. He even watches Lori's favorite aerobic exercise show as she follows along in her leotards each morning which she finds more than a little disconcerting. During his most recent visit, Jeremiah had hinted broadly that it was beginning to be a bit much. Maybe, he wondered aloud, a short commitment might come to some good after all.

Franz loved riding through the countryside on the back of the Harley almost as much as watching television. He wore a suit, as always, and a pair of goggles that Jeremiah had found for him among the clutter in the garage. If Jeremiah rolled the bike out he was sure to find the guy standing beside him, goggles discreetly situated in his jacket pocket, in hopes of a ride.

One day, shortly after he arrived, Franz asked to go to the railroad station. Jeremiah hadn't been to that part of town in quite some time and figured "Why not?" He took him to the Main Street Station. Franz did not so much seem impressed, Jeremiah had said, as 'at home'. He stood across the street for quite some time looking up at the clock tower, said it reminded him of a similar tower in Prague. The three story chimney drew his attention, as well, and the arches over the doors of the balcony above. Once inside, the marble floors and columns brought out a different side of him. He was almost giddy as he inspected the second floor platform.

The station is in one of the many historical districts of Richmond, and, train schedule in hand, he looked with great interest out of the windows. He tried the doors to the balcony but they were locked. It would be a while before the next train. Jeremiah walked with him through the streets below with their old fashioned storefronts. Those that had not been renovated interested him most.

He stood peering longingly into their windows, ran his hand over their doors. Jeremiah explained that the covered area between two streets was the location of an open air produce market. Perhaps, Lori would like company the next time she came to shop there and Franz could return to explore the neighborhood a little more. As they walked wherever the moment took them, a train rumbled along the overhead trestle. They had missed it. But no matter, another would arrive in 15 minutes or so. They turned and made their way back.

Back on the platform, the two took a seat on a bench. Franz pored over the train schedule, and, after a short time, looked positively glum. Then he could hear the train approaching in the distance. He stared up the tracks not quite knowing what he would see. When the slowing engine passed, his eyebrows shot up. "Trains here," he informed Jeremiah, "are much sleeker than in Bohemia."

As the train came to a stop, he looked as closely at the structure of the cars as he had at the old storefronts, from time to time shaking his head. As passengers disembarked, he inspected every detail of every person or as many as possible before they entered the station. He momentarily boarded together with the handful of passengers that had been waiting on the platform. The train lurched slightly and he leapt out of the exit. "I can see you don't waste time here," he cried. "Trains remain much longer when they stop in Prague. Even the Germans at least allow 5 minutes."

As Arthur was recalling Jeremiah's description of the excursion, a group of young guys entered the parking lot, outside his open window, and loitered about, aimlessly looking around. One approached a middle-aged woman, painfully struggling with arthritic hips, who happened to be walking to her car, and asked if she had any money. A large black gentleman emerged from an apartment several doors away and told the young men in no uncertain terms that they did not belong on the property. They glared after their most menacing fashion as they turned and walked down the street. It would be dark before Arthur returned from the party. He did not like being away from the apartment at night.

Jeremiah pulled up in the car and gently tapped the horn. They were soon on the way to his house, quietly chuckling about this or that ongoing conversation.

Soon they were in the house. Guests were milling about, Vichy waters in hand. As usual, those who met Arthur for the first time began their conversations with "You look just like your brother." Most he had met before and had managed to be sufficiently social on those occasions that they offered handshakes and "How's it going?" After the greeting, they returned to the conversations that had been underway when he entered.

The table was filled with a range of meat and vegetarian dishes, the refrigerator with bottles of Vichy and soda. Of course, there were also deviled eggs. A regular stream of people gingerly picked with their fingers from serving plates and scooped from bowls onto paper plates. Arthur was soon among them. He had barely eaten all day.

He set his plate on a butcher block counter, on the far side of the large space, and enjoyed the food and the bustle. "Did Anne make these stuffed cabbage rolls?" asked one guest. Answered in the affirmative, she declared them 'delicious'. She simply had to get the recipe. One guy asked another whether he was getting out on his 'bike' these days as they walked out toward the living room. Another guest called out: "I know who made this. I always look forward to Diane's pecan pie."

Lori gently worked to keep the conversation lively: "I know. Isn't it the best!" It being a special day for her daughter, Donna, she wore a long skirt and a blouse in lieu of blue jeans. Most of the guests wore more casual clothes. The birthday girl was accepting congratulations, in short shorts and a pullover top that celebrated a maturing body. She sat in a corner of the room, near the door, as she chatted *sotto voce* with a girlfriend presumably from school.

As all of this proceeded, a remarkably thin young man in a dark suit, made of impressively sturdy fabric of some kind, entered through the passage from the living room. His dark brown hair was impeccably groomed, his complexion light olive in color. He hesitated before the food. Lori encouraged him. "Go ahead, Franz. You better take some before it's all gone." He looked in her direction out of the corner of his eye and bowed slightly. The birthday girl and her friend whispered rapidly back and forth glancing toward Franz, and giggling as they did so.

The young man was stooped until he received his hostess's encouragement. As he straightened slightly he teetered, almost imperceptibly, before the food. He crept up to the table, with glances from side to side, and picked out a small number of items setting them on his plate. All of this left Arthur with the impression that he was quite timid.

As he finished his selection and turned around, Arthur noticed that the dark blue suit was made of an impressive tight-weave tweed. The narrow-lapelled jacket was cut in the style that used to be called a 'strolling jacket'. He was wearing a wide sky-blue silk tie. It was tied like a cravat, broad and bloused out. Such clothing did not come cheap. More than this, Arthur was impressed with his face. He looked exactly like the old pictures of Franz Kafka. The resemblance really was quite striking. Lori handed him a Vichy water from the refrigerator which he again accepted with a slight bow.

Once the Vichy was in his hand, Lori took him by the elbow and sat him down next to Arthur. Both men felt her action a bit shocking, being entirely unexpected. Arthur could not help but be thoughtful about the development. "Franz, this is Arthur, Jeremiah's brother. Arthur, this is Franz." With that, she returned to her duties as hostess.

Each nodded his head toward the other. Arthur returned to the table for a second helping of the food. Franz flinched as his neighbor rose, then began eating, head down and eyes riveted on his food. Arthur returned. As he sat back down he said "So you are Franz."

This seemed to make Franz acutely uncomfortable. "I am..." He paused in a quandary of some sort. "Yes, I am... *Franz.*" He said his own name as if he had to force it out against his will.

"I'm Arthur." Arthur extended his hand being careful not to make any sudden moves. Franz accepted it and limply returned a handshake. "I hear you're from out of town." He could not hold back a smirk as he said it.

Franz continued eating. He lifted a paper napkin, fastidiously dabbing at his lips, and carefully inspected his suit jacket for crumbs, after which he replied. "Yes, from as far out of town as could be."

"How are you enjoying your stay so far?"

"Jeremiah and Lori have been most kind. I have not seen much beyond their neighborhood. Most sights are at a considerable distance. I prefer not to bother them any more than can be avoided."

Lori was removing the serving plates for the dishes that had been finished. The two ate quietly as she placed a large cake in the space thus made available and began sticking small candles through the frosting on top. Franz glanced up as she did so, brow slightly furrowed. There was some mystery for him in her activity.

The kitchen was filling with people. They complimented the cake in the highest terms. A conversation was struck up about where it was purchased. This was followed by more compliments. Several people regretted aloud that they could only have 'a small piece'. Still more people entered until the entire party had gathered around the table.

Soon everyone was singing the happy birthday song off key. Arthur sang along. K looked on bemused. As the birthday girl blew out the candles K vaguely smiled. The rest of the party gently clapped. Both waited until the others had taken their slice of cake. Arthur then picked up a cake-laden plate from the table. Lori carried a plate to K who acknowledged her kindness with a slight bow. The next half-hour was taken up with the opening of brightly wrapped gifts.

Some ten minutes in, Arthur eased out the kitchen door to take a bit of fresh air. He was soon followed by Jeremiah who nonchalantly started talking. "So what do you think of Franz."

"He seems harmless enough."

"We've told him he has to get a job and find his own place. There are problems, though."

"I'm sure there are," said Arthur, evasively. He had a sense that something was in the air: something Jeremiah wasn't sure he would like.

"The people at the Roach Motel say that his tests there came back inconclusive for tuberculosis. It's possible that he has it but it's not active. No one should be able to catch it from him. Not even in close contact."

"Kafka did have tuberculosis," Arthur added.

"Lori's holding up pretty well but the TB thing is a whole different level. Especially with kids in the house."

Arthur was not one to beat about the bush. "You want me to put him up in my spare room."

"We live too far out of town for him to be able to hunt for a job. He doesn't have any way of getting an ID until he admits he's not Franz Kafka and remembers who he really is so he can get a birth certificate or something. He might be able to get a job under the table, though — he's pretty smart — but not if he isn't close enough to knock on doors."

"So you want me to put him up in my spare room."

"If they send him to the bug-house it'll be hell for him is my bet. He needs to get out on the street and be knocking on doors."

"I don't even have enough money for me," said Arthur. "It costs money to have a houseguest. I doubt he will want to cut corners the way I have to. With the suit he's wearing he would fit right in as a guest at the Jefferson Hotel."

"He barely talks. He wouldn't bother you. I can't see how he would. And he wouldn't cost anything. Just let us know what you need. Of course, don't get crazy about it. He'll need to understand that we can only do so much. He needs to get a job as soon as possible."

"He's a vegetarian."

"Lori and her friends have agreed to each make up a few meals for him each week. He'll just have to heat some of them up. He has gotten pretty comfortable with using a microwave. We'll bring them to your place once or twice a week."

"I don't know," said Arthur in a leery tone.

"Well, think about it and let me know."

"By when?"

"By the end of the party," said Jeremiah looking sheepish. "Lori is giving me fits about it."

Back inside, Arthur chose to take a seat in a corner of the living room. It was his habit to put a bit of distance between himself and a crowd and enjoy listening. It was Franz's choice, also. He had been sitting in another chair a few feet away. He, too, was intently listening in silence.

Some minutes passed before either spoke, Arthur being the first. "So, I understand that you and your father had a particularly difficult relationship."

Minutes passed again, K not seeming to have heard. At last he replied. "I am not used to the habit people have here of asking the most personal questions — even upon first acquaintance — without the least sense of transgression. I suspect, however, that you are playing amateur psychoanalyst, searching for an answer to how I can think that I am Franz Kafka. This, you may be interested to know, is not all that new to me. I considered amateur analysis equally impertinent in many of the people in Prague. Fascinating as your Dr. Freud is, I see far more harm than good coming from his theories."

Arthur could not help but smile. "Freud is considered seriously passé now."

K's eyebrows rose noticeably. "A brief conversation with the psychoanalyst at the Roach Motel strongly suggests that he continues to be very much in vogue, not to mention your own query."

Arthur found himself smiling once again. "Is it a surprise that the staff psychiatrist at a place called the 'Roach Motel' might be there because he is not the finest in his field?"

This time, it was K who could not help but smile.

"The talking cure itself," Arthur went on, "has not been put entirely aside, but, rather, the theories of how to interpret the replies. The professionals tend to depend upon standardized questions now and administer them as written tests. The amateur does not have this option."

The college football game that had been playing on the big screen television, on the opposite wall, with the volume low, was turned up now. Some key part of the game must have arrived. The volume of the various conversations increased accordingly. Neither Arthur nor K was pleased to think of yelling. Both silently watched from the corner. From time to time cheers went up or groans according with the results of a play as the two looked on like extraterrestrial observers.

The television cameras panned over the crowd in the stands. There obviously were many thousands in attendance. K struggled to put it all in perspective. He could only think of the Roman Coliseum, the men in the helmets gladiators. He looked for the President's box (for America did not have an Emperor) but could not make it out.

The thought came to him (not for the first time) that this Richmond, and the places he saw on the magic screen, were somehow remarkably Roman, the life Pagan. With much lighter building materials, it was clear, and with electricity and magic screens and Smartphones and Harley-Davidson motorcycles instead of horses.

He struggled to make the pieces fit together somehow. The Sunday before, he recalled, he finally felt that he could no longer refuse Jeremiah and Lori's repeated invitations to attend morning service with them. But the building they arrived at bore no particular emblems of Christian worship. The only symbol inside was a single bare cross, about the height of a man, situated behind a stage. All of the interior, including the cross, was finished with a clear lacquer of some sort. This gave it all a fresh pine appearance that was admittedly quite uplifting but entirely without the least sense of the soul's struggle with sin.

Only the rare Bible verse was cited during the sermon, nothing of Christ, only 'Jesus of Nazareth'. The humble Nazarene shared the stage with the Buddha, Gandhi and someone named Cat Stevens. Healthy living was the dominant theme: eating a proper diet, budgeting, opening oneself up to the joy in life, putting oneself in a position to have positive outcomes. In that church, life needed not be a burden. Prayers were for God's help to save one from poor personal habits. Repentance seemed to have been replaced by regret there and regret was openly discouraged. While it was not what K's limited studies of the Pagan temple might have led him to expect either, he could not now help but wonder if the place bore a consistency with the massive Coliseum and the warriors on the screen before him.

But, in the end, what did it matter, this desperate effort to put the pieces of it all together as if it were a grand puzzle? He was sitting in a 'living room' somewhere that he could not have begun to imagine as he traveled on the train to Matliary. He had no idea where he was or how he had gotten there and even less idea how long he would remain — when next he might wake from a nap to find himself god-knows-where-else. Yet still he felt compelled to try. He had never felt remotely so compelled before.

While K sat considering, the television was once again turned down in response to lingering complaints by some of the ladies present. A series of vignettes (which he had since learned were called 'commercials') appeared in place of the Coliseum. He watched as sleek, colorful 'pick-up' trucks accomplished remarkable feats and people ate chicken from a large paper bucket, which appeared, from their wide-eyed expressions, to be the most delicious food ever eaten.

"How," K asked, "do you presume to know about my relationship with my father?" He was sure he had mentioned nothing about it since he arrived wherever exactly he was.

"It is common knowledge," Arthur replied. "You are quite famous now."

"Jeremiah does not seem to attribute any such fame to me. While I was surprised Lori knew of my story, 'The Metamorphosis', it has been published and that seemed to explain the matter. That it is much more widely known than I could have imagined, or, perhaps, touches in a distant way upon my relationship to my father, can hardly explain your confidence."

Arthur hesitated, not knowing what best to reply. The permutations that might arise out of any of the answers that came to mind left him unsure. There was nothing to do but to simplify matters. He must choose. He must either pursue the conversation as if he were speaking to a harmless psychotic or with a displaced Kafka. "Your work has become quite famous since your death."

"Yes. Well I suppose that the impossible passage of nearly one hundred years, in the space of an instant, can only mean that I disappeared long ago. Perhaps I was presumed to have died?" The commercials having ended, he stared vaguely toward the Coliseum. He wasn't even aware of awaiting an answer.

"You died of tuberculosis a few years after your stay at Matliary."

"Yet another conundrum," K absently replied. "Still, none of this explains your presumption regarding my relationship with my father."

"After your death, Max Brod published your unfinished novels."

"What unfinished novels? Quite impossible."

"*The Trial, The Castle, Amerika.*"

K was visibly shocked. "How do you know about *The Castle*? I have only written a few notes toward it. How do you know about any of them?"

"You will work on it during the time you have left. *The Castle*, I mean."

"By *Amerika,* I assume you refer to *The Man Who Disappeared.* Either way, it is impossible that it could be published. It is a total failure, mere fragments. Max knows my thoughts on the matter. He would never do such a thing. It is almost as unbelievable as *this* America."

"While I might agree with you somewhat about the quality of *Amerika* — if you will forgive my continuing presumption — all of your work is quite popular." Arthur hoped that the news would provide some consolation. "Now your novels would probably best be described as cult classics."

"How do you presume to know about my father?" K firmly persisted.

Arthur hesitated. He looked up and noticed several people nearby obviously following their conversation. K followed his gaze to discover the same. "I think I'm going to get a little fresh air," Arthur said. He rose and walked out of the front door.

K was at his shoulder a moment later. "Am I expected to give chase?"

"Every word that could be found was published," said Arthur, "your novels, your stories, your notebooks, dairies and the long letter you wrote to your father."

K was so stunned that he stood looking wildly around. For what, he did not know. "Do you know anything about comas?" he asked at last.

"What?"

"Nothing," K replied. "What can it matter? It must have killed my father to have it made public."

"I'm pretty sure he was already long dead. The letter did not come out until many years later. I can look it up."

K stared toward the little decorative bird feeder on the other side of the lawn. Arthur thought that his mind was elsewhere but soon noticed that he was intently watching something. The small figure of a female hummingbird hovered and flitted before plastic blossoms filled with sugar water.

K stood rapt. "Your Lori tells me they are called 'hummingbirds'." He seemed about to weep with joy. "I have no idea whether or not I am in a coma or have died and somehow inexplicably arrived at... Heaven." The two of them stood marveling, all other thoughts were momentarily forgotten.

After quite some time Arthur felt he must break the spell. "I'm sure you can come back and visit often, if you wish."

K shook his head slightly in order to clear it. "Am I going somewhere?"

"Jeremiah has asked me to give you my spare room long enough for you to find a job and pay for your own place." Arthur felt it was important to provide the entire plan, to point out that it would be necessary to get a place of his own, somehow, as soon as possible.

"I have been a burden."

"No. Not at all. But they have children living here and the blood tests they took at the Roach Motel were inconclusive regarding your tuberculosis."

"Do you not fear that you will catch it?"

"They say you're not contagious for the present. You will need to find a way to get your own place, though." There was more, of course, and after a moment more looking towards the hummingbird, Arthur added: "I am a very private person. And the apartment is not large."

"Why have you and your small apartment been chosen?"

"Oh, I always am chosen for these kinds of things. Also, I have a great many books and know who Franz Kafka is. I am afraid you will find the apartment unconventional."

"Unconventional?"

"Yes, cluttered with equipment and books. If you want a spotless bathroom, you will have to budget time each day in order to clean it. It's a low rent affair. No amount of effort will make it sparkle. You can borrow any of my books you wish, though, as long as you return them before you move to your own place."

"I am not in the habit of cleaning bathrooms."

"Well, that makes two of us. But, if I'm not mistaken, you *are* in the habit of *having* a clean bathroom."

"Will I be staying on a bookshelf in your small, cluttered apartment?"

"Jeremiah and his friends will have to make arrangements for moving the things out of my spare room and a bit of furniture in. I have no television but I am sure you can easily convince him to find one somewhere for you. It will sooth his conscience. In fact, his conscience is likely to be especially tender. I would ask him for whatever your sense of the possible suggests. They're doing alright."

"If I have lost anything since my arrival at the Roach Motel, it is my 'sense of the possible'." They both gently laughed.

"Trust your intuition. I have a feeling it is still a good guide."

"What is 'doing alright'?"

"Not important. Just keep the fact that I said it under your hat."

"Do people still say 'under your hat'? I can only be surprised that the saying survives given the fact that no one wears a hat here."

"It is only used anymore by people who live in apartments filled with books."

On the way back to the apartment Arthur and Jeremiah worked out the general outlines of the move. Jeremiah and his friends would arrive as soon as he could arrange it. He would call to set up a time. The items stored in the spare room would be placed in his garage. Everything would be taken care of as Arthur directed. His daily routine was to be impacted as little as possible. It would be appreciated if he could let Jeremiah know of any special preparation that might be necessary before the group would arrive.

With any luck, the crew would be big enough that they could set up the bed and other furniture the same day. While the back room received limited sun, it would otherwise be functionally furnished and comfortable. Franz's travel trunk was designed to serve as his armoire. The ladies would bring linens and a week of prepared food that needed only to be microwaved. A small refrigerator would be part of the bedroom furniture in which would be placed the meals and associated items. Franz would be consulted about his needs. Jeremiah or Lori would visit weekly, at least, to replenish the prepared meals and to collect the soiled clothes and linens for Lori to launder.

For the duration of Franz's visit, Arthur's laundry would also be collected and done by way of thanks. Arthur fully expected a few other such spontaneous acts of thanks but that all would take care of itself in time. For the moment, he spoke only of the matter at hand.

Chapter 4

K arrived in the parking lot, a couple of days later, on the back of Jeremiah's Harley. In spite of the fact that it was an unusually cool early October afternoon, Jeremiah was wearing a leather riding-vest. His heavily muscled, tattooed arms, and fingerless leather gloves made a striking contrast with his stick-thin passenger in a suit and tie.

K dismounted and removed his goggles, settled his fedora on his head and turned slowly, where he stood, to take in his new neighborhood. On the way there he had passed many small storefronts all with colorful signs but otherwise nondescript cinderblock buildings. There had also been some longer buildings housing several nondescript units in a row. The bigger units featured large picture windows many of which stared blankly altogether empty of attendants or wares. Each building had a motorcar or two in a small parking lot in front.

Behind these concrete shops were streets with single detached houses much like Jeremiah and Lori's. Much bigger than cottages and smaller than villas such houses were rare in Germany and Bohemia and K was impressed with the general wealth they suggested. Here they occupied small lots on both sides of long streets apparently designed to serve no other function than to provide access.

Now, as he looked around, he was unsure what he was seeing. The large stone church across the street was familiar enough and something of a comfort. The rows of doors, everywhere he looked, vaguely suggested the old Prague ghetto but somehow with more space and decidedly less character. In another direction there were the remains of single houses such as he saw a mere block away. Some were simply boarded up behind lawns overgrown with weeds. Most appeared to be inhabited though poorly maintained.

It was not all entirely new to him. In some ways it merely confirmed what he had seen on those few excursions he had made, together with Jeremiah and Lori, to the church and the Main Street Station. He wished that he had found himself in the neighborhood of the station. It was a place he understood more or less. The pieces did not fit here in any way he was familiar with.

Once inside he was shown to his room. It was small but promised to be comfortable. His travel trunk first caught his eye, in the far corner. Next his gaze fell upon a modest second-hand flat-screen television on top of a second-hand dresser. While he was pleased to have a place at all, the details were more promising than he had expected. Once he had opened the refrigerator and travel trunk, to learn what was inside of them, Arthur walked him back toward the front entrance stopping in each room to point out its features and the simple rules he hoped K would find agreeable. While Arthur stressed from almost the first word that privacy was his essential need, K was positively encouraged, with the next word, to ask any question he had at any time.

Jeremiah began restlessly to tug at the wrists of his gloves. He had fulfilled his responsibilities and wished to ride for a while more before he returned to the home life he had known before rescuing his guest. When exactly he left, K did not know. At some point the man and the Harley simply were gone. He hadn't even heard the roar of the motor starting (a thing that seemed quite unlikely). The next chapter of life had begun.

Arthur noticed his new roommate's consternation at discovering he was stranded. "It seems your boat has left without you, Hunter Gracchus."

K stared at his new host like a deer in the headlights of a car too close to be avoided. To follow that, he blinked furiously, each flutter representing an attempt to determine how to account for the remark he had just heard. "What could you possibly know about 'The Hunter Gracchus'? Surely Max did not finish *that*, too."

"It's much more popular, actually, for being unfinished. It gives it a greater mystery: a man sailing from shore to shore unable to complete his voyage to Death. It is just the kind of tale that is more intriguing for being left a fragment. A friend of mine once wrote an essay on it. The essay is on that shelf down there, if you're interested."

The reply was so matter-of-fact that it gave K time to recover somewhat from his shock. Then came the next jolt. "Shall I call you 'Gracchus'? It is the Latin equivalent of 'Kafka,' after all. You could call me 'Arthurus'."

Was he Gracchus, doomed to travel in the realm of the undead perhaps for eternity? Was this Richmond, in this 2015, just the first of many such stops? Could such a thing be possible? Had he written his own fate? Sentenced himself to his own penalty? It was too cruel to think so... and too fascinating. He would love to have thought to write a story about it. "I would prefer not," he replied.

As the supper hour approached, K walked along the bookshelves at every hand trying to make out titles and the miscellaneous stored items. The rooms were like a maze of mining tunnels. The limited light that could find its way among the stacks required that he adopt various strategies in order to make out the printing on the spines. Surprisingly, many of the titles and subjects were familiar. He would not have been surprised to find the books on friends' shelves in Prague. Others referred to events of which he was unaware some with reference in their titles to dates long after his nap on the way to Matliary.

Eventually Arthur realized what his guest was doing and extended a long orange chord, from somewhere out of sight, to an electric light attached to one of the bookcases. With a flick of a switch, the light-level increased considerably. "Along these walls is history: from ancient here to modern at the other end." He gathered up some cushions and bedding where they lay between shelves and tossed them into a large walk-in closet.

"Will you be sleeping there?" queried K, nodding toward the spot the cushions had occupied until just then.

"Yes."

"Have I Taken your bed from you? Was there not another to be had? And your bedroom? Have I taken it as well? Somehow I understood that I was merely being moved into a spare room."

"I slept here before you arrived," Arthur explained.

"On the floor?" asked K, incredulously. "Between bookcases?"

"Yes."

"What occupied the spare room before I arrived?"

"Books and tools." Arthur pulled back the sliding doors of the walk-in closet. Where he made a sweeping gesture with his hand, There rose a clutter of metal boxes and satchels from out of which poked wrenches, screw drivers and the like. Articles of clothing on hangers were draped over them here and there. K blanched slightly at the sight.

"I understood that you had moved the contents of the spare room into Jeremiah's garage."

"What wouldn't fit here in the apartment, yes."

"Couldn't more have been stored? Couldn't you have made accommodation for a bed?"

"I always sleep on the floor. This section is sociology. This one is psychology and this philosophy and the last religion and anthropology." Next he walked into the philosophy tunnel, gesturing for K to follow. Midway through, he gestured to a particular shelf. "You will find the Kierkegaard here."

An involuntary laugh escaped K. "How could you possibly know that I read Kierkegaard?"

"Every word that can be found by and about you has been published and translated into many languages." It was so unbelievable that K could not think of a reply. Not sure that he could find his way back through the maze of bookshelves, he selected a volume and deposited it in his room for reading after they had eaten. When he returned to the philosophy tunnel, Arthur was no longer there.

As K brought the plastic container with his evening meal to the kitchen, he caught a glimpse of Arthur through yet more bookshelves. The perspective made his host seem far in the distance like something viewed through the wrong end of a telescope. In fact he was only a few meters away.

As K entered the 'kitchenette' (the name by which Arthur had introduced it) he was carefully reading the directions taped to the top of the container. When he looked up he could not help but stare. There were dirty dishes in the sink. Some of them apparently had been there for a considerable time. The stove was mottled with spills, the microwave hardly less. In fine, all of the space was covered with a layer of what he could only describe as 'filth'. He was soon beside Arthur, jaw clenched and a white ceramic plate in hand. "Is it appropriate to microwave my meal on this plate?" he asked.

"The plastic container should be microwave safe."

"You have only a few dishes in your cupboards and no dishwasher. What will we do when we have used all of the dishes?"

"We will have to wash our dishes at the end of each day," Arthur replied, without looking up from the screen from behind which he spoke. "Um…"

The *um* seemed to suggest that something more might be about to be said. K waited until he wondered whether he might be mistaken. Unsure what to do, he began inspecting the machinery that surrounded his host. He could not imagine what any of it did or how. Then it came again: an "Um…" followed by still more waiting. K moved absently toward the sound.

Arthur typed a few last characters, as evidenced by a flourish of his hand, like a pianist finishing a musical passage, and peered deeply into the screen. At least it appeared to be a species of typing. "I don't have a dishwasher. It's sort of a Survivalist thing."

Arthur had still not looked up from the screen and therefore could not see the quizzical look on K's face who hadn't the least idea what to make of the phrase 'Survivalist thing'. "I wash my dishes by hand. Let me know when you're done and I'll show you the drill."

"You wash the dishes with a hand drill?" Now K, as well, was hardly paying attention to the conversation. He was discreetly trying to peek at the screen which so absorbed his host. He was much too timid to press the matter.

"No," Arthur replied while typing gingerly and looking even more intently at the screen. K drew back as if he'd received a shock. It was a moment before he realized that the 'no' had been in reply to a question. He was only half aware that he'd even asked one much less what he'd asked.

"My magic wand will not work here," K went on. After what threatened to be an interminable length of time Arthur realized that something more had been said. K could sense that he was already having his doubts about the new arrangement.

"I'm sorry. What?"

"I've tried to operate the... *television*... with the magic wand but I cannot access it." Jeremiah and Lori had found it so amusing that K called the remote a 'magic wand' that they had positively avoided correcting him.

"I don't have cable."

"Cable?"

"Yes,..." Suddenly, Arthur stopped, looked up and himself looked quizzical. "You do know what wireless is, don't you?"

"It is used to communicate with ships at sea."

"It has come a long way since your day. The television is actually not a magic screen. It receives wireless signals coded to create the pictures and sound you see and hear. It's a lot like moving pictures were in your day except now there is color. Instantaneous transmission allows you to see the scenes directly rather than wait for them to be processed onto film and shipped to a theater. Jeremiah gets his signals from a company which sells him an insane number of channels for an even more insane price. It's called 'cable'."

"Yes. In my day... It is quite different in my day. If it is wireless, why is it called 'cable'."

"In ancient times — maybe 20 years ago — the signal was sent through a cable so people who hadn't paid for the service couldn't get the signals for free. They had to be connected to the company's transmission cable. In some places it is still delivered that way — through cables."

"Why can't you get the signals for free if it is wireless now?"

"A cable signal is transmitted in code now. The code can only be turned into usable signal by leasing the company's decoder box. Such things are much too expensive for me. I don't buy television signals through distribution cables. I get my channels over the air, through an antenna." K stood looking every bit as confused as before the explanation. Distribution cables? Over the air? But hadn't Arthur said...?

"I'll run a coax to your room and hook you up to the antenna tomorrow. You will only be able to get a dozen or so channels, but, for my money, even that many is too many for anyone's good. Kierkegaard is a far better use of time."

K was quite surprised at the sharpness of the pang he felt over the prospect of going for an evening without the magic screen. His distress left him thoughtful. Only a few weeks before, he felt no loss over not having that which he could not have imagined. Now, it felt like a crucial part of his life. It was not a pleasant feeling and he promised himself to watch a good deal less in the future.

Still, he could not help but sidle up beside Arthur in order to see what was on the screen in front of him. His host somehow transferred back and forth between a great many channels at a dizzying rate. The coordinated movements involved were not unlike those of the loom operators the Insurance Institute sometimes sent K to observe. Both were nimble and composed, a secret skill that visibly empowered the operator with a confidence that went beyond the task at hand.

Occasionally, K felt it not inappropriate to ask a brief question. During a half-hour, he learned that the object Arthur guided along the surface of his desk was called a 'mouse'. The arrow it choreographed on the screen was called a 'cursor'.

K wasn't sure he approved of this mouse. It reminded him of the Dadaists and their excesses against which he quietly warned anyone who would listen. In the wake of the Great War people hardly needed to add more craziness. They needed artists like Capek. The best new work encouraged order and healing. Perhaps order was struggling after so great a shock but it was very much to be regretted that it was being pushed out of the public view by Dada's soulless, irrational patter and clattering disarray. It was time to rebuild, to heal; not to fling the matter of daily life every which way. The world had had far too much of that already.

The screen was 'not a television exactly'. It was called a 'monitor'. The little screens at Jeremiah and Lori's house were not tiny televisions but rather tiny 'computers'. The channels were not called 'channels' but 'tabs' like the indexing tabs on the folders in the filing cabinets at the Insurance Institute. In fact they were intended to represent files in just such a cabinet. Somehow, at the same time, however, tabs appeared in 'windows' once they were retrieved from the cabinet. The mouse, however, was not originally intended to be a representation of a mouse. It just happened to have a vaguely similar profile. K said nothing about Dada.

"Do you receive your Internet… over the air?"

"No. Very powerful companies prevent it so they can charge a lot of money for it. It is pretty much impossible to flourish nowadays without the Internet. There is no choice but to pay."

"So they code all of the signals."

"Mostly they bribe the government to prevent laws like those that apply to the magic screen."

"So then, in America the wealthy still do entirely as they wish." K had never been to America but it was a regular topic of conversation in the Prague Cafés. He attended them often when he was young and it would have been unhealthy always to stay at home or to look to the synagogue for his social needs. He was a writer, however misbegotten, and the café was now his synagogue. His struggles with the social situations that he met there were his studies of another mysterious Torah of sorts.

But now he felt much older. He was trying to learn Hebrew but he was making little progress.

"America is nothing like you portrayed it in your novel of the name, I'm afraid. It wasn't in 1920 either. I can still hardly believe that you wrote it."

"I assume you refer to my notes for the American novel *The Man Who Disappeared*. I can hardly believe I ever finished it much less that it was published and is still read. I instructed Max to destroy all of my papers."

"You *didn't* finish it."

"How, then, was this *Amerika* published?"

"You seemed ambivalent. Max finished it as best he could from what you left behind."

"Have you ever *not* been ambivalent, Arthur? I shudder to think of people who are not ambivalent."

K received a wry smile by way of reply. At least he thought the smile was a reply. But this Arthur so often proved to be thinking of something unrelated.

As the conversation continued in short bursts, K managed to insinuate himself over Arthur's right shoulder in order to observe the computer screen. Arthur 'clicked' on Xs and folders vanished. This clicking actually made a tiny clicking sound. He clicked a folder tab and turned slightly toward K.

"This is the Google Search engine site," he said. It wasn't at all like the magic screen. It seemed to be a list written in typeface of every color and interspersed with tiny color photographs. "You type in the information you are looking for in the space here," he went on. "Just a few representative words most closely related to the topic or object or person. Here. I'll type in 'Leonardo Da Vinci'." Pictures of Da Vinci appeared. But mostly the screen was a grand confusion of text that K could not begin to understand. A half-hour later, he still stood beside his host, white plate in hand, his head swimming with directions about 'search listings' and 'rankings' and 'pages'. Photographs, writings, biographies: this world of computers ('Internet' as people called it) seemed filled with nothing but Da Vinci. Next it seemed filled with nothing but Dostoyevsky, Kierkegaard, Pascal, and Dickens, as K called-out their names at just above an astonished whisper. Even Max and the Capek brothers had a few pages of listings. Among the photographs of Max, there magically on the screen, were several together with K. He lingered almost unnoticeably before them, for the merest instant, at the same time urging Arthur on to the next lesson (for all of this was a grand, fascinating lesson). Much to his disappointment, the search results for Dada suggested that it was more popular than ever. But then that was hardly surprising given all he had seen in this Richmond.

When K suspected that Arthur was in the process of entering the name 'Franz Kafka' into the search engine, he looked only at the white dish in his hand. "It is late. I must put my meal in the microwave." He quickly walked to the kitchenette and busied himself with the preparation.

K looked out of the smallish window in his room as he slowly ate, chewing each mouthful exactly 50 times. It looked out upon a walkway high with grass, defined by the back wall of the apartment and a chain-link fence some two meters further on. Behind the fence was a lot for parking motorcars and another apartment building almost identical to the one he now occupied. Perhaps there were 20 apartments. A number of chairs were scattered, one or two each in front of several of the doors. They were clearly made of the hardened rubber material people in this Richmond called plastic. Plastic was everywhere and itself a kind of a miracle. The magical screens were all largely made from one kind of plastic. Some chairs were made from another kind, motorcycle seats from another (but never, Jeremiah had informed him, *Harley* seats). Most storage bins were made of it. All of it was light enough to pick up easily with one hand, and, he had been informed, cost much less than wood or metal. Left in the rain, it did not warp or rust.

In fact plastic broke more easily than most other materials but it did not decay at all. Lori was very concerned about all of the plastic piling up in the world. She had informed him that there were giant piles of cast-off plastic, everywhere throughout the world, that would never decay. But still she used many items made of plastic, of every description. Still, plastic chairs were scattered in her yard and in front of the apartment doors.

After his meal he did not feel quite ready to return his utensils to the kitchenette. He set them on top of the refrigerator and sat on the bed reading from Kierkegaard's *Either/Or*. He had read it many times already but it felt comforting to have it available in a place in which so little was familiar.

After perhaps an hour he grew anxious about the unwashed utensils on the top of the refrigerator. He marked his place in the book with a stray piece of paper and carefully opened his travel trunk. Inside, among a great many items, he considered a pile of silk loincloths. These he set aside, and, placing his suit carefully on various hangers, he lifted a red union suit for inspection. It seemed the best choice and he donned it carefully settling it in place. Next he lifted the dishes. In the kitchenette he found what were apparently Arthur's dirty dishes on the counter. Setting his own in the small remaining clear space he returned somewhat sheepishly to the computer station.

Arthur was reading from a book. Around him was playing a piano concerto that K recognized as Mozart. He stood a moment transfixed. Jeremiah and Lori had also played music on rare occasion, mostly on a machine of some sort in their motorcars. They called it "classical rock". It certainly wasn't Mozart. The present music seemed to issue from the computer. It gently filled the room.

All at once, this grubby apartment #16, filled to bursting, floors poorly swept, and apparently lacking that other miracle called 'air conditioning' (which K so appreciated at Jeremiah's house), seemed a remarkable place. He could not help but linger thoughtless of his errand. The longer he stood there the more he realized that there was something more but he couldn't quite put his finger on it. Then it came to him. He smelled beer. Arthur was drinking out of a soda can as he read. (K suspected it must properly be called a 'beer can' in such an instance.) He was at ease for the first time since K had met him.

Still, there was nothing to be done about it. "We must do the dishes," K said with what seemed, the moment the words were out of his mouth, perhaps just a little too much firmness.

Arthur took a deep breath. He did not look up. "We'll do them tomorrow," he said.

"If you show me *the drill*," said K, with a look of disbelief, "I will be pleased to do them now."

"I am settled in for the night."

"Surely," said K, as if speaking with someone who perhaps had left an armed explosive device in the kitchenette, "it will only take a minute to show me *the drill*. I will be pleased to do the task myself once I know how." Actually, he was less pleased than he suggested. He had never found himself doing dishes at Jeremiah and Lori's and certainly not at home in Prague. Lori had asked him to load a few dishes into the mechanical dishwasher once and the request was never made again. He had felt sorry that his attempt had apparently caused her considerable psychological trauma.

Arthur looked up from his book in order to click the computer mouse several times and vaguely scan the screen. With that he returned to his book. K's new home was clearly fraught with unseen dangers. His eyes were lowered in consternation and confusion. He could not help but notice the careless state of the floor. His host had no concern whatsoever for hygiene, it was clear.

He turned and entered the kitchenette. The countertop was textured with crumbs of varying age. The working of the water faucet promised to be simple enough. Presumably the sink must be filled. The dishes were beyond a rigorous rinsing. They could not properly be cleaned without a supply of standing water. Suddenly K violently flinched and stood listening with great intensity. Had he heard scratching inside the wall?

After long tense minutes he balled up a plastic bag and tried to plug the sink drain. It was quite obvious that the strategy was a poor one at best. He picked up a slimy strainer basket with two fingers as if inspecting a plague rat. This he settled in an obscure corner as far away from the sink as possible, struggling to suppress a wave of nausea. The situation was impossible but he would not sleep a wink if the kitchenette remained in this condition only a matter of meters away from his bedroom.

For a moment he felt that sanity had prevailed. Arthur entered. K looked at him imploringly as a sinner peering into the gaping jaws of hell. His host took up another small metal basket — this one with a rubber plug on the bottom — and settled it in the drain. He did not betray the slightest expression as he did so. Once the basket was in place he opened a bottle of some sort of yellow chemical and squeezed out a portion into the sink. With that he opened the refrigerator door and extracted another can of beer and was gone again along with all hope.

K gingerly tested the yellow chemical with his finger. He had entered yet another strange world — more disconcerting even than the Roach Motel — and he no longer knew what to expect. He was soon satisfied that the liquid was a soap of some sort, harmless. The glint of light off of the yellow liquid called back his attention. The Kafka family cook would have been gladdened in her kitchen without plasticware or mechanical dishwashers, he reflected, had this glowing yellow color alone welcomed her each time it came into view. He imagined her breaking spontaneously into a little song from time to time sung very quietly with the hint of a smile. Then the scent of lemon began to reach him.

Soon the sink was filled with water and suds. The garbage can was industrially large. He had no difficulty figuring out where to scrape off the residual food from the dirty plates and a bowl which seemed to have been dirtied during some earlier geological age.

Once the dishes were settled in the sink and the first item washed, thoroughly inspected and washed again, K stood frozen with the item (a fork) poised to deposit it he could only guess where. A brown plastic contraption to his immediate left first suggested itself but surely it could not be a place to settle dishes so that they could dry. What appeared to be a plastic drain board, directing fallen water back into the sink, was caked with a thin composite of substances only to be guessed. The small compartments in which one might have surmised the flatware would properly go were even worse.

The plastic contraption must be thoroughly washed first. K removed the dishes from the sink, placing them at as safe a distance from contagion as could be managed. That done, he explored the plastic drainer until he had managed to dismantle it into pieces and to fill the sink with them. The scrubbing of the drainer alone took quite a long time. Inspecting the results he drooped with disappointment and repeated the process with a new squirt of yellow soap, then another and another and then a new sink of scalding hot water. Or at least the stream of water began hot. A moment later it was lukewarm at best.

Two hours later (and two appearances of Arthur to get another beer turn and leave), a dish drainer that was worrisome in spite of all efforts was filled with dishes that simply would not gleam. The festive yellow bottle of soap was empty. Otherwise K might still be washing and rewashing. Between the exhausting emotional effort and the fact that he had managed what cleanliness was possible, K felt he would be able to sleep.

As he exited the kitchenette he found himself in a completely dark apartment. The computer screen was dark. A few tiny lights remained lit around it. They gave the front room an unsettling look. He could not form the least guess as to what they might represent. He stopped frequently as he attempted to feel his way toward his bedroom, straining to be sure that he had not interrupted the steady breathing coming from the other end of the bookcases. It was hard going but he eventually closed the door of the bedroom ever so gingerly behind himself and managed to find the light switch. He peeled off his union suit, folded it and settled a night shirt over his head, breathing a sigh of relief as he did so.

As K sat on his bed, he stared blankly past the copy of Kierkegaard's *Either/Or* he held in his hand. He tried to review all that had happened to him during the day. Every day was so utterly new that he found it difficult to feel confident of his observations.

People were somehow the same as always and completely different. As vitally important as it all was, however, he could barely keep his eyes open.

Strangely, since he had been in this Richmond he had not once suffered a night of insomnia. As he prepared for sleep each night he almost felt his new situation a precious gift. To be free of that curse for weeks on end was no small matter. At the end of each day he was so exhausted that there could be no doubt whatsoever that he would sleep from the moment his head touched the pillow.

He dreamed always of Prague. But how could he dream? The only explanation that seemed to make the least sense (and it not much) was that he was in a coma. Did people dream in comas? How did they conjure magic screens and computers? What else would he conjure tomorrow? Had Arthur been angry? If he had to leave, where else could he possibly go?

At least the dishes were clean. K put aside the book and lay back on his pillow.

Chapter 5

Arthur slowly woke to the sound of a persistent fluttering. It must have been going on for some time for his last dream before waking was about a white bird trying to escape the apartment. It was the source of a mysterious bright light. He struggled to keep his eyes closed, to remain in that better world. But somehow they were open and he gradually began to see the real world around him. The pale quality of the sunlight making its way through the blinds suggested that it was about 7:30. He stretched fully awake and a look toward the clock verified his estimate. He had overslept. But then yesterday had been an unusually trying day.

While the bird was gone, however, the fluttering was not. Slowly the sound came into focus.

K was perched on one foot vigorously swinging the other when Arthur, eyes red and hair sticking out from his head in random directions, the color of his shorts and tee-shirt random, and never having learned the meaning of the word 'ironing,' eased open the door. K was naked but for a black loincloth. His hair was perfectly groomed. His thin hairless chest glistened with tiny beads of sweat.

"Join me," he called out, flushed with his effort. "It's called the Müller Regimen. Highly recommended by all the best experts."

Arthur straightened to his full height, poised carefully on one leg and let out a highly musical fart. With that he turned and proceeded to the kitchenette where he filled a bowl with heavily sugared, imitation fruit flavored cereal. Next he extracted a large white plastic jug from the refrigerator, removed the top, sniffed the contents, screwed up his face and smelled it again. With a shrug of the shoulders, he doused the cereal with its contents. Breakfast was served.

K continued his morning exercise routine however much the joy had gone out of it. He could not help but reflect that what had promised, at first, to be a solution to a daunting problem, now was itself every bit as much a problem. How could this be the same person he had met at the party at Jeremiah's house? How could he be the only person that he had met, since arriving in this Richmond, who had read the books he was so painstakingly writing? Or was even the supposed existence of the books somehow another crude joke about which he would find himself deeply disappointed in the end?

After his exercises he donned his suit and once again settled his hair perfectly in place. The hair required several attempts before it was satisfactory. Following this, he chose to stay in his bedroom until he felt more up to what he might find outside of it. He was absently perusing a collection of the letters of Kierkegaard when a knock came at the door. He hesitated, looked toward the door, conflicted. There was nothing to do for it. He must call for his host to enter.

Arthur entered pulling a white cable behind him. He attached it to the back of the television on top of the dresser and directed K to try casting with the magic wand. Instantly the television was on. "Press '6'," he ordered. Nothing changed. "Now press the 'up' arrow." With that the screen was bright with activity.

It took some time for Arthur to explain how to make the magic wand work without cable. He disappeared for a time and returned with a piece of paper restating in writing the instructions he had given and the numbers of the available channels. Why his host was taking such pains on his behalf he could not begin to understand. It could not be reconciled with his inexcusable behavior of the morning or of the night before. For now he would assume the best of him and be always prepared to be shocked and even offended without warning. The prospect of the shocks was not at all a happy one. It was sure to linger constantly in his thoughts. Hopefully, time would clarify matters.

K sought some further comfort from watching the television, Kierkegaard beside him on the bed. Around midday a forceful knock came at the door. He called for Arthur to enter. "What is this?" the man cried as he entered. He was holding up the empty bottle of yellow soap from the kitchenette. "There was almost a full bottle, yesterday! I can't be replacing this stuff every day! It should last weeks!"

K sat frozen. It most assuredly did not seem the moment to confront Arthur with the implications of his completely unacceptable behavior of the night before. It happened at that moment that a vignette came on the television about the world's best dishwashing liquid. An impossibly peppy young woman was holding up a yellow bottle and beaming an impossible television smile. If K was unsure of what to do when Arthur had objected, he was beyond unsure now. What could this mean? Could Arthur be taunting him? Trying to make even the magic screen a fraught experience? His head swam with the implications. His strongest impulse was to flee and it took all of his courage not to bolt past the figure in the doorway. But where would he go once he was past the immediate source of anxiety?

In Prague, he wouldn't show the slightest hesitation to quietly order Arthur to leave and never return. His behavior was abominable, after all. Or, should the apartment be Arthur's, even then, he would turn on his heel without a word and leave with a perfect determination never to mention the man again. Except perhaps to his sister Ottla as an object lesson after which she would have a few choice words to say.

"I've set out my last bottle. It is made to use a squirt or two at a time." With that Arthur turned and left. The door gaped open where he had stood.

K quickly rose and shut it. It was all too much. He cast about for ideas but nothing came to mind. For the first time since he had arrived at wherever exactly he was, he felt utterly lost. The apartment was a place of hugely erratic mood swings. The bedroom was only the most imperfect shelter from it and he could not possibly spend all of his time there.

By the time a knock came at the door again, K had already decided that he must do as he always did. He must act no differently than he would have if he and Arthur had been getting along well. In this way he might buy the time necessary to better understand the situation.

People could not have entirely changed even in 95 years. Jeremiah and Lori, for instance, had seemed quite normal. For all that they were very different from most people he had ever known, they were not so different as the Italians he'd met during his travels in that country.   He did not for a second think that they were different in the sense of being eccentric to their own place or time. They moved easily among their fellow denizens. They were at ease at home, so much so, and so naturally, that it was undoubtedly an introduction to how all in this Richmond lived. He was slightly pathetic and they had taken care not to startle him. He was careful not to stare, asked no question that might be interpreted to his disadvantage, and the standard emotional bargain was struck even more easily than it would have been as an extended houseguest in Prague.

But here things were different. Not only compared to the Prague he once had so carefully observed, at some little distance, in order to pass as quite normal, but different even from the commonality of the world in which he now found himself. Surely few people resided in libraries even now. Thinking back over the past several weeks the time had passed as if libraries might no longer exist.   Here it seemed that dishwashing machines and air conditioning didn't exist. Even television only barely existed. It had been clear without commentary that these things defined normalcy, were expected, taken for granted.   The mobile telephones that Jeremiah and Lori and each of their children kept beside them at all times were an astonishing development from the big clunky telephones in the office and the better Prague homes.   But they bespoke not so much a radical change in social relations as a predictable development of the *homo telephonicus* that he could not help but notice had begun to make its appearance even during his own time.

For all of his own peculiarities — and K was only too well aware there were a great many — his new situation promised to be even more impossible due to Arthur's.   At least that was his experience so far. However ironic, on the face of it, it could not be denied.

A knock came again at the door, this time with more firmness. K lifted the volume of Kierkegaard from where it had lain unheeded all morning and called out "Do come in." As the door opened he sat on the bed, the book open in his lap, finger poised at a passage. An attentive look greeted his visitor.

Arthur was gazing thoughtfully toward the floor when he entered. He looked up as if he had only just realized he was standing just inside the bedroom. "I'm going out for a walk. Would you like to go along? It's a good idea for you to get to know the neighborhood."

K always loved walking in Prague — especially prior to his tuberculosis — and the thought was appealing. He could not help but wonder whether his struggles in that way might have disappeared together with his cough. That he had barely coughed and had not brought up so much as a single spot of blood since he had arrived in this Richmond was yet another of the surprising number of unexpected blessings that had come along with his new circumstances. He asked for a few minutes in order to prepare and emerged into the front room, shoes on feet and suit jacket and fedora added to his leisure ensemble.

At first the two walked silently side by side. It was a dance of sorts and Arthur led via nods and extending his hand to apply gentle pressures. K took in all around him: the looming gray stone church next door to the apartment, its large parking lot vacant except for two motorcars, the small unadorned park just beyond the church, the great many trees lining the roads and the occasional groups of fleshy women rapidly walking in march-step. As they approached a larger thoroughfare, he noticed the signs and lights at the nearby intersection. Knots of motorcars somehow arrived at the crossroads together. They stopped and waited as one. When the light poised above the traffic turned green, they accelerated as one. It was quite impressive. When he lagged behind in an attempt to understand the mechanics of it better, Arthur kindly slowed his pace as well and observed K with every bit as much interest.

Soon K noticed a small number of persons at various locations around the intersection holding signs. One sat in a wheelchair, disheveled, unshaven. His sign read "Iraq Vet, Please Help". He looked thoroughly downcast. A couple on the side of the street nearest held a sign reading "Stranded Need Bus Fare". Across the street, partially hidden behind low hedges bordering a gas station lot, a man held his sign under his arm and swiped his finger across the screen of a Smartphone. From time to time he peered intently apparently having come upon an item of particular interest.

The man in the wheelchair wheeled down the center mall, moving away from the traffic signal, holding out a small can toward the driver-side window of each car in the left-most lane. One window opened and a hand placed something in the can. The man in the wheelchair nodded his head, and, proceeding to the next car, held out the can. When the light turned green, he returned to his position beside the traffic signal and made ready for the next queue of motorcars that would form behind the next red light. While he had a moment, he unwrapped and ate a small frosted cake. He threw the wrapper on the street and lifted a beverage can from a makeshift holder on the arm of his chair. Just as he settled the can back in the holder, the light turned red and the first driver came to a stop to see the can held up outside of the window.

K seemed to find the intersection overwhelming and Arthur thought it best to urge him toward the crosswalk by gently taking his arm. There would be time to understand the whole picture during the walks to come.

What is 'Iraq Vet'?" asked K as they waited for the light to turn.

"Are you familiar with the country 'Iraq'?" K shook his head 'No'. "It had only just come into existence as you boarded the train to Matliary. That's a big part of the problem."

"Problem?"

"Not important at the moment." The light changed and Arthur once again gently urged K to cross the street. K resisted his partner's lead this time. He imagined fearful possibilities with so many vehicles careening past. "There is no danger," Arthur said, in an attempt to comfort him. "Time is allotted for pedestrians to cross while the light is red." He pointed to the "Walk" signal. "When that signal shows a little white man you can safely cross."

The two crossed when the signal next showed the little white man. Soon they were walking along a less frenetic, tree lined street. Along one side were individual homes and along the other large public buildings. There was only the occasional sign alongside the road to identify the public structures which sat well back in the midst of well-groomed multi-hectare lawns. The scene conformed quite nicely with the descriptions he'd heard of the vast country of America. He half expected to see a coal mine or a gleaming manufactory in the distance.

"That one's the Children's Hospital," Arthur volunteered. He pointed out several buildings as they walked along. "That's an administrative building of some sort. That one's a school."

K was happy to think that such buildings were well away from busy intersections in more genteel surroundings. With their bright red brick facades they almost looked inviting. The luxury of so much space, it seemed to him, spoke highly of the schools in this Richmond.

"I would like to have gone to school in such a place," said K. "In Prague there are no such spaces."

"The school here is a private school," Arthur replied. "We will pass the public schools on other walks. In the poorer neighborhoods there are no such spaces and no pressure-cleaned walls."

That his host foresaw future walks was of considerable comfort. The thought brought an ease to his gait. He wasn't sure how he felt about the fact that he and Arthur were the only two walkers in sight. He could see almost a quarter of a kilometer in either direction and the sidewalks were deserted. The yards of the homes were also deserted. If motorcars did not occasionally pass he might have imagined they were in a life-size diorama.

They turned right as they reached a large complex of buildings to their left with blue signs reading 'Veritas School' and another to their right declaring itself a 'Presbyterian Seminary'. The side of the street was lined, for an entire two blocks, with well-tended grounds and red brick structures suggesting a single entity. If the buildings had been of white brick rather than red, and the roads around it cobbled, K might have felt almost as if he were looking at the grounds of the Emmaus monastery near the center of Prague once more. Numerous white signs, further on, identified a 'Presbyterian' church of some sort. Arthur said the site was a 'Presbytery,' if he recalled the term aright. It did seem a little unusual that he did not see a single human being during the length of the entire complex, only two motorcars in a macadam lot. Even in the monastery there were generally people walking across the grounds.

"We'll be passing a lot of churches in our walks. They're pretty much everywhere."

K had made no mention of synagogues since arriving in this Richmond. He was in the habit of being circumspect about such matters. "Are there Lutheran churches?"

"I'm sure there are but I couldn't say where."

"The church beside your apartment?"

"Catholic."

"Do you attend?"

"No more than you attend synagogue."

"And are there synagogues in this Richmond?" The subject was a risky one and K regretted almost immediately that he had been so indiscrete as to ask the question. His throat constricted causing his prominent Adam's apple to bob. Arthur could see that he was anxious.

"A few."

"This complex is quite large and beautifully maintained. So is the Catholic church. Yet I see no activity at either."

"Churches are no longer the center of the neighborhood in which their members live. That has steadily changed since cars became commonplace. People travel to their churches. It has changed the experience as you have noticed."

"But they do have worshippers."

"On holy days churches can still be quite active. The weeks between not so much. At the Presbytery, here, I imagine the schools pay the freight. The Catholic church probably has large trust funds. Maybe it owns rental properties."

As they turned the corner to head back to the apartment they were back on a busy road once again motorcars of every description careening past with abandon. There were also people walking on the sidewalks. Generally, they seemed to congregate on benches alongside the road. As they passed one such bench, someone called out "Got a smoke?"

Arthur shook his head and said: "Sorry. Don't smoke."

"Got fifty cents? I'm short of bus fare."

K was becoming comfortable with the fact that nearly everyone in this Richmond seemed to wear t-shirts and the footwear called 'sneakers'. Even mendicants, he was quickly learning, dressed in the same fashion, although the beggars at intersections showed more wear and tear to their persons and clothing. He tried, while furiously absorbing every detail, to look like he was quite familiar with all that was happening before him.

Suddenly he had to steady himself from a whoosh of air followed a moment later by a gargantuan vehicle something like a railway passenger car bearing directly down upon the little knot of people. He cried out reflexively and quickly backed away to a considerable distance. It seemed utterly inexplicable that he was the only person to do so. Surely they would all be killed in a horrible accident.

The railway car came to a stop directly in front of the bench faster than could be imagined possible. All but Arthur climbed aboard and the metal beast lurched forward and was half a block away before K realized it. He staggered in place momentarily and tried valiantly to steady his feet under him again. Looking toward his distant friend, Arthur lowered his head in an attempt to hide a broad smile and turned to continue the walk.

"It's called a 'bus,'" he said as K caught up to walk beside him. "They are everywhere around town. They run along main roads so the poor can get to work and the market and such."

"We have the tram for that," said K. "But it is much smaller and moves at a much more civilized speed."

"Richmond used to have a trolley also, many years ago, much along the lines of your tram. Nowadays there are far too many passengers and they must get where they are going faster. The buses need no tracks so they can run everywhere."

"We have no markets like yours. Not in the least. Lori took me to one once. I've never seen so much food. She didn't know how it came to be there." Intent on the conversation, Arthur stumbled on a heaved-up slab of sidewalk that he had not noticed and cursed aloud.

"It is shipped in on trucks. Not like any you are likely to have seen in 1920. They are much bigger even than buses. Many of them, anyway." They stepped aside for an elderly woman to pass, a little girl holding her hand and squirming slightly. "They often come hundreds or thousands of miles."

"But how does it all arrive looking so fresh? I have never seen such vegetables."

"The trucks have refrigeration systems inside. And the food is treated with preservative chemicals."

"Even the trucks have refrigerators?" The surprises simply never ended. As K was reflecting upon this, they entered back into the parking lot of the apartment building. Arthur greeted a woman he addressed as 'Rhonda' and chatted briefly. Two young girls rode bicycles around the lot, the older calling out imperious instructions to the younger. In some ways people, it seemed, never changed. For a moment, K felt like he was in a familiar world.

"Why does food have no odor in Richmond?" K asked as they entered the apartment. It was a question that had occupied his thoughts on and off since he woke to find himself in the town.

"The fruits and vegetables in stores are bred to stay fresh as long as possible. They must travel a long distance before being put out on the shelves. It happens that the longer lasting the breed the less taste and odor it has. The preservatives, used to make them last even longer, mask what little taste they have left." Arthur turned on the power to his computer. "As for the rest of the food, it is highly processed, also to remain fresh, and the processing chemicals reduce the odor and the taste."

"Does no one miss food with savor?"

"People put some of the flavor back in with spices," Arthur replied, half paying attention, as he clicked and typed. "They've never known what food tasted like before it began to be manufactured. They would be offended if food arrived in their markets with the tastes and odors it had in your day. They would think it was somehow tainted." With that he raised his eyebrows meaningfully. "Often enough it was."

"Nothing is as bereft of its customary pleasure as eating here in Richmond. As it was, I took little enough pleasure in eating in Prague. I miss the aromas, nonetheless. There were always aromas of every description in the air. For all that is done to enhance pleasure of every kind here, there seems to be surprisingly little of it."

"It's not just Richmond. It's everywhere: everywhere in the civilized world."

"I've never been much of an eater anyway," K absently repeated. His thoughts were already elsewhere. "Why do you live among Negroes, Arthur?"

Arthur's head poked up like a deer that has heard a twig snap. "First of all, you need to lose the word 'Negro'. It has not been appropriate for many years now. This should be the last time I hear it or else you need to find somewhere else to live."

K stood blinking. All of the gains of the walk seemed to disappear in an instant. This characteristic of his host was not going to be mastered so easily as a single excursion, if it would be mastered at all. The prospect was a daunting one. He could not imagine what might be proper to reply so he stood silent.

"Blacks are called 'Blacks' or 'African Americans'. I'll ask you to use 'African-American'. With a suit and a fedora and a formal way about you, it's the only right choice. Agreed?"

K nodded his head forcefully 'Yes'.

"An even better choice is not to mention race at all, black or otherwise."

Again, K nodded 'Yes' with vigor.

"In *The Man Who Disappeared*, why did you have Karl refer to himself as a 'Negro'?"

K froze in place, not knowing what to do or answer. But the reference to his book was too much to resist, even in the face of such fearful possibilities. "Because he had sunk to be a common laborer of the lowest type. One hears of the... *African-American*... still slaving away for little benefit. Karl felt reduced to the same level."

"It seems you've answered your own questions."

"But don't the African-Americans here generally have motorcars? They must be quite expensive, being as fast and colorful as they are."

"So then, even in impoverished circumstances many people can afford cars nowadays. Matters have improved. But still they live squeezed together into impoverished neighborhoods, yes? Still many have only the buses to get to the market, yes?"

"And their public schools do not have great lawns or shining red brick walls."

Arthur was staring daggers into the computer screen. "You're getting it."

"But the people begging at the intersection, they were all…" K stood at a loss for how to continue. Words were unusually evasive. He offered a best guess. "Caucasian-American?"

"Crackers."

"Crackers?"

Arthur found his own joke so amusing that he could not help but chortle as his guest stood at a loss. "No, not Crackers. Definitely not Crackers. It's another word that you should strictly avoid. Just call white people 'White' or 'Whites'."

"They were all White."

"It a long story and I'm not sure myself that I know the answer. There are Black panhandlers at some intersections. We're not going to figure out all the world's problems in one walk. Or ever. Even if we could, no one would listen. It's best just to leave all that alone. A person is a person."

With that, Arthur beckoned for K to look over his shoulder at the computer screen once again. K hesitated, not knowing which version of Arthur was beckoning, but obeyed when the gesture was repeated with slightly more emphasis. There, on the screen, was a colorful map.

"This is Google Maps," said Arthur. "Here is the apartment, where we are now." He pointed the cursor at a small orange inverted teardrop of some sort. When he moved the cursor to the teardrop and clicked, a small block, presumably of information of some sort, appeared. Another click and the screen was filled with a picture taken from directly outside the window.

"So then," said Arthur, "go to a Google search page, click here on 'Maps' on the little bar at the top of the screen and enter any address in the little slot on the upper left. I've written down the address here, and the telephone number, and for Jeremiah and Lori's house for you to carry in your wallet."

"Wallet?" asked K, leaning down to inspect the screen.

Arthur reached inside K's jacket and pulled out his billfold.

"*Brieftasche*," K explained.

"Yes. Whatever. Place this slip of paper in your wallet. If you ever lose your way, you can tell people where you live." This time, K guarded against any optimism regarding how the arrangement might be working out.

"Tomorrow I will install my back-up computer in your room. You need to familiarize yourself with how Google Maps works. See. Here's the children's hospital." Again Arthur clicked on the teardrop and clicked to make a bright picture appear looking just as K had seen the hospital an hour ago. Two more clicks and he was back to the map. He entered in the address of the apartment and the name of the Children's Hospital and a bright red line connected the two locations by a circuitous route. "Watch where I click now," he commanded. With the click, a printed set of step-by-step directions came into view.

"Now you will be walking or taking the bus," said Arthur, as he handed K a small card. "Jeremiah and Lori have bought you a bus pass. It means that you can ride for the next month without paying a fare. Just step into the bus and ask the driver how to use the card. You'll get the hang of it in no time. When you want to know what bus to take and where to wait for it, you put in the address here and the address to which you are going. Next you click this little bus symbol. The directions that appear will tell you which buses to take and where to get on and off."

"I've entered in the destination of the old Beth Ahabah Synagogue, by way of an example." Arthur clicked the bus symbol and clicked for the printed directions. K read them over his shoulder, only half understanding what was meant. "I'll show you how to print the instructions onto paper, from your room, with my back-up equipment tomorrow. I'll also go with you on the bus for a test run, to make sure that you understand the basics of all this. Ahabah is near the Public Library and I need to return some books."

"The day after tomorrow, you must begin looking for a job."

"But how shall I know where to look," asked K, in a very controlled, emotionless voice.

"I don't know," Arthur replied. "You have no papers: no license or birth certificate. Unless you remember now that you were born in the United States, that is. We could send for your birth certificate then and get your papers squared away." K remained silent by way of reply.

"That means that you cannot apply for employment listed in the classifieds. Perhaps the owner of a small shop downtown will be looking for someone to work under the table."

"Under the table?" K asked with as little alarm as he could manage. Certainly the shocks kept coming. It seemed that nothing was too much to believe.

"Off of the books. Without official records of payment or employment."

"You will be going with me?"

"Only the once: tomorrow. You will need to learn quickly. I'm running out of time as it is. I can't be accompanying you during my days." K stood silent. "You're a quick study. You'll pick it up."

"Might Lori be able to accompany me?"

"Sometimes maybe. I don't know. You have her number in your wallet. You can use the phone to give her a call after supper if you wish." A knock came at the door. "You need to start fending for yourself."

"For what are you running out of time, may I ask?"

Arthur answered as he opened the door. "It's not important."

There in the doorway was the retired widower from two apartments down. Arthur had grown in the habit of chatting a bit with his lonely neighbor most days, as he looked up information for him on the computer or talked about the police dramas the man had watched the night before. Soon the widower began showing up at the door every week or two with a plate of hot food that he explained he could not otherwise use in time because the date on the packaging was about to expire. Having noticed that Arthur now had a roommate, he stood in the doorway holding two plates.

No mention was made that K was a vegetarian. Arthur called out profuse thanks behind his neighbor as the man walked back toward his own door not wanting to be a bother. The second plate went into the refrigerator to be reheated the next day.

Chapter 6

The going was difficult at first and several days passed before K was able to operate the back-up computer that stood, poised like a sphinx, on top of a multi-colored collection of milk crates covered with a piece of plywood, beside his bed. Arthur had to spend many more hours than he had budgeted in order for his guest to grasp the rudiments of the machine. It had also proven necessary to accompany him on several bus rides, each route selected to highlight the various skills he might need. The more complex task of judging where in town work might be available threatened to be more time-consuming still.

K did choose to call Lori. She arrived to ferry him about town on a couple of occasions as well. Neither of those occasions resolved themselves into lessons in public transportation. They seemed designed more to comfort him, or perhaps her. Thankfully laundry was collected, food delivered.

In spite of his frustration, Arthur knocked on the bedroom door each afternoon to invite him for a walk. K realized that his host had shown remarkable patience in the matter of the bus and computer. He could only appreciate the mild tone with which he was addressed during the lessons. At times it was clear just how much self-control Arthur was calling upon in order not to express a periodic anger and impatience.

Encouraged by this development, K ventured other wider ranging questions at times when Arthur was away from his computer station. He learned that so few people walked the streets because they had grown used to doing all of their travel by motorcar. He learned that commercials were so frequent on magic screens not because they were popular (which they decidedly were not) but because they worked well to convince people to buy the products that were featured.

"I have noticed that Jeremiah and Lori rarely look at the screen during these commercials," K interjected, with a mild sense of enlightenment.

"As you have seen, each is shown repeatedly. The effect is largely subliminal."

"And no one finds this troubling?"

"The first generation or two debated the matter."

"And they decided to keep these subliminal messages?"

"No. They got tired of debating it and went on with their lives. That is how most decisions are made these days so I suppose you can say that 'they decided'."

K also learned that very few people read Dostoyevsky or Kierkegaard anymore because they required too much time reflecting on other things than buying products. Dickens novels were made into popular moving pictures rather than read as the rule. The same was true of someone called 'Jane Austin'. All of K's beloved writers were all but unread in this 2015.

But mostly what K learned was that, for Arthur, everything had a reason and the reason was precise. Not that Arthur claimed to know every reason (however much it felt like he did whenever his answers grew tiresome) but rather there could be no doubt that there was always a reason and that it was precise. It seemed ironic to K that his roommate should be one of some very small minority of people who still read Dostoyevsky and Kierkegaard. For Arthur the conflicted soul was merely a soul without sufficient information to understand its precise reasons.

K couldn't imagine Mrs. Smith or Jeremiah or Lori or any of the other people he had met since arriving in Richmond reading such works. Perhaps it was the magic screens or the Smartphones or the computers or the plastic or all of it together that made it seem a foregone conclusion that Arthur's analysis was sound: that no one read them any longer. No one any longer knew who they were.

Stranger still, K reflected, it might be the light. It was so bright everywhere and so white. There were so few shadows, either in houses or in the people who lived in them. Only here in the apartment, divided as it was by so many tall shelves, did he find the shadows that were everywhere in Prague. He thought to ask Arthur whether he was aware of it also but he did not wish to have even the shadows made precise.

As the two walked one afternoon past an industrial park, tucked away in a corner of Richmond, Arthur directed K's attention toward it. "You'll need to keep your eyes open for such collections of buildings. There are many small offices in such places. Being inconspicuous, they are more often in the habit of offering work under the table."

K stopped and carefully took the measure of the nondescript cinder-block complex. It impressed him as being singularly unpromising but he said not a word. Instead he slowly nodded his head as if he had come to the same conclusion after careful consideration.

"Remember what I've told you about 9/11. Keep in mind that you have no identification to present and people will be wary. Speak only English and don't speak it too formally. It wouldn't hurt to mention that you're a Christian."

"But I am Jewish."

Arthur shook his head at just how hopeless the whole exercise seemed. "To offset the fact that you have no identification or work history it's better that everything else about you suggest that you're just a regular guy." He looked K up and down and shook his head again. "As much as possible, anyway."

The two walked several blocks without speaking each deep in his own thoughts. Analyze the situation as he might, Arthur could not think of a single strategy to increase K's likelihood of success. Looking at the matter rationally, there was a significantly greater chance that the man would be carted away for questioning as a suspected terrorist than that he would be offered employment.

"In my father's house," said K, "I am in the habit of staying up all night. It's the only available time in which to write. A busy house is no place to write, not during the day."

For all that Arthur could not see the connection he nodded his head. If he had learned anything, it was that nothing was simple in the mind of his guest.

"Since I've been in this Richmond," said K, "I do not think of staying awake all night. The effort of merely getting through the day exhausts me to the point that sleep has become not only a certainty but a necessity. I've become used to waking refreshed. I can no longer imagine arriving at work of a morning, grimly prepared to meet my responsibilities in spite of a mere hour or two of sleep."

"You wish time to write?"

"No. I could not possibly write here. I could not imagine for whom I was writing. I have no readers here. The few I have ever had are all somewhere else that I cannot inhabit now and one must share the world of one's readers. Don't you agree?"

"Me? Do you think I write?" asked Arthur.

"Your computer says you do. The search pages indicate that you write quite a lot. I find that you have just recently begun a novel about Franz Kafka. Is it how you make your living? Taking in strangers until one proves promising as the subject of a novel?"

"It pays the occasional grocery bill. Nothing more."

"But you do not seem to be looking for employment yourself. How is it that *you* can afford an apartment?"

It had never occurred to Arthur that K might be putting the computer to his own uses between lessons. In part he felt encouraged that his guest was learning more than he had expected. Mostly he felt vulnerable. Most of his acquaintances showed no interest whatsoever in anything he might be writing and he had resigned himself to the situation. For all it wasn't, it *was* comfortable.

Anyway, this was no time to get confessional. "I thought you said that you *weren't* writing a book."

Present matters needed attending to without further delay. They were passing a row of two story commercial properties fronting a small triangular plaza between the road beside which they were walking and the much busier main road that they were approaching. He pointed these out as also promising places to apply for a job.

As they turned the corner to head toward the market, K returned to the thread of his ongoing conversation. "Last night there was a great thrumming noise in the next apartment... a great thrumming noise until all hours."

"The neighbor is 50-ish," Arthur replied. "He's trying very hard to remain young."

"And this thrumming is a badge of youth?"

"I'm afraid so."

"Can there be no alternative badge?"

"I did knock on his door around midnight. He turned down the music. Next time I'll knock earlier."

"I would hardly call the inconsequential reduction he made 'turning down the music'. Is this being 50-ish somehow an overriding consideration in this Richmond?"

"No. The music has been an issue for months now. After I knocked on the wall he turned it down further."

"Midnight having long passed."

"If I complain to the landlord it should help, at least for a while."

"It *is* music, then?"

Arthur turned his head away and suppressed a smile. Sometimes he quite liked his new house guest. He wasn't sure he wouldn't be happier in some ways if it had been he who had been whisked away to the 1920s.

"Does this 50-ish... *youth*," K went on, "feel that there is no need to accommodate his neighbors? And what of the residents of the building opposite the bedroom window? Are they also 50-ish that they are allowed to chatter outside of their doors until the break of dawn? Or the woman upstairs who heavily paces the floor at all hours? Is this somehow not an infraction of common decency in this Richmond? Is it simply understood that persons who are 50-ish are to have a privilege of keeping their neighbors distracted all day and awake all night?"

"Were such intrusions uncommon in Prague?"

"They were less intrusive."

"Yet, as I recall, you constantly complained of the noise from other family members and the least noise especially of neighbors. You were quite clear that you found any intrusion on your silence unbearable."

"So this argues, in your mind, that it is I who am being disrespectful of the noise of others?"

"I told you, I'll knock earlier from now on. There's nothing more to be done. As for the rest of it, there's nothing to be done at all except to get used to it. Once you find a job perhaps you can rent a place better fitted to your needs. Besides, you said you've been sleeping through the night."

"It's a miracle that I have. What I have not managed is to read so much as 10 pages of the wealth of Kierkegaard you have at hand. I reside in the midst of a library and cannot read."

"You've been watching plenty of television."

"What else is there to do?"

Arthur laughed. "I somehow manage to read plenty. You've just become addicted to television."

As the discussion was coming to an end, Arthur and K approached a small corner storefront, its door propped open and ringed by a semicircle of gleaming Harley Davison motorcycles. Within the ring, a half-dozen men and women sat, with hunched shoulders, on battered spindly-legged chairs, and spoke in tones too low to be made out. K paused momentarily to look intently toward the bikes before Arthur firmly took him by the arm and forced him to continue along in the direction they were walking. It was hardly noticeable that they had broken stride.

This was quite extraordinary in K's estimation but he sensed the matter must wait to be addressed until they were out of earshot of the dour and heavily tattooed group. "What danger was so great that it necessitated dragging me up a street like a child its ragdoll?" he asked once he gaged that they were at a great enough distance not to be overheard. "Are they American Indians?"

It took most of the three block walk, until they approached the grocery store, for Arthur to explain biker groups and their protectiveness of their motorcycles and tough guy reputations. As they approached the turn-off to the store, K noticed a group of young men gathered glumly together at the entrance to a parking lot below a large sign bearing the name 'Lowe's'. The men spoke little as the two approached. The little they said seemed to be spoken in a foreign language.

"Are these, perhaps, American Indians?"

"Latinos," replied Arthur. "It's rare to see Indians in Richmond, or much of anywhere actually."

"Latinos?"

"Latin American immigrants. They're hoping some small contractor who shops here for work supplies will want to hire them as inexpensive day-labor."

At the other entrance to the Lowe's, just beyond where they turned to approach the grocery store, was another group of men. This group spoke quite volubly and appeared to drink from brown paper bags. They only attracted K's attention for a moment, however, as he and Arthur were approaching colorful signs above a block of small shops at the end of which rose the facade of a much bigger store. Suddenly the two were no longer walking along streets otherwise deserted of pedestrians. Motorcars and bodies were disconcertingly rushing about in every direction.

A shabbily dressed man sidled obliquely up to K and called out "Got any change? A quarter?" Dickens, it seemed, survived not only on the magic screen. Arthur once again had K by the arm and was directing him toward a broad glass entryway flanked on one side by a great number of pumpkins, and, on the other, by little girls in uniforms of some kind offering small boxes to passersby. He wished that his sister Ottla were with him to see the unimaginable profusion of color. There were no markets remotely like this in Prague.

Inside the store K was once again amazed at the wonders of the 'supermarket'. Apparently the individual markets resembled each other closely, as he could hardly tell the difference between this one and the one to which Lori had taken him. He did note a particularly astonishing difference when he walked along the frozen food section. As he turned the corner, he discovered that the freezers were dark behind their glass doors. He stood wondering what to do in the face of such an obstacle. As he did so, another customer brushed past him. As she approached each freezer bright interior lights blinked on. As she continued to the next freezer the lights turned off behind her. It was a most remarkable phenomenon.

Suddenly Arthur was standing over his shoulder. "It's done with electrical sensors," he offered. What precisely were 'electrical sensors' would have to wait a better moment. A young woman in a blue uniform, pushing a flatbed cart of some sort, passed by with a cheery "How are *you* today?"

The opportunity to speak with a welcoming stranger was too attractive to pass up. K turned and called out an equally enthusiastic "Well!" only to see her rapidly disappear into another aisle. He staggered slightly with the surprise of it.

"It is part of her job to greet each customer with a friendly smile," explained Arthur. "The duty comes second to stocking the shelves as fast as humanly possible, though. If the greetings become actual conversations she will fall behind. She's just doing her job."

As K walked through the store he received three more identical cheery greetings. In one instance the greeting was given as a man, a few steps away, with a slightly different blue uniform and demeanor, looked up from some sort of mobile device perhaps an enormous Smartphone. (It seemed to K that he must be a supervisor.) Noting the greeting without a change of expression, the man returned his attention to the device in his hand. The greeter fairly ran up the aisle, careful not to notice the supervisor, and began stocking shelves with a fervor K had never seen in such tasks.

Arthur browsed the shelves in order to give K time to explore. Their paths next crossed in the seafood section. "I was not aware that this Richmond was near the sea."

"We're not." Arthur replied. "Refrigerated trucks make it unnecessary." After a long pause he asked if K ate seafood. "I know you're a vegetarian."

"I hardly know," said K absently. "I have only rarely had the opportunity." He stood, brow furrowed as if evaluating something. "It seems to me there might be the distant suggestion of the scent of a seafood market here."

"Actually, most of this seafood is imitation. These here," said Arthur, pointing at a row of gleaming cellophane-wrapped packages, "are molded to look like crab. Flavor molecules have been developed that make them taste like crab. You're smelling the scent of lobster, though. They can be grown in farms so sometimes they're still real."

"Imitation?"

"Yes. The most popular kinds of seafood have almost been fished out. They're prohibitively expensive now so other inexpensive types of fish have been altered to look and taste like them." Arthur lifted a package boldly labelled 'Crab' and pointed out a tiny word immediately above it: 'Imitation'.

"Are there no longer crabs in all the earth's vast oceans? No lobsters?"

"Not many. Markets in the pricier neighborhoods will offer more real seafood. It's time to go. I'm ready to check out."

As K followed Arthur toward wherever this 'checking out' was to occur, he could not help but wonder if anything in this remarkable place was real. That the market was astonishingly colorful and filled with what purported to be food was so overwhelming that the details hardly seemed to matter. The greetings one received were so buoyant that one did not care that they were not genuine. The vegetables were so flawless that it hardly mattered whether they had taste or not. Tiny print on a label might tell one that the food in a package was an imitation with genuine imitation flavor molecules added. It did not seem likely that the pattern ended there.

But as usual there was not sufficient time to properly begin his thought much less to complete it. He found himself standing behind Arthur in a queue. Before them was a crowd of people taking groceries from blue plastic carts and placing them on what looked like yet another kind of computer. From their motions it was clear that some sort of ritual was involved which each person and each machine understood. It involved small plastic cards and a pattern of gingerly touching the screen. On the far side two women in employee-blue uniforms stood languorously surveying the scene.

To the left of this swarm of activity, a few elderly customers could be seen slowly having the prices of their purchases tallied by cashiers not much changed since he'd seen such arrangements during his visits to Paris. They were the height of modernity then. The cashiers had clearly lost their pert sense of celebrity now. Their pace was rapid, their posture stooped and their faces expressionless. The disparity between the two areas for 'checking out' could only remind him of his own tiresome predictions that 'frictionless thinking machines' would soon replace the workers in the factories he inspected. Even so, he could not have imagined such eventualities as these.

As Arthur stepped up to a machine that had come vacant, and pulled out a badly tattered wallet, a klaxon sounded through the store. It did not seem that such could be a propitious omen. K froze in place but Arthur continued unaffected. Comforted by his companion's lack of concern K looked over the shoulder of the woman at the next machine to try to understand more about what was going on. Letters and numbers blinked as she placed each new item on the desk top.

She abruptly looked back over her shoulder with a surprising suggestion of violence. "You *mind?*" she shouted at a volume to compete with the klaxon which had just ceased blaring. The tone suggested more command than question. He rapidly withdrew to a distance that, while it did not feel safe, was all that could be managed. The move momentarily placed him in the flow of traffic between the machines. Another woman, whose path he now partially blocked, swept him aside with the back of her arm and a look of exasperation.

It could only be attributed to random chance that he found himself once again beside Arthur who had completed the ritual and bagged his single item. They headed toward the big glass doors but again found themselves waiting as a man in a supervisor-blue uniform stood beside a bright blue cart reading from a small slip of paper and peering at the grocery items the cart contained. At last he called the shopper and the cart aside. Arthur and K walked out past the pumpkins and the little girls. One of the girls approached extending a box toward them. Arthur smiled and bowed toward her slightly, replying "Sorry. Not today." With that, they continued on their way.

As they walked back toward the apartment, Arthur had to wait continually for K to catch up. From time to time, as they briefly walked side by side, he pointed out aspects of the Virginia Union University campus past which their path took them. On their right the school football team was going through its daily drills. On their left a fitful stream of students passed on their way back to their dorms from the last class of the day.

As they next traversed a long block of small auto repair shops, the grease-stained mechanics steadily at one sort of work or another, none of which he understood or cared to understand, K kept pace. Something was happening about which he was highly ambivalent. "I am wrong to remain. I see it now."

"In the apartment?" asked Arthur.

"In Richmond."

"Do you have a choice?"

"I've never known anything in my life that I did not choose, at least in part. It has always been a matter of struggling to admit to myself that such was the case."

"But doesn't it seem clear that all the rules have changed since you woke up to find yourself here? The rule that you always choose what happens to your life may be as incommensurate with your present circumstances as everything else. You may have left the rule behind in Prague."

"Since I learned that I have the tuberculosis I have found in it a long awaited deliverance. My doctors understand my weakening lungs as entirely a medical fact. They sometimes find my replies confusing as I forget to answer from their perspective that illness is an act of nature quite beyond will or lack of will. Yet I know beyond all question that I choose to have my disease as I chose to have all my other afflictions before. Finally I have come upon a disease that will allow long periods of writing, a disease that makes it impossible for me to be sentenced to a normal life."

"But you aren't able to write here. You said so yourself." Arthur's interjection seemed to go unnoticed.

"I felt such relief as I rode toward Matliary. My family understands that I must be away from them even if they don't understand that somehow I must remain away for the time I have left. I have a doctor's excuse. At last there is a reason that all of us can accept. There can be no further accusations from my father. The Institute has approved an extended leave with pay. The long nearly sleepless nights and the headaches may soon prove to be unnecessary. The days of exhausted daily drudgery — the office, the plans to marry Felice, which, had I surrendered to them, would have put an end to my life instantly — are behind me for the time being. I suspect they may be behind me forever. It is an attractive prospect."

K began to slow again. Intent now on what his companion was saying, Arthur slowed to match his pace. The two walked on silently for a long block.

"My desire for escape can only have been greater than even I understood; I who feel that I have learned to face some small part of the realities of life, its perverse deceptions, while inextricably trapped in the midst of them."

"Is it possible that you are over-analyzing?"

"Oh, it is certain that I am. I always do. I cannot see that people think overly much in this world. I can only assume that this is the reason I have chosen to come here."

"That's another thing you might not want to go talking about to others."

"Actually, there was not much thinking in Prague either. In both worlds people merely seek to adopt behaviors that promise a life like all others. The difference is that there one must pay great attention to the past in order to navigate the obstacles it presents and make one's escape. Here, I can hardly imagine that there exists a past."

"The railway station?"

"Well, yes. For a moment it seemed like there might be a past."

Dusk was just beginning to settle as they approached the main road that led to the apartment. "And you?" K continued "Do you have a past to satisfy?"

"The less you know about the past the more it controls your life."

"And so you live in a library?"

"There is a past there."

"Perhaps you are under-analyzing."

"That's hardly likely. I am, however, under*stating*. 'How can a critic judge the performance of the actors if he's part of the play,' isn't that what you used to say? What's the use of a long presentation?"

K raised his eyebrows at hearing himself quoted. It was still disconcerting to think of himself as being read in this 2015. But if he *was* in a coma it was quite explicable. It struck him that he rarely thought of the coma any longer. It was almost as if it no longer mattered. "Are you pleased to live as a critic?" He hadn't realized that he'd asked the question until he'd caught the mental echo of it. He had asked himself the question so many times that it emerged with a will of its own.

The two were waiting to cross the busy intersection as the question was asked. Arthur continued to eye the flow of traffic and he led the way across when the little white man appeared. Perhaps it was better that he hadn't heard. After walking silently for a long minute, it became clear that he had.

"One does not always have the choice to do as one is pleased to do. In fact, one rarely does. Though I suppose it's as much a matter of choice as not. Do you feel as if you always know what you want?"

"Not regarding any matter worth asking the question. I'm surprised that you cannot quote me to that effect."

"Desire does not fare well in your work, it seems to me. Even in your letters to Felice, you seem to be torn between a desire to be able to desire things and a dread that you might surrender to that desire."

At the mention of his letters, K let out an audible gasp. "They have been published?"

The answer seemed obvious enough. Arthur continued. "You did not love Felice so much as you loved the possibility that you might be able to learn to love her."

"I love her. We would certainly be married if it weren't for the tuberculosis."

"You only just pointed out that your tuberculosis is a choice you've made in order to free yourself. In spite of all of the explanations you made to her over the years, it was you who you were trying to convince. She struggled to understand but she just wanted a normal life: the last thing you wanted, the thing worse than death."

"I dearly wanted to have a family, children. Nothing could have been better for me. No life is complete without them. I would have been dedicated."

"Feeling guilty for not being able to want something is not the same as wanting it."

"It is the height of presumption to read someone's private correspondence — Private, I say! — and to think you know them better than they know themselves."

"For the moment, though, you were able to be a part of the play — however perversely. You clearly kept matters alive well after you were aware that no possible arrangement could give you the assurance you needed. She did try to let the correspondence lapse, more than once, and you protested that she was ignoring you. She didn't want to be unkind and that was your hold on her in the end. That and the hope against hope that she might become the wife of a respected official."

"I swear to you, I meant to marry her."

"In the end you drove yourself into a deep depression. You could not bring yourself to care that you might drive her into one as well. Your needs were overwhelming, impossibly contradictory."

"Another amateur Doctor Freud," said K, almost meekly. His defenses were collapsing. "The neurologist said it was a 'coronary neurosis'."

"He was trying to cajole you. He prescribed a regimen of electro-shock treatments."

"For *coronary neurosis*."

"There was no more such a diagnosis then than now. You were having hallucinations, Franz. Electro-shock is a treatment for profound intractable depression." K cast wildly around as if desperately looking for a route of escape. Arthur regretted that he had said such things. His companion could only find his revelations excruciatingly painful. At the same time, for all K knew Kafka's life as his own, for all he seemed to know every detail as intimately as someone who had lived through them, this man could not possibly be Franz Kafka. Arthur had only accepted the persona as a practical matter, little more, he'd originally thought, than a form of address. Still, he felt he'd been unkind. "No Franz, one does not *choose* to be a critic."

"I wanted a family. It is unhealthy to be alone." K sounded utterly defeated.

Arthur sounded hardly less so. "If your desire hadn't been profound you would not have nearly destroyed yourself in the struggle. One does not choose to be a critic. It's hard to be alone. Anyway, for now you are not alone."

"Things are so much simpler here."

"Isn't that only because you have no history here? Perhaps that is why people have chosen to go on without history."

"You have already explained that it is in order to free people to buy more products."

"Yes I did, didn't I."

For the first time since he had arrived in Richmond, K did not sleep during the night. It was wrenchingly disappointing to return to that. Arthur did not sleep either.

Chapter 7

Arthur dragged himself out of bed two hours late after refusing to go without at least an hour or two of fitful sleep made still more fitful by the flutter of K's morning exercise regimen. His own morning regimen was equally established. Hair all akimbo, he went to the front of the apartment and turned on his computer. Next he raised the blinds on the front window. Finally, he popped the remains of the previous night's final cup of coffee into the microwave to serve as the morning's first. Soon he was scrolling down the morning newswires with a breakfast of peanut butter and crackers waiting beside him and sipping extra-strong black coffee.

The long summer of California wildfires was over and Texas was now battling several of its own. California had been pretty much entirely on fire or so it seemed. The droughts in both states continued with no end in sight. With Pacific Ocean temperatures historically high, torrential rains were now in the forecast in both states. Unfortunately, occasional torrential downpours are of limited effect on droughts. California was already cleaning up from the flooding and mudslides that go along with such storms. "Hail the size of golf balls" was reported. The tops of cars peeked out of brown sludge in photo after photo from the area.

As he watched videos about the forest fires in Texas, a flock of crows noisily settled into the towering elm across the street. A dozen or so others perched on the peak of the church roof scouting the neighborhood for promising feeding sites. As a result, several pigeons found themselves jostled toward the cross at the front edge facing the main road. The woman from the apartment several doors up passed on her way to the dumpster with a small bag. Her young grandson must be visiting elsewhere or the task would have been his. He was always properly dressed as he held the bag well away from his crisply ironed clothes. It was as if the sixty years since his grandmother had herself been a 'properly dressed' little girl had left that one apartment unchanged in all the world.

Days of heavy rains had stunned South Carolina two weeks before and stories about the historically unprecedented inundation were still followed by stories about the aftermath. The cleanup and repairs were expected to cost vast amounts of time and money. Grim-faced homeowners standing among piles of soggy drywall and waterlogged kitchen cabinetry were all over the news. Most were finding that their insurance policies covered little of the damage. Phones in lawyers' offices were ringing off their hooks. Hundreds of roads and bridges had been closed. The state had already been 40 billion dollars short of the monies it needed to repair its crumbling roads and bridges and now the shortfall would be much bigger still.

A scientific study had just been released that declared that neither Miami nor New Orleans could be saved from rising ocean levels. Miami's low-lying areas flooded now with every high tide. Small amounts of money had been allocated to install pumps and raise some road beds servicing high end commercial areas. The states were tallying their losses and projecting even greater in the years ahead. Insurance companies were tallying their losses and warning that they would soon have to dial back on the coverage they offered. There was only so much they could do and stay in business.

Every bit as troubling, Russia was rapidly building up a military presence in Syria. Its military fighter jets were still regularly being escorted out of European air space. The country was playing a grand game of chicken in an attempt to remain a dominant player on the world stage. They possessed an enormous and aging nuclear arsenal. The implications were becoming worrisome.

News of presidential candidates and the new movie about Steve Jobs was everywhere. Not that anything was being reported about the candidates' policy positions. The Clinton email scandal was still much in the news. It was the only available bold headline relating to her campaign (and bold headlines there must be). Everyone had to have a say in the matter sternly wagging their fingers at every revelation from one or another 'unnamed source'.

The Trump candidacy for president was being treated more seriously every day by everyone except Donald Trump and the late night comedy shows. The real estate magnate had managed to turn the Republican presidential primary into a personal free advertising platform. Not averse to having a little fun at the same time, he was gloriously turning his media events into rambling free-association sessions. His sense of what the extreme right wants to hear had given him a lead over the serious Republican candidates in the polls. He constantly used the media attention this garnered to point out how victoriously wealthy he is and to advertise his business ventures. His sense that he'd have to end the charade at some point, and that it hardly mattered when, left him free to indulge in jibes and politically incorrect rants such as the others could not afford.

Richmond was quiet as usual. That was welcome news as news is always more interesting at a distance. Better locally to dawdle over stories about road closures for bicycling events scheduled over the weekend and a local woman who has made the bigtime as the star of a new television sitcom. The most troubling news this day was that residents of the crumbling Creighton Court projects fear their rents will be increased in the wake of scheduled renovations.

He cleaned his ears with a Q-tip as he read about the inevitable overnight robbery or fire or two. The pastor emeritus of one or another local church had died. He was remembered kindly by all who had known him. A small downtown haberdashery was closing its doors after many years, its owner retiring to Florida. Some drivers in the area were refusing to remove license plates bearing the image of the Confederate battle flag from their cars now that the plates had been made illegal in the wake of the recent mass shooting during a bible study at the black Emanuel A.M.E. Church, in South Carolina. For some reason, his ears were producing quite a lot of wax lately.

Arthur was laughing at the day's "Non-Sequitur" comic strip when he heard K gently rummaging in the kitchen. He apparently found what he was searching for and returned to his room. For a moment, the silence he left behind him sounded accusatory.

His guest was undoubtedly questioning the wisdom of present arrangements as much as he. For all the discomfort he had already experienced, however, he could not imagine putting K out. Nor could he imagine either of them changing their ways. The important thing for the moment was not to let the situation spoil his morning. It was his apartment and he could ignore what he wished. Opening a computer folder of saved items, he clicked a video on Network Theory, just the thing to watch on a cool, sunny morning.

As noon approached, Arthur gently knocked on the door to K's room. He found him seated before the computer. Given the uncomfortable ending to the walk of the day before, he could not choose to mention that his guest had not gone job hunting in the morning. Instead he announced that he was about to call Jeremiah and wondered if K had any requests to pass along. It was meant as an apology of sorts and taken as one however much it could not possibly be sufficient.

As Arthur walked toward his guest to see what he was perusing, K blanched noticeably and quickly pointed and clicked with the mouse. Arthur took the liberty of gingerly sitting beside his guest on the edge of the bed. On the screen was the home page of the Edgar Allan Poe Museum. Behind the museum page was another page tab. It displayed a title obviously associated with a pornography site. He could not help but raise his eyebrows. K could not help but notice.

"Pornography sites have a lot of computer viruses," Arthur observed. K blushed furiously. "I'll be going for a walk after lunch."

K's eyes darted from one direction to another searching for a proper reply. At last he said, "I will go along if you will be pleased to have the company."

Arthur nodded. His own eyes could not help but wander back to the computer monitor. "So then, you are a reader of Poe?" he asked in an attempt to defuse the situation. Or maybe it was meant as a wry joke of sorts.

"A few things. Years ago." The answer was brusque.

"I'm not the only person who has noticed the appearance of a relationship between your works. It's often mentioned but I've never seen any proof. I understand he was quite popular in Germany when you were young."

Embarrassed to be caught out about the porn site, K could only think to suppress a reaction. He was stern. He was silent. Perhaps his reaction had to do with Poe, perhaps he was being careful not to be caught off guard again. He closed the porn tab and began to scroll through the news indicating that he considered the conversation at an end.

After Arthur fixed a lunch of homemade mini-pizzas on sandwich bread and K picked at a salad in the kitchenette the latter returned to his room in order to carefully brush his hair and don his suit jacket, tie and fedora. He returned a half-hour later to find his host checking email by way of waiting.

It was a fine Indian summer day. The sun shone brightly and the temperature hovered around 80°. Among the delights of Richmond is the fact that the streets in the older parts of town are still lined with trees. Elm, oak, maple, magnolia: the leaves had already turned various colors. Most remained stubbornly on their branches. A dog barked from behind a tall white picket fence as they turned onto Seminary Avenue. It was impossible not to feel especially alive.

Arthur lingered over a carriage house along their route that had been converted into a garage, presumably during the 30s. A number of the yards dotted throughout the area featured such outbuildings with broad swinging doors just beyond a large main house. On rare occasion the original hayloft door was still intact and the loft turned into a kind of storage attic. Most carriage houses around Richmond were painted white, but a few, like this one, were white with bright green trim. Standing there it was possible to forget that busy thoroughfares, apartment complexes, minimarts and all the maddening rush of the modern world existed only a block away.

As they stood admiring the structure, K thought for a moment to ask if the Jewish Quarter was close enough that they might walk through it one day. Arthur knew that he was Jewish. Still long experience had taught him to be wary of asking such questions.

"What is a computer virus?" asked K, breaking a fine silence. "It is said that the... um... *Internet*... is plagued by them."

His question brought an end to his companion's reverie who could not help but wish that the question had waited. "It's a malicious code that an attacker tries to inject into people's computers. Once inside the computer, it can act much like a virus in a human body."

"For all they provoke anxiety, I am surprised that no one seems to avoid the Internet on which they are so common."

"People have become dependent upon their computers. Many are even addicted. Some do try to avoid the sites where they might be suspected to be present. Mostly people know no more than that they exist. They buy anti-virus programs to protect themselves as best they can."

"Anti-virus?"

"Yes, another kind of code that detects and inoculates against viruses. It's like a vaccine."

"Like a smallpox vaccine?"

Arthur could not help but reflect that smallpox was the only vaccine used on the general public around 1920. For all that K could only be a crazy man, he was a well informed and a quick thinking one. "There are lots of vaccines to prevent different maladies in humans now."

"And in computers," K added. "Can humans catch computer viruses?"

Arthur could not help but chuckle. "Only computers can catch the kind of computer viruses we're talking about."

"There are other kinds that people can catch?"

"Nothing that you need to worry about. Being born in the 19th century is a 100% effective vaccine to the others."

As they talked, a 30-something man followed close behind a little girl on a bicycle heading in their direction. The child sported elbow and knee pads and a pink and white helmet. K stopped to take in the scene, obviously charmed. He tipped his fedora as they passed. The little girl wobbled slightly and her father rushed up to position his hands at the ready a few inches from the bicycle seat and the handlebars until he was sure she had regained control.

"Why must it all be done in codes?"

Arthur explained that computers were just enormous banks of electronic switches, all but a few thousand set to 'zero' at the factory. Before they were offered to the public, programs were loaded in. The 'programmers' positioned banks of switches in patterns of zeros and ones. A computer without programs was just an expensive doorstop to all but a very small number of specialized programmers.

"Code then is a pattern of zeroes and ones corresponding to tiny switches being opened or closed?"

"Everything is composed of zeroes and ones, in the final analysis, but code is a formal language of sorts made from words. The patterns of zeroes and ones are combined to make symbols like letters of an alphabet. Those symbols are then combined into words of computer language. Arranged into the equivalent of simple 'sentences,' the words direct the computer to perform actions." The conversation about how computers worked and what was 'code' lasted almost half of a mile. For all K interrupted the explanation to ask surprisingly insightful questions, it was clear that he was struggling with the concepts.

"So codes are languages in which letters represent arrangements of zeroes and ones and viruses are malicious codes meant to take over the original codes and control them towards maleficent ends," he announced by way of recap.

"If it sounds complex, in reality it is a million times more so."

"Even the... um... *videos* I watch are made up entirely of zeroes and ones?" he asked with a tone of disbelief.

"Yes. A section of registers codes for a color. Another section codes for where exactly a dot of that color will appear on the screen. The images on the screen are made up of a great many of such dots."

"They are not a succession of photographic images?"

"No. A great deal has changed since those days."

"Are the images on the television created in the same fashion?"

"Yes. In order to be compatible with computers. It was required several years ago by law."

"Are the images created by these zeroes and ones real?"

Arthur pondered the question. Simple though it was, the answer was anything but. "You've seen a Charlie Chaplin movie before?" As he replied with his own question, a squirrel crossed the road halfway and patiently waited on its hind legs for an oncoming car to pass.

"Yes, several," K replied, as he stared in wonder after the squirrel. "They are quite destructive really, for all their charm. Have you noticed what the moving pictures do to people? How they are hypnotized?"

"Those movies were the videos of your time. Were the people on the screen real or characters? Or were they both? And what exactly does the distinction mean?" K watched as the squirrel scampered up a large oak. He'd half expected it to take a seat on the green bench, on the other side, and pull out a tiny bus pass.

"Perhaps you saw a newsreel, prior to the movie, in which a public figure was speaking with his words roughly paraphrased printed below him. Let's say a newsreel in which a high government official told the German people that Germany was winning the first World War when they were losing. Let's say he was making a great deal of money through the sale of armaments. Maybe even to both sides."

"Did you see the squirrel?" K interjected.

"A fascinating example of natural selection. Maybe he has a reputation,…"

"*What?*"

"The high government official… Maybe he has a reputation, as a morally upstanding family man, which is part of the image called immediately to mind upon seeing his face, but, in actuality, he is seeing a mistress as often as possible on the pretext of working late at the office. Is the figure you are seeing real or a fiction?"

"We should invite him to tea."

"*What?*"

"The squirrel. I'm curious about his table manners."

"I do not serve teas."

"But I have learned much of what I know about this Richmond — about this 2015 — from videos. How can I tell what is true and what a lie? Are there no longer lies? When we walk out together what I see appears to be generally in accordance with those videos. There is a great deal more than the videos portray, it is true."

"The Internet is definitely a convenience. It's obvious that you've gained a good deal of familiarity from it. The world you see on it must bear some meaningful relationship to the real world, then, don't you think?"

"I could not have imagined."

"No illusion can succeed that does not hew closely to reality, no lie that does not resemble the truth, none that is not crafted to fit a realistic context. And no lie is so believable as the lie that the liar him- or herself deeply believes or desires to be true. Oh, lies still exist. A great many more, to my understanding, than in 1920." Arthur paused and quickly inspected his companion out of the corner of his eye for a reaction. "The German official is real. His image on the screen represents his physical reality. But his public image is a lie and movies are all about images." As Arthur finished his sentence, the distant sound of a rescue truck approached near enough to make conversation difficult. The vehicle sped past as they walked quietly side by side. Another siren approached behind it.

K was deep in thought his eyes fixed intently on the sidewalk before him. After a police cruiser sped by and he could be heard he spoke. "How then can I tell what is real?"

"Perhaps you can't. Perhaps you can only learn to tell what the world has agreed to call 'real' and perhaps that turns out to be enough. Anyway, it is all that one has available in most matters."

"So even you do not know what is real?"

"I live in an apartment full of books..."

"Full of history."

"And computers. I leave it as little as possible."

"For the occasional walk."

"And to do marketing."

"So then, you do not concern yourself with reality?"

"With little else, actually. I do not hide out attempting to escape from reality." Arthur paused, in search of examples. "I am widely reputed to be able to repair pretty much anything..."

"I overheard Lori say so once. She and her girlfriends are quite impressed with the trait. I had pictured you quite differently before I met you at the birthday party. I expected you to arrive in overhauls, like Edison emerging from his laboratory."

"Not every library implies impractical bumbling or escape from the real or worse. Not every computer is used to play video games. Fixing a dishwasher can be a test of the quality of a library every bit as much as a knowledge of Kierkegaard or of Kant's categorical imperative."

"I once took up carpentry," interjected K. "It seemed to me I need something in my life that requires my body as much as my mind."

"As the result I may have written some pretty good books that no one reads. I've even made discoveries that have been quietly appropriated. I've stayed in decent physical condition." Arthur hesitated, building a sense of suspense. "But I am utterly unemployable and almost as unpublishable. I find it painful to be in general company for more than an hour or two, excruciating to be tethered to a cell phone. Not only do I have no business connections but I attend no parties beyond the occasional family celebration. No publisher would think of looking at the work of so poorly networked a person much less publishing it. If I might know something about reality it has come at a cost. More to the present point, it has come at a cost that no normal person could choose to pay."

"One does not *choose* to be a critic."

"No. One does not choose."

"Aren't you just being uncharitable to speak of human foibles as 'lies'?" asked K.

"Actually, you are the one who introduced the word."

"I suppose I must have."

"I assumed you were trying to employ the vernacular."

"You wielded the word with such assurance I'd remembered it as your own." As K said this they crested the gradual incline up which they had been walking. Below them, several blocks ahead, the pulsing lights of the emergency vehicles marked the scene of a motorcar accident.

K hesitated at the sight of the police cruiser. "Don't worry," his companion said. "The officer won't be checking papers. They have other things to occupy their thoughts."

"Why not build another Internet?" K asked as they continued toward the scene. The concept of what precisely an Internet was had not yet been fully grasped by him. But, then, most people who nominally belonged in 2015 did not understand it either. "One without viruses."

Arthur began with a simple explanation of how the Internet worked, what nodes and service providers were and redundancy. "The Internet is more or less a tangled ball of string. It almost builds itself. To try to replicate it would arrive at the same problems but not the same resilience. Not to mention that it would cost a fortune. People do build miniature networks all the time though but they must be attached to the Internet in order to form connections to the rest of the world. The moment they are, viruses are a constant concern again."

"And all of it is created from zeroes and ones?"

"Difficult to believe, isn't it?" Arthur could not resist a smile. "It seems impossible. Sometimes I almost think I must be in a coma or something. That I'll wake up and the real world will be back."

The ambulance must have approached from another direction. A middle aged woman in a neck brace was being strapped onto a gurney as they approached. She answered questions from the emergency technicians in an unaffected tone of voice. Another was standing outside the police cruiser giving information to the officer who was entering it into a computer via a keyboard attached to the dashboard. From time to time she looked over toward two lightly damaged vehicles in the void between two sections of the center road-divider.

K strained to catch every detail. The sense of order was comforting. As he watched, a yellow leaf pirouetted past his gaze and settled on the ground some small distance away. His gaze lingered on it as if it too had something to teach him, some meaning.

"Will we be inviting it to tea, as well?" Arthur asked. The two men returned to their walk.

"Is 'Network Theory' also a matter of these codes? You seemed to say that 'networking' was somehow associated with publishing."

"How could you know about Network Theory?"

"It is difficult to miss the fact that you are often watching lectures on the subject."

"Of course. You've been eaves-dropping."

K was as shocked at the playful accusation as Arthur had intended. "Your accusation is unfair, the expectation it implies unreasonable. How must I be 'eaves-dropping' to hear a course of lectures to which you listen night and day."

"The videos of sexual intercourse you have been watching…"

K fairly stamped his feet as he blushed this time. "I prefer we leave off with the subject, if you please. It will not happen again."

"*Any* video you might watch — or book I might write — can only get to its audience because there is a path available to do so. In order to acquire the equipment to make the videos, the originating party must establish personal and professional connections. In order to acquire the expertise to create the visuals another set of connections must exist and another in order to acquire actors. In order to advertise to the world that the resulting videos are available another set of connections is necessary. Before all of this, there must be connections to planning expertise and funding expertise. All of this interconnectedness describes the network necessary in order to be able to accomplish the moderately complex task."

"And there is some sort of theory attached to this?"

"Network Theory is the study of the form and function that networks take. Your present network, for example, is very simple. You are at its center. Mathematically speaking, you are a 'node.' Lori, Jeremiah and I are also nodes. Your direct connection to each of us is called a 'first degree' connection. Lori's network has a great many more connections. The ladies generally do. Her first degree connections are your second degree connections. As the result you are poor in first degree connections and moderately richer by virtue of your second degree connections."

"So I do not have the connections to make a video."

"You've only just begun to assemble the connections to *watch* a video."

"One needs connections simply to watch?"

"When you first watched the 'magic screen' it overwhelmed you."

"Yes."

"Now that you have made connections in 2015 you are able to more fully understand what you are watching."

"Because I have met Lori?"

"And because you have learned what some of the pieces of life are now and how they fit together. Your brain has formed the connections necessary in order to better understand. This forming of new connections to modify existing networks to function at a high level in new circumstances is what makes the brain far more magical than the magic screen."

K tipped his hat to a gentleman in shirtsleeves who was trimming hedges. The gesture went without acknowledgement. Half a block further along Arthur returned to his thought. "The brain is also a grand network. The nodes are called 'neurons'. Are you familiar with the term?"

"I suspect I have given it far too little thought, but yes."

"Those neurons know nothing more than their version of zeros and ones. They know no more about being part of the brain than an individual wire in China knows that it is part of the Internet. Yet together they are the stuff of conscious thought. More rapidly than the videos on the Internet, they composed your thinking about the 'land surveyor' in your novel *The Castle*. They were able even to invent him from generalizations, developed from long experience, stored on other neurons, about what a land surveyor might be like. They knew intuitively that he would have to establish... connections... in order to be accepted as the land surveyor. Such 'rich' connections were only available through the officials of The Castle."

"I'm sure that a good deal must have been discovered about the brain since I dozed off on the train to Matliary. Does this have to do with Network Theory, or has the subject changed without my being aware?"

"The brain is far more wondrous even than the Internet but the two are proving to obey the same laws of Network Theory. Your computer terminal is a node on the Internet. Through it you have an effect but neither you nor it can know what the effect is. Through it the Internet affects you but neither you nor it can know what the effect is. A neuron is a node in the brain but it cannot know what its effect is. The brain affects it but it cannot know what the effect is."

"It is impossible that something so complex as a human being can be a mere node."

"It turns out that no one person or neuron looks any different than any other when millions are considered at once. All are essentially points on a graph. This is confirmed by the fact that the distribution of the nodes follow exact mathematical laws — or rather our understanding of the mathematical laws is becoming ever *more* exact."

"The Internet is reducing people to mere points on a graph?."

"No. They always have been points on a graph. The Internet has made those points so much more interconnected that we now have the capability to see that people are such points and that all networks obey the same mathematical rules."

"You hardly look like a point on a graph to me."

"Each point taken individually remains an individual. Each individual values his or her connections as interpersonal connections. It is when very large numbers of people — or of computer terminals or neurons — are considered in relation to each other that they become points on the graph and obey mathematical laws."

"So then, our brains are now Internets and neurons now the wires and switches by which they compute?"

"They always were. Your prediction of the 'frictionless thinking machine' was the product of a frictionless thinking machine. It can hardly be a coincidence."

Having had enough of nodes and graphs. K sought to steer the conversation elsewhere. "Is it difficult to find publishers in this Richmond?"

"I suppose there are none to be found here at all. Commercial publishers set up offices in major cities like New York City or Los Angeles or maybe Chicago."

"Or Berlin. Yes?"

"Smaller publishers tend to publish the owner or the owner's friends. Not that it matters."

"Surely it does matter."

"As hard as a land surveyor found it in your day it is much harder now, I'm afraid."

K smiled. "Is The Castle more impenetrable now? Can that be possible?"

"You may have noticed that there isn't even a castle any longer. A land surveyor need only walk in an automatic door and look up the office number of the appropriate official on the register posted in the lobby in order to present oneself for work. What could be more accessible?"

"I have not studied lobbies much, as of yet."

"The fortifications are still stronger for the fact that they are now invisible. All of the administrators know now that a land surveyor is positively not authorized. They have their orders. If he enters the doors that he is so free to enter, the professional qualifications they will find when they retrieve his official file will be listed as 'organ grinder' or 'rag-picker,' anything but 'surveyor'."

"Are there still organ grinders? I've yet to see one."

"A license is strictly required for which nobody qualifies and no application form has been printed. The Castle has enough to deal with without the problems that a survey brings."

"Is there an actual license involved?"

"To be a metaphorical land surveyor? A metaphorical one most certainly."

K gave his companion a sidelong look indicating he was not amused.

"I've always had the impression that your surveyor never could have succeeded. That you had decided as much from the first."

"It is the fate of the land surveyor to fail. Should I make my notes into a novel, at last, it will be integral to who he is. I cannot imagine that I would change my mind about that."

"But you succeeded. You did write the novel — more than one — and the stories. They managed to make their way into the hands of appreciative readers."

"Did I? And is this the world that my survey brought about?"

"It's impossible to say. As popular as your work has been, I have to think that the answer in some small part is 'It did.' All of your works together being collectively your survey. Perhaps the point is more that they entertained millions of readers while they failed to affect the world much."

"You must know that the point of the land surveyor was that his ironic talents, as much as they marked him out as a promising candidate for his quest, achieved nothing. Even when success was within his grasp his limitations prevented his reaching out to take it. After all, it was he who prevented his own success." K's features looked drawn. "All his spirit gained him was the inability to quietly settle into some corner of the village and inconspicuously live out his days."

"What other option was there but to try?"

"None. Or tuberculosis, perhaps."

"Then he is a tragic character."

"No. He could only be tragic if his reach had not exceeded his grasp, if the cause of his failure could have been overcome. I am sure that I will never come to a different understanding of the matter. All of my work keeps turning out to be low comedy. I imagine the same would be true of *The Castle*."

"The difference between the two of you is that you understand that. That may be all the difference that is possible."

"I instructed Max to destroy all of my unpublished manuscripts."

"I've already told you that there is a copy of *The Castle* in the library. The translation would seem to be solid at least. Why don't you read it? I should think you would be more than a little curious."

"I have stayed strictly away from anything that relates to me. I do not want to know. Who could wish to return to a life from which they already know the central incidents? Who could bear the responsibility of choosing whether to preserve or change it? If I am to remain here — wherever 'here' may prove to be — how could I bear to read the life that somehow becomes less my own with each word I read?"

Matters were in danger of becoming impossibly convoluted, a danger that Arthur was determined to avoid. It was this he took walks to get away from. He turned toward the apartment. Slowly the pleasure of a silent walk in the golden late-season sun returned to him. As they passed the houses, peaceful back from the busy street, the low shrubbery of one shook at irregular intervals with the gleaning of a small flock of sparrows. Both men stood entranced as the tiny beings went about doing a thorough job of it.

"You mentioned," said K, as they approached the apartment, "a 'first World War'. May I ask to what you were referring?"

In a flash, Arthur saw the danger at hand. K could hardly have failed to notice that he was blinking furiously as he searched for a way to deflect the question. A first World War clearly implied that there had been at least a second. The topic was far too dangerous to engage in. "Another day, perhaps," he replied, trying to sound as if it were a matter of no particular importance.

Chapter 8

Early next morning, Arthur pumped up the back tire of his bicycle and pedaled away. As there had been more music from the neighbor's apartment again, the night before, K remained late in bed. He was unsure whether to complain more strenuously, but, the apartment being empty when he sallied forth for breakfast, the decision made itself. Instead he imagined what he would have said. It was really quite impressive what he would certainly have said: unanswerable.

In his host's favor, it did have to be admitted that the volume was noticeably reduced on two occasions. The fact would suggest that he had knocked on his 50-ish neighbor's door. But each was followed by a gradual increase until the music was louder still. More guests would seem to have arrived, as the accompanying laughter and boisterous talking grew even louder than it had been before the momentary reductions.

It seemed particularly unwise for him to go himself to knock on the door and remonstrate. Instead he lay miserable in the dark, periodically turning on the light beside the bed and browsing a few pages from the Kierkegaard volume he was presently reading. This went on until well after 1 AM.

In the dark, however, his thoughts went where thoughts can so easily go at such times. How did one press one's case when their host thinks them crazy? K himself could only wonder on occasion whether he really was somehow deluded, whether it might be possible that his real name was 'John Smith' and that he only imagined being Franz Kafka. Yet his memories were so real, so much a part of who he was. Of course they *were* real. He had to hold onto that. Still, what was the rational reaction to waking up 95 years after what was supposed to be a short nap? To waking up in a place called 'The Roach Motel' not having aged regardless? With vivid memories and identification papers intact?

Putting himself in the place of his host, what could the man possibly think? There indeed was proof. How could John Smith wake up in 2015 with Bohemian identification papers dated 1920 in his pocket? For all such details seemed clearly to make the case, what really did it mean? What could possibly serve as proof in such a situation? Even to K himself? What precedent could be drawn upon? The likelier answer could only be that he was John Smith. From that it only followed that he had contrived the evidence in his favor. That he was a con artist, or, worse, a mad escape artist.

How had he come to know how to speak English? He barely knew a few words of the language in Prague. If he was suddenly able to speak English because he was a psychotic American, how was he able to speak German? Czech? Equally a mystery, why was he no longer struggling to breathe? No longer coughing up blood? On the other side of the ledger, how did he remember having had a coughing fit the day before his departure? Quietly laughing with Ottla in the water-closet? His mother's embrace on the platform?

His mood was considerably improved, however, when he found a French toast casserole in the sealed plastic bowl that he opened. It was already one of his favorites, almost like eating strudel for breakfast. Again, he could not help but return to the unanswerable questions. How could the memory of his mother's strudel come back into his mouth? The sight of it on the sideboard? The smell of it through the flat? It was maddening to be helpless before the onslaught of unbidden thoughts.

He was Franz Kafka. He was in a coma. It was the only possible answer. But he could not fend off the other thoughts. The experience of his days was simply too real. He would have imagined a coma might result in a dream-like experience, with all the discontinuities and magical transpositions one experienced in a dream state. He could detect no such discontinuities here no matter how closely he inspected the world around him. The sealable plastic bowl from which he would eat the French toast casserole was perfectly in place however much he could not possibly have imagined such an amenity as short a time as a month ago. It did not blink in and out of existence or transform into a bird and fly away.

Every time he looked into the refrigerator in his room at random intervals to see what he might find, the stack of bowls that held his meals appeared precisely as before.

The microwave was utterly inexplicable he had to admit but perfectly consistent with the more explicable advancements. (As he thought this, he could not help but notice that it was filthy and begin absently cleaning it while his thoughts took him where they would.) The CDs of the music of Mozart that Arthur so kindly handed along to him were so much an advance on the gramophone records he used to listen to at Werfel's apartment that they were unimaginable. Yet such a progression was consistent. They were perfectly consonant with a world of flying hotels that had been developed from the aeroplanes he watched with such fascination at the Brescia air show.

What of the CDs of the music of Janáček that Arthur had handed along apparently as a kind of apology for having been insensitive about Felice? He had met the man. Knew almost nothing of him or his music. Only that Max translated his operas from Czech into German between days tirelessly promoting half the Jewish writers in Prague to the publishers in Berlin. Max with his endless energy, and his refusal, it would seem, to destroy K's manuscripts. How could he possibly be dreaming all of this? All of these denouements to histories most of which he only knew a few vague details at first hand?

Normally he would despair of ever having such an unfettered and facile imagination. Perhaps that was it. His dream was his way of getting to that place that had always proved discouragingly far beyond him. His soul had always been maimed: a bird that was, at the same time, its own cage. Perhaps the fact that it all seemed so real meant that he was learning to be free. That the bird was escaping the cage. Perhaps this was the feeling he had always despaired of having.

His breakfast nicely warmed, K. returned to his room and turned on the computer. Being an older model it took some time to boot up. Being new to the experience he did not notice. Soon enough the miracle of the Internet was before him on the screen and the struggles of only a moment before utterly forgotten. A group of figures looked angry. Their skin was hanging in shreds. The frequent appearance of these 'zombies,' as they were called, on the television and Internet, was another mystery. Almost assuredly, they were only fictional creatures but why the obsession with them?

Anyway, he was becoming more practiced at 'clicking out' these 'advertisements' for all they tried to make the means of doing so as confusing as possible. Arthur had explained that it was becoming almost impossible to read text for all the various styles of ads that were launched while one tried to do so. He had explained not to click in the blank portion of the pages unless this might release full page 'ambush ads,' not to click anywhere near expandable ads that were programmed to deploy if the cursor inadvertently traveled over them, to mute the sound unless it was needed, to always click "No. I don't want access to the finest news being published today." It had ceased to be a game any longer, the initial sense of challenge having descended into wholesale disruption and frustration.

All of that said, when the impressively lithe young woman appeared, lightly clad, in a short shift of some sort, the length of her stretched yearningly along the surface of a bed with the coverlet turned down, K could no longer resist. She had been appearing on a small video screen on the side of virtually every other page he'd clicked on for several days. He turned the volume on. As he did, she looked directly at him and explained that older men often suffered from something called 'erectile dysfunction'. She assured him that, whatever precisely it was, it was not at all his fault. She ran her hand across the glistening sheet beneath her. In most men, this erectile dysfunction could be overcome with a simple pill. An erection would again be possible and her desires could be satisfied. The viewer was warned to contact a doctor if he should experience an erection lasting more than four hours.

Four hours! Well, again this would be consistent with the advances in the other facets of life. But no. Surely not. He looked at the little window in which the video had played. It was now playing a news story about someone named Trump who said he was very rich and constantly repeated his own name and how he could be trusted and promised to build a wall to keep Mexicans out of somewhere. Although he was so rich, the Mexicans would have to pay for the wall themselves. He kept repeating 'trust me' and 'believe me'. He would make it happen. When the story ended, the woman appeared again. K could not detect the least sense of coyness about her but only a hint of brazenness. She and others like her simply desired sexual intercourse from men with powerful, long-lasting erections.

The only possible explanation for all of this was that he was in a coma. It was the clearest confirmation yet. The psychologists would say this was a psychic reflection of the frustrations that his hapless attempts to engage women had caused him. It made perfect sense, however much it galled him to submit to the amateur psychoanalysis he so much despised. Yet the perfect woman in the ad was nothing like the shop girls and bordello women with which his needs so shamefully involved him from time to time, and who, riddled with sores, haunted him in his nightmares? She was certainly nothing like the inscrutable women at the cafes either. How could this all be the result of a coma? How could this lithe woman have been hidden somewhere in his psyche without him having the slightest clue? Where had all of these Internets and microwaves and beckoning sirens been hiding inside of his mind until the coma?

As he struggled to escape the inextricable web of these questions — to get free of the constant internal dialogue that threatened to become crippling — he forced himself to think of the French toast before him. His breakfast had grown cold while he sat staring into the screen seeking his inner depths. He carried it back into the kitchenette to be warmed again.

The casserole was delicious, much sweeter than anything he'd ever eaten in Prague of course. He lingered over it as the Google Maps site popped into view. He would begin searching for a job on Monday. The prospect was somewhat daunting. He printed out a number of 8 ½ x 11 maps of the different areas he hoped to canvas. That done, he traveled each virtually, making his way on the 'Street View' function. That having become tedious he had a thought. His sense of trepidation suggested it might not be a wise idea. Nevertheless, he entered "Prague, Bohemia" in the search box. The search engine demanded 'Czech Republic' instead of Bohemia. Soon he was making his way through the streets of his hometown.

For all he had convinced himself that it amounted to nothing more than a minor transgression, the sight of modern motorcars lining the narrow cobbled streets he knew so well reminded him that he was farther away from the city than he could ever have imagined. People were dressed much like the people he passed during his Richmond walks. Only a single woman was wearing a dress. It ended above her knees as if she were a young girl who suddenly found herself grown like *Alice in Wonderland* while her clothing had remained a child's. The rest were wearing casual trousers. The men all wore casual t-shirts and jeans. Nearly everyone wore sneakers. A surprising number were consulting Smartphones at the moment the photograph was taken.

He found the Insurance Institute office building much changed. It was now a hotel surrounded on every side by colorfully painted shops such as had most certainly not existed during his years of working there. The central doors were made of glass rather than the heavy dark oak that greeted him each morning and the front was festooned with flags. They were flanked by full-length glass windows. A small sign on a lamppost left him stunned. It sported an emblem showing the golden double arches he had come to recognize as the symbol of the cheap hamburger restaurant called 'MacDonald's'. These restaurants were pervasive in Richmond, and, apparently, ranged much further, even to Prague. He did not know whether to laugh or to cry out in anguish. More coincidental still, a small shop was built into the hotel front, on one side, called 'Felice'. Stunned by one and then the other, he felt a mounting surge of anxiety. He struggled for breath for the first time since he had found himself in Richmond. Neither was a mystery he wished to pursue.

It was the sight of the trolley that buoyed him and encouraged him to go on. The cars were no longer green, it turned out, when he saw the fuzzy image of a moving car further along on his walk, but the rails embedded in the street and the wires overhead were exactly the same. He embarked on a new tour the moment he saw them, a memory tour through, not this Prague, festive though it might be, but the darker, dingier Prague that he loved to tour in the green streetcars that stopped outside the Insurance Institute doors. He stepped up into it again, at the end of his workday, as the sun grew low, and rode it in his mind, through all the quarters of a city he once knew intimately well. Over there had been the Louvre Café where he attended so many Yiddish theater company plays, waiting always to see Mrs. Tschissik make her appearance on stage. Down this narrow street was the Arco Café, on this plaza the Continental and the Savoy, where he'd spent so many nights searching for the self-confidence that his father's expectations always denied him, studying to be one of the fellows, falling in love with every pretty woman to the point that some found it uncomfortable and he felt even more impossibly maladroit. While it was a daunting task, especially at first, the nights were fondly remembered. In time he seemed the gayest, most confident of all. Or perhaps it came across as a bit forced (he was never quite sure). As supper hour approached, he stepped off and walked across the plaza toward the family flat. It would not do to be late. Perhaps there would be the opportunity to stop in at the cafes to say hello to his friends later in the evening. Or perhaps it would prove possible to write.

After a few comforting moments — amounting to some fifteen minutes — the revelry wore off and he was back in front of the computer screen. Looking up the street toward the Alt-Nieu Synagogue and the old town hall with its reassuring clock tower, he felt a pang of regret. At the same time he could not help but be fascinated by the colorful traffic signs. He could not remember a time that the buildings were ever all at once so freshly painted. Rarely could he remember the sun having shone so brightly.

As disconcerting as the strange pervasive changes were, he was somehow sure that there was something more that he had yet to notice. Half of him felt sure he should see it. The other half wanted to close the tab. He even began the motion several times and poised the mouse over the little X. He knew the dangers of the temptation to which he was succumbing but something would not let him leave the streets he'd walked so often before. Suddenly it came to him. No one was walking along with their eyes focused on the pavement before them. He saw no fear. That must be it. With a sigh, he typed "Richmond, VA," in the search box, looked one last time, then hit "Enter".

Arthur felt himself breathe normally for the first time in days. As he biked toward the downtown, the morning air was cool and the sun bright. He could feel his body relax. He was free once again. The world was a friendly place. Virginia Commonwealth University students walked briskly along Broad Street intent on their Smartphone screens. Some few stood outside the bicycle stop quietly chatting.

Back a block, on Grace Street, the grand old houses were all divided into university offices and student apartments. The going here was a bit more perilous. Cars launched out of street-side parking spaces often without bothering to check for bicycles. Other cyclists flashed by on far better equipment also paying little attention to any of the various forms of traffic darting in every direction. Small groups called out to familiar passersby from second floor balconies asking why they hadn't been at so-and-so's party and shouting out the news of the social day.

Back a couple blocks more, Franklin Street skirted Monroe Park, and more of the same but a bit more stolid, more offices and fewer balconies. Newer architecturally more functional buildings began to dominate the Federalist and Greek revival office buildings around them, indicative of the university's search for space into which to expand. On one corner or another, a church might sport a banner advertising God's love and a party of its own.

At Harrison Street, the college atmosphere abruptly changed. Arthur continued toward the Public Library, ahead. He had a half-dozen books in his backpack to return, all of them relating to Franz Kafka. The Jefferson Hotel rose up before him. The glass-enclosed ground floor dining room was empty and the tables bore pristine white linen laid out with gleaming flatware. A valet drove up to the main door in an also gleaming Mercedes and held open the door for the owner who emerged in tennis togs after a short wait. Whereas the side streets in the VCU campus area were completely occupied with small exotic shops and eateries, the storefronts here were largely empty, the rest open only during limited hours or by appointment. A few less prominent lawyers and real estate agencies chose the area for their offices rather than pay much higher rents around the capitol area a few blocks ahead. There was little traffic. Two blocks over, on this end of Broad Street, unrented buildings slowly fell into disrepair waiting for new occupants. Small stores selling used and cheap goods held on for a few years and then closed. Around the hotel, even vacant buildings were maintained in better condition, almost prim.

Franklin Street itself remained a well-kept, pleasant, tree-lined street. A couple of blocks past the library, all the store fronts were occupied again, many with fast food outlets suggesting a lunchtime clientele. The Times-Dispatch office building was almost monumental. (The print newspaper itself was unimpressive, scaled back by Internet competition.) Just beyond it, bank buildings and modern hotels towered over the scene. The capitol itself lay out of sight a few blocks on the other side.

After returning his books and perusing the 'New Books' shelf, he carried his bike back down the porch stairs and started back toward the university. It was much too early to surrender his freedom. As he simply enjoyed pedaling back through a world in which the worst trials were midterms and boring meetings, the world of panhandlers and roommates held no attraction whatsoever for him. Beyond the campus was the museum district and more subdivided grand houses along wide boulevards in which young professionals lived.

Beyond the museum district was Carytown, a redeveloped area featuring small shops and narrow streets designed to invite pedestrian traffic. He dismantled his bike in front of the little Chop Suey Book Store and chained the pieces to the tree there. No one would choose to steal the duct-taped seat so he left it in place. The plan was to browse the books and window shop his way to the plaza on the west end and then retrace his steps. There was no need to hurry. In fact the whole point was to do quite the opposite.

This was the place to which he took all of his out-of-town guests (this and the Fine Arts Museum). Not only did it possess some inevitable charm but one or two of the eateries here were surprisingly inexpensive. He could even afford to pick up the tab for a round of coffees from time to time over which they would reminisce and catch up with recent developments. Later they would treat for dinner. It was an old pattern and one that they had recently begun to find wearisome he suspected.

Yes, he had been taken advantage of by his last employer and the one before that but everyone was taken advantage of these days. Sentences would haltingly be interjected to that effect — as previous coffee shops, in previous small cities, were fondly remembered — and be broken off with a wistful smile. Arthur was no longer young. He had never been a social networker, found it almost physically painful to put on a manufactured smile. Yes, everyone still mentioned, with a sense of wonder, that he could "fix *anything*," but others who could fix less, if anything at all, were out trying to ingratiate themselves with contacts who might be able to help them. They had jobs.

Some of the guests he brought there had known him since he was a child and had yet to 'figure him out'. His presence there beside them was a reminder that somehow he'd always been a puzzle. As the years passed, all of the other children had grown to be much the expected adult; each year expressed the same personality one year more established. But what had the child Arthur been expected to grow up to be? Looking back, it seemed that the puzzle had always existed. If he'd had a distinguishable personality, they had long forgotten what it might have been, forgotten what they might have done to encourage it to develop into steady employment and a family. They would have wanted to do that much.

Others had met him perhaps 20 years ago. They had been impressed. How had so talented a guy ended up making shift from day to day, trading conversation and laughter for burgers and beer? The conversation was so engaging. The abstruse knowledge he brought to bear added to the impression that he was brilliant. The observations on human behavior were nothing short of revelatory. To talk to him was to look at life in a fresh way. He was stimulating. The next morning he was refusing seven dollars an hour to work under the table repairing a commercial air conditioning system and spending the day at a picnic table in the park his small satchel beside him filled with books they'd never heard of before.

He could understand their growing hesitation. Revelations no longer seemed to any point. Even he did not know how the worst could be prevented this time. Somehow he had always survived, even flourished in ways, but the world was changing. He had grown too old, and it too cold, to make shift in the ways he once had. Still he spoke as if barely a year had passed since they'd first met. They spoke of doctors' appointments, cancer scares and he nodded and shook his head on cue. Anyway, he was glad to hear that they were "as good as could be expected." Still he was not 'good,' but 'well'. He had still been 'angry' at an acquaintance, not 'mad'.

The Chop Suey was a quaint little book shop of the sort he always loved to seek out in the obscure little corners of cities. The first floor was the domain of Won Ton the cat-in-residence, his worshippers, and his servant the store clerk. It was also incidentally shoehorned full of gleaming new books. Arthur ascended the narrow stair to the second floor. It was a less social space than the first floor featuring only unfinished bookcases on natural-finish wood floors and a gratifying number of used books for company. It was the perfect place to let his mind quietly graze. An inexpensive used paperback was all he could afford and he took his time finding it.

As he left the shop he settled the book in his backpack and slowly headed west. It was particularly pleasant to see others walking, as well, and seated at café tables, beneath colorful awnings, talking over light lunches.

About half way along, however, there seemed to be a disturbance of some sort ahead. People were hurrying away from the parking lot of a small, nondescript strip mall that had escaped the redevelopment. As he came to the point where he could look into the lot he saw three young men walking in his general direction bearing military assault rifles and ammunition belts. The weaponry appeared to be quite real.

Arthur was so unprepared to see such a sight that he merely stood in place, his head tipped slightly to the side, watching intently. The young men exhibited all the confidence their equipment might provide. There could be little doubt that their stern expressions and actions were intended to assert their perfect right without any apology which might suggest that they were acting in the least inappropriately. While all of this might suggest a threat, he hoped that they were intent only on asserting their right to 'open carry' anywhere they should wish, even amongst popular boutique and linen shops. There had been at least one other such incident in the news recently. Residents did not dare to complain.

The young men strolled away east with their shoulders thrown back and fingers on their trigger guards, very much aware, and more pleased, that every eye was nervously upon them. Nothing was so clear as that they were positively unconcerned for the implications of what they were doing. If anything, city police cruisers would be warned to be scarce in an attempt to avoid the inevitable onslaught of local NRA lawyers to protest that their members were being harassed for doing nothing more than walking lawfully down Cary Street.

Arthur looked after them as they walked away. Not because he feared they might use the weapons but because he was curious. What would the street look like as they walked it? It was clearly changed in the mere minutes since he had strolled along it to this point. There were fewer pedestrians. They had suddenly become interested in the wares of one or another shop and lingered inside. The bulk of those who remained looked furtively in the direction of the machine guns carried demonstratively past them on the other side of the street. Some few made it a point to go along as naturally as they could manage, positively failing to notice that the least thing was out of place. They had no intention of being intimidated. A UPS delivery truck began to pull over before he saw them and immediately realized his delivery was somewhere further up the street.

There quite possibly was a degree of sophistication behind the actions of these heavily armed young men. If they had asserted their rights in the VCU area they would have been surrounded by police cars and security people in short order. The surrender of their firearms would be commanded and their permits checked in hopes of discovering that they failed to satisfy the law in some way, however small. If they had done so near the capitol, it is quite possible that there were special exceptions to the open carry laws the NRA had purchased that would find them arrested on serious charges. Here in Carytown, however, there was unlikely to be an established protocol. They had the element of surprise.

Arthur, too, proceeded to the far side of the street, the side his bike was chained on, and walked casually along trying to recover the feeling of freedom that had made the morning such a pleasure. A television transmission truck passed as he did so, stopped alongside the gunmen and rolled down its driver-side window. The young men gestured back toward the strip mall, by all appearances discussing the matter of where would be a good location to do an interview. They turned back the way they had come and proceeded to retrace their steps. The television truck turned onto a side street and reemerged to pursue in the same direction.

No. The morning was over. He would stop at the supermarket for a few odds and ends to bring back to the apartment. He returned momentarily to the parking lot where all had begun and where now the television truck was parked, a long vertical antenna topped by a satellite dish deployed. There, astraddle his bike, he watched the inexpressive faces of the young men as they explained, with all the nonchalance they could muster, the reason for their walk — or, actually, the reason they didn't need any reason. He turned north for home.

Chapter 9

Arthur could not explain why he always felt supremely optimistic when he woke each morning. The world, of course, had probably changed no more than a jot overnight, and, that being the case, was unlikely to greet him having changed for the better. The greatest blessing, then, was that it was unlikely to have changed for the worse more than that tiny jot. For the first few minutes, the sun shone without subtext or the rain simply and soothingly rained. The sun invited a bicycle ride. The rain gave a perfect excuse to stay inside and organize his thoughts and world.

Often enough, reality brought... well... *reality* to his mood within those minutes but this Monday morning he rose to a world that only wished to go its vague way as if he did not exist. Every item at the computer station had been left exactly where it belonged and no curse-laden search was required for one or another essential tool left out of place. Nor did he knock one or another small part to the floor that rolled to some obscure location under a bookshelf. No software alert took over his monitor with a call to spend his first 15 minutes downloading a safety patch. The milk had not soured. The butter knife did not slide off the plate and onto the floor when he took it out of the refrigerator. Grounds and water awaited the touch of a button to become a fresh pot of coffee.

This morning was going particularly well. The news ticker was almost bland with stories of recovery work in the various areas devastated by fires and storms. Donald Trump was accusing ex-President George Bush of having left the nation vulnerable to the 9/11 attacks in his continuing shock-jock approach to presidential campaigning. The Chinese were still hacking into the computers of US companies after signing an agreement that had promised that they would cease to do so, blah, blah, blah. The Russians had hacked the New York Stock Exchange looking for inside information, blah, blah, blah. The Far Right press was uniformly running a syndicated story that accused Hilary Clinton of having mishandled cybersecurity when Secretary of State, blah, blah, blah. The area weather was expected to be clear and cool for some time to come. Only a handful of articles tempted him and only a few of *those* did he read. It looked like he was going to have some time on his hands, a rare event of late.

His Facebook feed was normally unexceptional. The poets had attended 'awesome' events over the weekend at which all the readers had been 'amazing' and were 'incredibly talented'. He scrolled without pause past several of the finest poems that one or another writing program adjunct had ever heard read before. The Shakespeare Authorship folks had each made a game-changing new discovery coded into the text of one or another Elizabethan play. Traditional scholars cried out once again that not believing in the man from Stratford was the moral equivalent of holocaust denial. The liberal blogs were declaring Dick Cheney a war criminal and the Right Wing blogs were blaming the recent extreme weather on God's displeasure with gay rights. The online community eBible Fellowship was apologizing for the world not having begun the Apocalypse two weeks earlier, as predicted, and announcing that the new date for the advent of the biblical Final Days would now fall in a window beginning shortly before Christmas. The exact date would be announced as soon as more precise calculations were completed. Joel Osteen's dial-a-prayer phone bank was manned and standing-by for the reader's call and donation just in case it wasn't time quite yet. The wealthier friends smiled and waved from the beach at St. Tropez, those less wealthy from the bar at their local Eagles Club.

Photos of everyone's children and grandchildren brought a smile and a sigh. He did have to wonder what kind of future they would have. It was difficult not to lose the optimism of the morning given the prospect. But long experience had taught him that there was little he could do and a great deal he could lose trying. He staved off such thoughts and simply enjoyed the moment.

Rautavaara's 'Cantus Arcticus' played on headset — in order to welcome the dawn without inconveniencing his neighbors — as he watched the world go by outside his door. The grandson of the woman up the walk carried the small bag of garbage past the window, dressed in crisp, ironed, button down shirt and brown denim pants. Neighbors in rumpled sweat shirts, heads down between hunched shoulders, pressed the buttons on their key chains to beep open their car doors and drive out of the parking lot, one by one, until only a few remained.

The lack of compelling news and family photos, on this fine morning, left him time to follow Rautavaara with a new open access paper on Network Theory — this one on Rich-Club Architecture. Such topics benefit from a freshly recharged mind. That and a fresh cup of insanely strong coffee.

The study covered in this particular paper calculated that 9% of brain neurons belong to highly-interconnected Rich Club networks. Arthur was in the habit of observing that for all the infamous 1% were constantly in the news, 5-10% of adult Americans composed the highly skilled allies that made their massive wealth possible. The 9% figure promised to provide a correlation once he drilled down into the numbers. He was not sure what portion of Internet web pages had sufficiently high connectivity to qualify for 'Rich Club' status. It was a number well worth calculating, although the general consensus was growing ever stronger that the percentage was the same as it was for brain neurons and all other social networks. He would have to set aside the time.

As he was slowly wending his way through the paper yet another development promised to free up far more time in his day. K passed with a slight bow on his way, presumably, to catch the 10 o'clock bus and begin his search for work. Arthur had wondered if this was the reason he seemed to be even more than usually attentive to his suit on this particular morning. A good deal of extra fluttering about and polishing shoes suggested that the decision had been made.

When the next day brought more of the same on all counts, Arthur began to feel a little guilty at the pleasure he took in the progress of events. After all, what was the likelihood of success? K had no identification to present unless he intended to try using the papers from 1920 that he insisted were his own. A potential employer was unlikely to find them a promising recommendation. And, come to think of it, what recommendations did he have? While quite a lot of work was available to those without papers, his suit and fedora suggested that he had no intention of standing outside of Lowe's waiting for a contractor to show interest. The Latinos were more than a little territorial about the place and unlikely to take his presence well. They had, after all, been the only ones willing to develop the idea and the location. It was their territory and they would not take intruders lightly. It was impossible, in any event, to picture him digging ditches or hammering shingles into place.

Arthur realized that he was demanding what he himself could not choose to do, and being persistent, perhaps, precisely for the reason that he was projecting onto K the resistance that he felt. K's issues were only variations on his own. They both were impossibly out of their element each in their own way. Both could present marketable skills but no marketable social networks in a time when the first (and the second and the third...) requirement for finding any job was a social network. He imagined his guest dealing with confusion and rejection by way of a workday. Job hunting was the most dispiriting kind of work and lacked a paycheck to make it half-bearable.

K had little to say upon his return and spent the evening in his room on the Internet. The next morning he was out the door again even a bit earlier. His determination in the face of all the obstacles was unexpected. Perhaps it was another import from a tougher-minded age (however exactly he had come by it). Whatever the source, it could only arrive at frustration and disappointment. The relief it brought Arthur was probably unfair. Still, he could not help but feel pleased to have his days, at least, to himself once again, and the prospect, however dim, of his roommate getting a place of his own in time was an attractive one. He imagined a small apartment nearby where he could keep a protective eye on his inexplicable friend.

The next day, however, K did his morning exercises and toilet and did not emerge again from his room until he furtively entered the kitchenette and placed his breakfast in the microwave. Plastic container in hand, he returned to his room. Arthur became slightly more agitated with each passing minute. He knew it was hardly fair but there was simply no other alternative but to stay with the effort. Yes, success promised to be impossible but K must try, try again. When K emerged, around noon, to heat a small desert cup that was part of the salad plate he had chosen for lunch, his host appeared in the doorway. K smiled wanly.

"Aren't you going out to look for a job today?"

The answer was so astonishing that he staggered slightly and steadied himself against the molding. "I have found employment. I begin on Monday morning."

"May I ask where?"

"I am employed in a small office downtown. I am sure you would not know it."

The answer was not a promising one. The unwillingness to provide detail smacked of evasiveness. "Perhaps I'll surprise you. I'd really like to know." Quite aware of K's concern about not having papers to present if he were stopped by the police, Arthur saw his opening. "I'd hate to have you get involved in something that might get you into trouble with the authorities."

"I am employed by a Mr. Mendelssohn. His family owns a small import-export business with offices downtown. It is a perfectly legitimate concern. Still, he prefers to be inconspicuous. His business is conducted entirely via the Internet and the mails."

"How did you come to find out that there was a position available?"

"I took your advice. I went into a small refurbished office building and knocked on the doors."

"Am I to understand that he offered you a job based on the fact that you wear a fedora?"

K could not help but scowl about being interrogated, much less made fun of. "We spoke, as gentlemen are wont to do, and it turns out that we have some things in common."

"Such as...?"

"Mr. Mendelssohn's great granduncle used to make deliveries to my father's shop."

Arthur could not help but emit a short burst of laughter such as expressed utter disbelief. "You knocked on a random door in a downscale office building and the knock was answered by the grandnephew of a man who delivered to your father's shop, ...in 1920, ...in Prague?"

"*Great* grandnephew, yes."

An involuntary, convulsive laugh escaped Arthur again. It was simply too much to believe. "And there is no chance that I might meet this Mr. Mendelssohn?"

"I ask that you not place my position with him in jeopardy. He has been enormously kind. I fear it would be received as a betrayal for me to allow him to be an object of observation."

Surely that was it. There was no Mr. Mendelssohn. K had simply grown tired of wandering aimlessly around town, on a hopeless mission, and invented a job. It would free him from the unpleasant task of looking for work for at least a week or two before the question of why he had not yet been paid arose. "But he might not be legitimate. I should know more. I'd hate for you to end up in jail because this guy was not what he appeared to be. I have to think that you are quite naïve to believe that the man can have known your father."

"Of course Mr. Mendelssohn was not even born then."

"You begin to see my point…"

"It was his great granduncle."

"Whatever. There are a dozen classic cons that start with similar claims. A lot of small import-export concerns are a cover for receiving contraband goods. Illicit drugs generally. It really is true. It could help avoid a very bad situation if you were to introduce me to Mr. Mendelssohn."

K's dessert cup had grown cold waiting in the microwave. Checking it, he placed it back inside, without comment, and started it heating again.

"Like not getting paid, perhaps, or being questioned by the police." When it was finished warming, he lowered his head and returned to his room. Arthur called out behind him. "Or even prison time. The penalty for dealing in drugs is many years of incarceration."

K passed his door and closed it behind him. The action brought the conversation to an end but not Arthur's doubts. After all, how was it possible that K could have met an acquaintance of his father? In Richmond? At the distance of almost a hundred years? It simply was not possible. But what to do? His guest's announcement left him in a quandary. He spent the rest of the day considering the situation. Periodically he entered search queries on the name

'Mendelssohn' and on Richmond import-export companies. None of the various alternative spellings of the name or similar names or related queries provided as much as a single pertinent listing. He considered speaking with K once more. But what would he say? In the end, he decided that he would ask occasional offhand questions the next day in an attempt to wheedle information out of his guest by which he could challenge the story of Mr. Mendelssohn. Possibly, no more than a day or two would be lost (along with the last shreds of his trust). But suddenly a day or two sounded like an eternity.

The next day, however, contained yet another surprise. As Arthur was scrolling through the morning news feeds a story about an attack upon a Swedish high school jumped out at him. That kind of thing rarely happened outside of the U.S. Such a crime was virtually unheard of in Sweden.

He was particularly interested to learn whether it had been inspired by Anders Breivik, the horrific Norwegian mass murderer. Until recent years, the scourge of mass murders was unthinkable in the idyllic Nordic countries and he felt that he personally had lost some bit of hope because of the change. Still information and distance gave him some little feeling of control, which, if it could be made real, was better than hope.

While he was reading the handful of articles about the knife wielding rampage, and the neo-Nazi paraphernalia rumored to have been recovered from the assailant's apartment, K passed once again, with his customary slight bow, and exited the apartment without explanation. Arthur rose, leaned over the low bookcase in front of the window and watched intently as he walked past the bus stop, and, for the first time, walked up the street entirely unaccompanied. He was soon out of sight. Arthur peered in the direction he had gone his thoughts tracing K's steps until he could no longer imagine which way he might have continued. He dropped limply back into his seat as if all the world had gone crazy. What had he gotten himself into? Nothing in the world made sense anymore.

Not having waited for the bus, it was unlikely that K was pretending to go to the import-export offices in order to avoid the continuation of the questions he knew would certainly be asked. Besides, he had made it clear that Monday would be his first day. Thinking about it, though, it might be an even cleverer move if he intended to disappear for the day with vague or no explanation as to where he had been. While it would be difficult coming up with excuses as to why he'd had to spend the day out, the thing could be managed. It would be impossible if he remained in the apartment, on the other hand, to avoid questions about an employer who somehow had known his family a hundred years ago.

Had K simply continued to look for a job, Arthur would not have felt he had any reason to interrogate him. The introduction of Mr. Mendelssohn, however, made it impossible to avoid, a fact which K was sure to have realized. What other response could have been expected? But why go out the next day, anyway, after having made up a story to avoid the unpleasant task of going out hunting for a job? Given the circumstances, could it be for any other reason than to avoid questions? He may have decided that a daylong walking tour was more pleasant than hunting for a job that did not likely exist. But, no. Even that theory did not quite fit together.

Arthur found this was one of the more frustrating aspects of sharing living space. It always seemed to devolve into evasions and mysteries. That they had begun after so short a time was disheartening. To find himself staring past a computer screen, again and again, oblivious to what he had intended to do, his mind calculating the likely permutations of behavior from which he could not simply click away, was as inevitable as it was exasperating (which was doubly exasperating). There was nothing worse. Well, it always felt as if there was nothing worse anyway… until still worse happened (which was pretty much guaranteed). He had no idea how others dealt with it so willingly and regularly.

By the time K returned, Arthur had lost an entire day in this way. Nor was that to be the end of it, for K was not alone. Again without a word of explanation, he walked inside pushing a yellow bicycle, edged it along until there was room to close the door, and continued past Arthur threading the maze of bookcases to his room. As he made his way past the beaten-up old bike behind the door, with its duct-taped seat, and rusty frame, it looked impressive indeed. Once the rider and bicycle were in their room, he closed the door. There had been no sign that he intended to emerge again until it was time to microwave his supper.

When K did come out of his room, microwavable plastic container in hand, Arthur was not yet ready to chance another shock. Not that he was managing to accomplish anything but to stew over circumstances he should have known better than to invite. The man claims to be Kafka, for God's sake. What had he expected? For all of this, and whatever might lie ahead, Arthur was receiving the convenience of laundry service? And the satisfaction of helping Jeremiah and Lori out of a difficult situation? What had he been thinking?

But it was not like this was out of character he had to admit. Somehow, for all he thought he'd changed, he found himself back in some close variation on the usual problems. No one else was fool enough to take his guest off his hands, that much he could depend upon.

Why had he taken the man in, after all? The decision had to be made quickly, that was it. When it came to making people decisions that had always brought disastrous results. It takes a few minutes to realize that one is destroying one's life. Several days at a minimum, actually. Jeremiah knew his weaknesses and had gone straight for them. Undoubtedly, it was *normal* to do so. But he had proven an easy mark. What about the one absolutely inviolate rule? No roommates. Keep the apartment inviolate and all the 'power-law distribution' dramas and elsewise cluster-fucks take place somewhere far away. He knew the rules. They were designed to do nothing so much as to avoid situations like this. He had no one to blame but himself.

Later, K emerged once again to wash his dishes and utensils. He'd borne up under the results of Arthur's pitiful attempts at cleanliness for days, while his energies went entirely toward the job hunt, but it hadn't been easy. He longed even more for the days his mother made so sure the maid kept a tidy flat and the cook a spotless kitchen. The pieces of life fit together so naturally then. He had arrived at a barbaric place. Civilization had been left behind, and, with it, the possibility of an uninterrupted hour rereading Flaubert (he'd stumbled across Arthur's copy of *Bouvard and Pécuchet* with a cry of joy). He took a deep breath and gathered all the other dirty dishes piled on the counter, as well, cleaned the various congealed spills at every hand and swept the floor. Mopping would follow dishes.

Squeezing the bright yellow dishwashing liquid into the sink and turning on the water, he could not help but notice how it all had quickly become commonplace. Even the microwave had ceased to be a marvel. As he reflected on all of this, he became aware that the quality of the light in the kitchenette had altered slightly. He turned to find Arthur standing in the doorway.

"Nice bike. Is it new?"

"I bought it at the Salvation Army," K replied, settling a glass into the dish drainer. "I was surprised that they existed in this Richmond. Google Maps informed me that there was one not too far away, near the sports stadium."

"Diamond Stadium. They've gotten pretty pricey there. It must have cost nearly a hundred bucks."

"Bucks?"

"Slang for 'dollars'."

"It appears to be genuinely in the best of condition."

The guy had escaped from the Roach Motel a couple of months ago without so much as an American penny to his name. He thinks he's the novelist Franz Kafka. Now he owns a bicycle to put my clunker to shame, Arthur reflected, more amused than offended (and more envious than either).

"Did Lori give you money for it?" He cringed noticeably in expectation of the answer.

"No. Mr. Mendelssohn gave me an advance on my salary." K held a plate up to the light and inspected it closely. "He suspected that I must need to purchase a few items given the circumstances."

"The circumstances?"

"Finding myself suddenly here with only outdated Marks for currency," he went on, as he dipped the wash rag in the sink water, now empty of dishes, and began wiping down the counters and surfaces. "I explained that I have already put you all to a good deal of expense. It didn't seem fair to ask for pocket money."

"You told him that you are Franz Kafka? And that you were napping on the train and woke up to find yourself in the Roach Motel?"

K scowled as he realized that he would have to use his fingernail to dislodge a particularly stubborn blob of spaghetti sauce from the top of the stove. He was very particular about his manicure. It was the kind of small sign that marked out a true gentleman. "I reflected, as I searched on the Internet, what might be the best thing to do. I could think of no justification sufficient to permit lying about such matters."

"So you told every person at every company that you were Franz Kafka."

"It was the only thing I could do in all honesty. They did, after all, ask who I was and whence I came."

Arthur laughed to imagine it. "Did anyone believe you?"

"I cannot say with certainty. By the third day, I *was* wondering whether the reactions I received indicated that I was being more honest than might be wise. Perhaps the saying 'When in Rome' is still current?"

"It's as much a lifestyle as a saying now. Did anyone inquire further? About your qualifications, for example?"

"Only one office, above a small bakery, where they were looking for something called a 'data entry clerk'. They seemed to think that, being from 1920, I would accept a wage such as your indoctrinations indicated was 'beneath contempt'. They were quite friendly and even a little excited to show me around until I declined their offer. Then they just laughed and said that they loved my 'book about the giant bug'. What is a 'fax machine,' by the way?"

"Why a bike?" asked Arthur, ignoring the question.

"I will be acting as Mr. Mendelssohn's personal assistant at times. He works from home as often as he is able."

It was all too much. Each new revelation (with the amusing exception of the office over the bakery) was more unlikely than the last. Yet somehow, astonishingly, the supporting details each taken separately could hardly be questioned. "You knocked on the door of an import-export office, that you had never even seen before, announced that you were Franz Kafka looking for a job, and the owner hired you on the spot to be his personal secretary?"

"I do have some demonstrable typing skills. I was perfectly dependable at the Insurance Institute until the onset of the tuberculosis and I seem unaffected by it here. Far more to the point, I may be the only person in this Richmond, according to Mr. Mendelssohn, who is fluent in both German and Czech."

"Mr. Mendelssohn does his correspondence in German and Czech?" Again, it was simply too much.

"A good deal of it, yes. The company is a family concern. He operates the United States branch office."

"Wouldn't you rather take the bus?"

"He lives somewhere called Byrd Park. He informs me that it is not along a bus route. Nor is it close enough to walk from any bus stop."

"The biking shouldn't be too worrisome there."

"I checked the laws relating to bicycling last night."

"Yes, well there's one thing to remember above all else."

"To obey all traffic signs?"

"No. To forget about everything you read about the laws pertaining to bicycling. There is only one rule of bicycling. Cars are much bigger than you therefore they always have the right of way regardless what the law says. When a car hits a bicycler, it is always the bicycler's fault or fault will not be able to be determined. Drivers know this and it makes them homicidal. If you are worried for any reason that riding in the far right lane might not be safe, ride on the sidewalk."

"But it is illegal to ride a bicycle on the sidewalk."

"Yes. And it is definitely *not* illegal to get run over while riding on the roadside."

K stood considering.

"That's a pretty wealthy area over there," Arthur went on. "Some of those houses weigh-in at just short of a castle. I assume, then, that his offer was not beneath contempt."

"I will be paid by the hour when my services are necessary. The amount seems fair."

"This will all be under the table?"

"Mr. Mendelssohn is an honorable businessman. I will appear on his accounts as an independent contractor."

"He won't look so honorable on his accounts if he is paying his contractor in cash."

"I will be paid by bank draft, of course (which I understand, these days is called a 'check')."

"How in the world will you cash it? Without identification you will not be able to open a bank account. If I were to cash the checks I could end up in an impossible position with the tax man myself. The same for Jeremiah and Lori."

"Mr. Mendelssohn's office will cash the checks. This is apparently sufficient to meet the requirements of the law on his part. As for my part, I could not venture a guess in such a matter. Each morning, the first thing I do is look around me to see if I have returned to my seat on the train or otherwise to Prague. I passionately hope not to have to worry about explaining myself to 'the tax man'."

Chapter 10

As long as K had a bike now, Arthur thought he might as well suggest taking a ride. The two men had been under a lot of stress lately. The mood in the apartment was tense and there was nothing Arthur found more uncomfortable. He was constitutionally unable to ignore tension. The effects would linger in the air making him struggle slightly with every breath and nothing was so unbearable as that. It was the primary reason he no longer took roommates... until now... and, of course, he straight away found himself in the situation. The prospect was maddening. For better or worse he felt he must be proactive.

This also made it necessary that Arthur trust K as a matter of expediency if for no other reason. Truth be told, he was feeling more than a little guilty which only made the situation more maddening. The only thing less rational than inviting Franz Kafka into one's home and to have him find employment with an old friend of his father's, was feeling guilty about it.

As with all matters these days, the employment search had proven to be an unaccountable affair. Stranger still, a realization had struck Arthur, the night before, as he struggled to regain his customary focus. Had he stayed with his original determination to treat K as if he were actually Kafka most of the discomfort of the past week would have been avoided. Once one accepted that K was Kafka, it was a bit late in the game to question the existence of a Mr. Mendelssohn. He groaned to think of it but it wasn't as if this kind of utterly irrational requirement only occurred when Franz Kafka was the roommate in question. He could think of considerably less rational circumstances on more than one occasion in the past. Now that matters had reached the present... whatever... there really was no alternative but to take K at his word in all matters once again. Otherwise the situation would be untenable.

For these reasons, he addressed K as "Franz" when he suggested the bike ride. It wasn't the first time but now he intended to make it a habit. His guest might take it as being overly familiar but the message would also be conveyed that upon reflection Arthur was choosing to trust him. Or at least to let the matter unfold as it would.

After lunch they were soon pedaling past Virginia Union College's Hovey Field on Lombardy Street. The bleachers and fields were deserted as the football team was playing an away game. As they passed above the railroad tracks, beyond the field, an elderly black man pedaling in the opposite direction called out, with a laugh, for them to reduce their speed to the posted limit. They waved and laughed by way of reply. K, who was always charmed by a spontaneous greeting that wasn't part of a job description, felt it was an excellent omen. The easy speed of the bike, the almost cloudless sky and the unexpected greeting gave the excursion a lightness that he hadn't felt since riding on the back of Jeremiah's Harley.

As they passed the supermarket parking lot on one side of the street and the Lowe's lot on the other, and approached the intersection with Broad Street, K found the large number of cars coming from every direction fearful to navigate. Arthur looked over his shoulder to find his companion well back walking his bike. He stepped off his own and stood waiting until they were side by side again.

"I cannot imagine how you ride here with such confidence," said K, once he was within range to be understood. "I expect to be run over every minute."

They walked their bikes across Broad and within a block were in neighborhoods of a decayed gentility K had not experienced in Richmond before. Turning onto Grace Street, they passed a pair of white granite sentinel columns mounted with carriage lamps that even he recognized as a throwback to earlier times. The route was lined with trees often of considerable age and spreading canopy. The houses regularly featured small front lawns and steps ascending to pillared porches and heavy front doors. As the rule, they were separated by just enough room for a single person to pass between. Occasionally, the space was wider and revealed exposed wooden stairways providing access to side doors on first floor and second. He could not help but notice that the houses had chimneys. Every feature suggested that they had ridden into a world that retained a sense of an earlier time.

Ironically it was also more contemporary in certain ways. Here, the road surface had no cracks or holes. The street and cross streets all displayed white painted figures of a bicycle augmented with directional arrows along the side of the roadbed. At every street corner the crosswalks were bold with fresh white paint. Fresh double yellow stripes divided each road perfectly in half. The roads and sidewalks were clearly better taken care of than in even the better neighborhoods through which K and Arthur had previously taken their walks. "There are many bicycles on the porches here," K noticed aloud.

"We're close to VCU. Some of the students prefer to rent apartments outside of the main campus area."

"VCU?"

"Virginia Commonwealth University. Most of this area serves it in one way or another. Many of the students ride bikes." The explanation was offered as they passed two more identical columns with carriage lights. The columns marked the beginning of an area of an entirely different character. On the other side of the intersection was the first of what would be a great many signs boldly featuring the initials 'VCU'. Large public buildings that K understood to display a more modern architectural style rose on either side. In the spaces between these large buildings was a mix of every kind of small obviously older building, mostly storefronts, no consistent pattern or purpose being discernible.

Ever greater numbers of students could be seen out walking as K followed his guide toward what could only be assumed to be the center of the University. The gray slab sidewalks became a herringbone pattern of red brick that felt somehow festive. Most of the buildings were also of red brick. Entire blocks were dominated by the color. It being a Saturday most of the students walked at a leisurely pace usually in couples or small groups. One or more among the group tended to be casually manipulating the small screen of a Smartphone then rejoining the general conversation. Those who were far more intense about their little screens tended to walk much faster, he noticed, and alone. While the expressions within the groups were vague, the brows of the intense individuals were furrowed, their lips pursed.

Arthur having slowed to a stop and dismounted, K did the same. He had not thought it necessary to buy a lock for his bike, so Arthur chained both their bikes together to a small tree along the sidewalk. K's being so much nicer, Arthur would normally have been uncomfortable about leaving it the least bit vulnerable but Grace Street at the Virginia Commonwealth campus was probably not much subject to bicycle theft.

The students now passed in every direction, K thought, much like a bustling Breughel painting of a harvest festival except that they wore t-shirts and jeans and the coeds were more expressly sensual. Whenever two coeds recognized each other their eyes sparkled especially and they smiled huge movie-star smiles and literally cried out with joy. "People are so free here! It's as if there was no such thing as sin!"

"Oh no," said Arthur. "Sin remains, only God has changed. God always does, of course, but the most recent change is..." he hesitated to use so grand a word, "epochal." As he spoke, Arthur turned right, down a side street, K tracking beside him. "The Network created by the 'frictionless thinking machine' is God now."

"By the 'Network' I assume you mean the thing you call 'the Internet'."

"More or less."

"It seems to be everywhere but hardly God."

"In each age, God becomes the sum of the prevailing culture and mores. Of course, the previous image of God remains part of it all for a while. Slowly, though, each successive image fades away into the next."

K looked toward a public park that was just coming into view ahead. "The Network becoming the new image seems hardly a matter of one image fading into another."

"The idea of 'fading' implies time for transition, but the time that used to be involved for historical transitions also implies long stretches of subpar productivity. The System began as a remarkably effective means of increasing production. That is still its core function. One might describe it as the 'tradition' of the System. The results have reduced transitions from centuries, or even millennia, to decades or years."

"So then, fading is no longer 'fading'."

"As in all things these days, the matter has been accelerated, made much more efficient. Transitions must be streamlined. Those programs that hinder optimum productivity must be transformed."

"Do people not feel imposed upon to lose all that they once held dear?"

Arthur nodded toward a young coed, thumbs furiously typing a text into her Smartphone. "History is not profitable. Therefore, it barely exists. They no longer remember what they once held dear." She walked briskly away alongside the park.

"I would protest that such things are not possible but then this Richmond itself does not seem possible."

"In the age of the Network, God has become the sum of the culture and mores that arise from out of the Network. It needs people to buy things now and to desire satisfaction of the flesh. Of course the details are, as always in such matters, quite complex."

"*It?*" K could not help but blurt it out.

"*He*, if you prefer to keep the old anthropomorphic God-father-concept lingering on a bit longer."

K was surprised to hear the clack of horses' hooves. He turned slowly around trying to get a fix on their location, continuing the conversation as he did so. "But the Internet is nothing more than a great many wires."

"So is the human brain. So many wires that the vast number allows for conscious thought."

At last he saw two riders in identical dark blue uniforms and white helmets passing leisurely into the park. His gaze followed the two. "This Network, on the other hand, cannot think."

"Actually, it is just beginning to do so," replied Arthur. He paused to give the import of what he had said time to sink in.

"How is that possible?"

"The brain is nothing more than a great many wires and *it* thinks."

"But unbridled desire for physical satisfaction is the realm of Satan, is it not? While, even in the more fashionable Prague cafes, Gods and Satans are rather passé, it is beyond thinking to do away altogether with the order they provide. Mustn't it eventually resolve itself in..." (it was K's turn to hesitate now) "...*epochal* destructiveness?"

"And if the profits from unbridled desire enrich everyone, pay for public works, extend the average lifespan? Asceticism is unprofitable. The destructiveness of desire is statistically supportable — theoretically, at least."

Horse and rider having disappeared around a corner beyond the park K turned back toward his guide again. "But God and Satan served civilization for thousands of years. How will decency survive without the majority of people believing in them at least enough to fear the possibility of them? What will not be allowed?"

"If memory serves, none of the characters in your books attend church, or, for that matter, synagogue. Had they it would have been spurious, it seems to me."

K smiled more broadly than he would have liked. He could not help but momentarily lower his head and wipe the palm of his hand across his mouth. "Yet perhaps they struggle with God... in their own way."

"Your characters are always impossibly entangled in an irrational world," Arthur went on. "Ours are always impossibly free with the illusion that our incredible technologies empower the irrational without the entanglement. Decency is being redefined as we speak. Anything that seriously introduces friction to the System will not be continued. It is already the new sin: introducing friction. Anything that expands the System, anything that reduces friction, is becoming 'the will of God'... the will of the Network."

"But we are just now passing a Catholic cathedral if I am not mistaken." As K said this his gaze turned back toward Monroe Park across the street to linger over the red and yellow foliage of the trees.

A small group of skateboarding students soon caught his eye. The sun broke free of a cloud as if their laughter was the cause of it. "It is quite impressive, don't you think?"

"Cathedral of the Sacred Heart."

"It would seem to have an entire city block for its administration buildings, K went on, his attention returned to the church. "Look, it specifies that its services are made available as part and parcel of the University."

"Look everywhere around us," said Arthur. "What do you see that is different than anywhere else we've walked through all these many afternoons? All of the places so gloriously untroubled by sin?"

"We have walked places much less pleasant. There sin still seemed to exist."

"Poverty is sin, then?"

K was embarrassed to have made such a blunder. He blushed noticeably and looked away in order to compose himself. Of course he thought no such thing. The two of them entered the park. "It is a sin that people are impoverished. Perhaps it is this I felt."

"Perhaps," said Arthur, not wanting to take advantage of an uncomfortable and entirely understandable lapse. It was an informal conversation, not a formal debate. "Less friction will mean more wealth. It is inherent in the whole idea." He was careful not to make his next statement sound like he was pressing his advantage. "But didn't the people in those places seem less well behaved? A bit more worrisome? Wasn't that why you could sense sin existed there?"

"Of course it is so," replied K, "but that is not a new misconception. Everything is so overwhelming. I am reduced to the understanding of a child here, and, it seems, I make a child's mistakes if I am not particularly careful."

"Those here at the University have reason to hope for a happy future. Moreover, they have the resiliency of youth to make their hopes seem brighter than their realities are likely to be. They have been born into the System and will not question it until disappointments encourage them to do so."

"Will they turn against it?"

"The Lord giveth and the Lord taketh away. Without God — without the System — what blessings can be expected? Some few will and they will live short lives of suffering and envy those who pleased God. Most will struggle and come to terms. They will think of the struggle as a matter of 'maturing,' perhaps, or, more likely, correcting an imbalance of brain chemicals. Studies are regularly undertaken, as a matter of course, to quantify the annual cost to the system and reduction in average annual salary at different points in life for the challenged worker. Returning the disaffected to the faith takes on a certain urgency given the demonstrable cost to everyone involved. Each day away from God has a quantifiable financial and social cost."

"Imbalance of brain chemicals?"

"Yes. At the moment, the most popular imbalances are called 'attention deficit disorders' and 'mood disorders'. 'Depression' is *always* popular. I imagine you are familiar with the diagnosis."

K scowled.

"Depression never goes out of fashion. Huge numbers of millions conform themselves to the demands of the System by taking drugs to adjust their brain chemistries, to correct their disorders."

"Why, then, is the Cathedral of the Sacred Heart here at all?" asked K. "Or any of the other churches that are so remarkably common in this Richmond?"

"They know more intimately well than anyone else that the old God is fading away. But life must go on. Like all large enterprises, they must continue to bring in customers or fail to cover payroll and this has helped them become analytical about their situations and prospects. The students already pay large amounts for housing and tuition. The various businesses we are walking past here entertain and feed them: this costs still more money. Should they find it all an unsustainable burden, the churches offer humbler, less expensive alternatives. Should the System feel unduly harsh — as is bound to be the case at times — the churches can soften the effects. Almost all of the old sins are quite bearable now in light of a new tolerance. The few that create friction remain sins. This describes the church's 'market niche'."

"Is nothing left of the old faiths? Is there no longer access to any of that?"

"The Medieval church burned people at the stake. The higher ranking clergy were often also fierce warriors who thought nothing of crushing an enemy's skull. The poor born outside of a parish were neither fed nor sheltered but shown to the city limits to survive outside of it as best they might. Luther himself acquiesced to the horrific punishments of the competing Protestant Anabaptist sect of his place and time with little sense of the grand irony of such an act. Yet still you seem to think that faith was somehow more real then."

K's brow was deeply furrowed as he listened. His silence made clear his resistance.

"The poor are friction before God now. The church remains connected with its mythical past by feeding and clothing them. Their compassion is as much a matter of tax laws that remain on the books since the Middle Ages as anything. Happily those laws can be recruited toward reducing the friction of poverty. Where the effort threatens to create more friction rather than less the churches are firmly encouraged to stop."

"If told to stop, they will stop? They will obey the new God?"

"Look around you." The sense of defensiveness K had come to feel over the past week was forgotten. He inspected the scene, as directed, with an intensity that bordered on the naïve. "Do you see anyone panhandling on the street corners?" His eyebrows rose with modest astonishment. The lack had not yet dawned on him. "Has anyone asked you for pocket change?"

"You're saying that this area is free of these things because there is an order forbidding it?"

"Such formal orders were not necessary, as the rule, in your Prague, were they?"

"No. Of course you are quite right."

"Still, there were places where the poor were not welcome."

"Yes, in the Christian quarters undeniably."

"It was not good for business there."

"But the synagogue made sure that our poor were taken care of. Discreetly: no one wished them to be unduly embarrassed. One should not give with pride or be forced to receive with shame."

"The Jewish Quarter was the home of outcasts and that taught you better how to give. There are no outcasts here. Not yet anyway. Those that will become outcasts will find it uncomfortable should they wish to return to stroll through these neighborhoods."

A thought came to K. "But, in Prague, God was not this System."

"No? Why were you in the habit of warning others about the advent of the 'frictionless thinking machine'?"

"So the System was God even then?"

"The new God didn't have the resources then that it has now. Even in 1920, the city was as much Medieval as modern."

"There is a charm to the combination that even residents such as I appreciate. I notice that your tourists find it particularly attractive in this 2015."

"What was only beginning in your day is now coming to its conclusion. Now God is no longer Medieval. The church is more and more a *product* of its times. Weddings and funerals and all their attendant *products and services* continue, and, of course, eternal life is the ultimate high-end product. Businessmen still sit on church committees, the résumé enhancement and connections being an attractive product. In these neighborhoods, relations are established with promising student prospects as a matter of propinquity. While the rules remain those of all products — production cost must be kept as low as possible and profits as high — perhaps there is nothing more in it to prohibit faith than any of the other accommodations with social mores at any other time. Faith has always required a convenient lack of self-awareness."

"Even eternal life can be a product?"

"It is the *perfect* product. The production cost is almost zero and the market price high. Churches could not survive without it. Change though God may, death remains stubbornly the same."

"Is it all so bereft of the *mystery* of God now?"

"Surely you have come to have a sense of how much more impressive mankind has become with the advent of the computer — 'the frictionless machine'. If someone had a terrible pain in the stomach, in the old days, their family prayed to God for a miracle cure. Now they go to the hospital, a surgery is performed. Results are almost guaranteed. No miracles are necessary. No mysterious will caused the illness. Only the ability to afford the surgery chooses who will be cured."

"There are greater mysteries than a stomach ache."

"Yes there are. But if you asked even the teachers of these students they'd be hard-pressed to say what they are. Their most likely answer would refer to illnesses that we cannot yet perfectly cure or something of the sort." Arthur had stopped walking. He looked around rather sadly, K thought. "The priest's answer would come to just as little; the priest, that is to say, who did not sell fervor as a kind of mystery."

K stood silently, his brows deeply furrowed in thought again. "It seems to me there would be considerable friction in fervor."

"Most definitely," Arthur replied, "but it is also deeply human. The Christian churches of Prague were at the beginning of a transition between the Medieval and the modern. Every time is also a transitional time (no matter how rapid the transition). Even God must have patience sometimes. Fervor is being channeled into more harmless, recreational directions. For present purposes it is enough that the religious version can be strictly kept from places like this campus at least."

"But what of the soul?" K regretted the question the second he asked it.

"The soul remains. It is a product, of course. If the System detects that enough people feel the need for a more satisfying soul-product it perceives it as a demand without a product to fulfill it. It will design a more effective soul-product to monetize the need. Soul will be analyzed, a digital approximation created, a system of production assembled. Like all manufacturing processes, the most successful product will have the lowest possible production cost and bring the highest possible price. The successful version of the product will depend on historical legitimacy only inasmuch as it enhances the ability to engage the largest possible customer base. There will be stockholders. The managers will be tasked to earn them the highest possible profits. Anything less will be a failure if not an outright fraud."

"Surely there are many who cannot be satisfied by such a concept of the soul."

"Yes: the immature and those with imbalanced brain chemicals."

The answer brought a gasp from K. "Can nothing be done?"

"About what? Life?"

"So this state of affairs satisfies you, then."

"If anything can 'be done' it will register as a matter of demand. A product will be created to do it." Arthur looked at the sidewalk at his feet. "It does not matter in the least whether it satisfies me or not."

"Do you always take your guests on bicycle rides on a charming university campus and discuss the identity of God?"

"You mentioned sin. It seemed important that you know."

"How could it possibly be important?"

"Actually, it is important that you are in no position to make trouble for me for explaining it. It is I who need to explain it."

It surprised K just how immediately he understood. It was as if a fact had instantly blinked into existence. *"You* are an outcast. How are you permitted to be here?"

"We both are outcasts. Can you think that you fit-in here having arrived on a bicycle in an old fashioned suit and fedora?"

"How are *we* permitted to be here?"

"We are White, unarmed, the bicycles are chained well behind us. I have shaved, dressed to blend in. I could be just another resident of a house, a few blocks from here, taking a stroll or showing the campus to my friend from some old fashioned corner of Europe. If the VCU authorities were to overhear me explaining this to students, I would be escorted off of the campus forthwith, I suspect, and forbidden to return."

"They do not share your assessment, then."

"Students are at an impressionable age. Strangers with unaccountable opinions might present any number of dangers."

"Yet you do not see your status as resulting from immaturity or an imbalance of brain chemicals."

"I prefer to think that I am an outdated model. My manufacturer felt I was not satisfying, not sufficiently user friendly. It long ago evaluated the expenditures it would require in order to keep me in service and determined that it was insufficiently profitable to continue to support my maintenance or my spare parts inventory. It no longer supports my operating system."

"Your manufacturer?"

"Society. The System."

"Are you a machine?"

"Of course I am a machine. One that was once considered quite promising. But that was product generations ago. It didn't work out."

"How can you mean 'generations ago'? Can one live many lives in this 2015?"

The two walked back toward the bikes. Students emerged from the apartment buildings, to left and right, generally in twos and threes, disjointedly laughing, chatting and peering into their Smartphone screens. The few who walked alone along the sidewalk did not smile. They looked still more intently into their phones.

"Sometimes it seems impossible not to... if one hopes to live any life at all."

A motorcar filled with chatting students pulled away from the curb as they walked past. Behind it, another screeched to a halt and angrily beeped its horn. Around them, the world stopped and turned to watch. For a moment, K wondered whether danger might not somehow be at hand. Suddenly, the students laughed and gestured out the open windows of the vehicles. Both continued on their way.

"People had yet to learn how to evaluate the likes of me then. There were many misunderstandings. They became the basis of decisions."

"There were poor decisions made?"

"I've since come to doubt that there is any longer a basis for judging whether a particular decision is bad or good. Users complained. As the result friction increased. Losses were incurred. Decisions were made. Narratives were created. A new model was purchased. Life went on."

"Narratives?"

"Yes. We no longer assess facts *per se*. The process is *much* too unwieldy. A situation arises, or is foreseen. Each of the parties creates a narrative explaining it in the way they wish the matter to be perceived. An attempt is made to incorporate at least something of each narrative (or so the narrative of 'narrativity' goes), in a kind of transaction, resulting in a balance to satisfy the various social and wealth hierarchies in play."

"And this succeeds?" asked K, more even than usually astonished.

"Whether it succeeds or fails, life goes on," replied Arthur. An especially fierce twinkle came to his eye. "We've grown in the habit of calling the results 'Kafkaesque'."

K lurched to a swaying halt.

"The permutations are many but the pattern is unmistakable," Arthur went on. "Of course, a great many very popular products have been developed based upon narrativity. They are pervasive."

"Surely you cannot be saying that there is no attempt at all to determine the facts of any situation?"

"Well, science and technology, of course, must proceed along more traditionally functional lines. But only a tiny portion of the population is needed for such matters. They must continuously advertise the advantages of their exception — such as extended lifespans, reduced physical pain, more satisfying stimulation of the senses, etc. — in order to avoid the ferocious prevailing punishments for intractable elitism. Even so, they are the subject of conspiracy theories and care must be taken for their safety."

"I cannot believe a bit of this."

"Too great an oversupply of rational thinkers would only be dangerous. Should anyone else be detected trying to put rational methods to inappropriate uses they are immediately decried as 'elitists' and ostracized. There is nothing more socially abhorrent than 'elitism'. God has made sure of that. The elitist has a long hard life ahead. He or she will need to be repeatedly demeaned until they learn their place. Recantation will be demanded under the most humiliating conditions possible. As the result, only the rare attempt is made, and the person who makes it, in spite of the widely advertised punishments, is almost guaranteed to be in some glaring way socially or mentally perverse. This reinforces the sense that profound realities are involved."

"Isn't this simply your own narrative? A deeply troubling one, I might add."

Arthur bent down to unlock the bicycles for the ride back. "Now you're getting it," he replied. "You're a quick study. But then your books indicate as much."

"It must be hard to be you."

"It seems that we have that in common. Nothing I can't handle. And *you?*"

"I must find my way back to Bohemia,… where, if you are right, I will soon die."

"I guess that's 'handling it,' in a way."

"At least I will not be a machine there."

The two riders turned back toward the apartment. Arthur seemed deep in thought as they made their way, this time along the more rundown neighborhoods along Belvedere Avenue. Beyond large new apartment blocks for VCU students they passed a procession of 24 hour stores, fast food restaurants and vacant store fronts. As they were about to cross a particularly perilous intersection — a heavily traveled fork in the road without a traffic signal — he felt K take him firmly by the arm. Two cars passed at a high rate of speed unconcerned for the presence of bicyclers. Even then no further word passed between the two. They merely nodded and continued on their way.

Back at the apartment the two little girls were both out on their bikes again. They rode to the opposite end of the parking lot and played there as their mother had undoubtedly instructed them to do when strangers were about. Arthur parked his bike behind the door and went straight to his computer station. The path now clear, K wheeled his own bicycle past on his way to his room.

"You were a machine in 1920, every bit as much as you are now." Arthur quietly said. "Then as now, it was one of the true mysteries and we are no closer to understanding how such a thing can be."

"Perhaps we really were created by God."

"Perhaps we were. But invoking a magic name doesn't change a thing. How can such a conjecture possibly have come down to anything but a narrative agreed upon among the parties?"

K stood silently considering. But the last thing he desired was more talk. He walked his bike past the kitchenette and into his room.

Chapter 11

Come Monday morning, Arthur watched out the window as K stood at the bus stop. Both men had been up early, Arthur to play the computer game N-Back and surf the morning news. It had been a while since he was in the habit of playing N-Back in the morning but he was feeling like his mental sharpness was not what it should be. As he struggled to reproduce the order of the flashing letters and lights on the game board he could hear the muffled sounds of K's morning exercises. He was even slower than he had expected and made a mental note to return to playing every morning again. Having a roommate was taking his edge off.

K was relentlessly brushing his suitcoat in the bathroom as Arthur turned his attention to the newswires. John Boehner, the Speaker of the House of Representatives, had resigned. He'd thrown himself on his sword like a good Roman, and, for a few weeks, until the new Speaker would be chosen, bills could be passed without need of cooperation from the obstructionist anti-government wing of his party. Reader comments spewed rage at the Speaker for having betrayed them yet again. Readers counseling moderation received worse treatment still. K brushed his trouser legs, occasionally picking at lint with his fingers. Arthur read about two students who had been arrested for collecting firearms and explosives to attack their high school nearby. K poured milk over a bowl of cereal and returned to his room. A House Committee hearing designed to politically savage opposition presidential candidate Hillary Clinton had failed and her opponents were alternately fuming and denying that any such thing had been their intention. Reader comments were raw with anger. Any reader who dared to advise civility was immediately excoriated in a choking rage of misspelled words delivered with an innocence of grammar. Back from breakfast, K washed his bowl and utensils. The Daesh terrorist group had put a young boy to death, in Syria, by running him over with an army tank. Two Klux Klux Klan members were arrested for carrying shotguns onto the University of Mississippi campus while protesting in favor of the Confederate flag. The article was illustrated with yet another photo of an enormous flag unfurled and flapping from the bed of a speeding pick-up truck. Such photos were now a staple of each day's news. Looking closely at his shoes, K scowled and brushed. The seemingly endless Texas drought was suspended for a third day as torrential rains flooded much of the state. High tides had inundated low lying areas on both U.S. coasts as homeowners, no longer able to sell their homes, or to get flood insurance, looked helplessly on or tried to drive to work through knee deep water. K inspected his fedora and brushed.

When K left the apartment Arthur watched behind him. An unkempt elderly woman sat on the bus-stop bench wrapped in a red blanket, a stark contrast to K's carefully brushed dark suit, fedora and shined shoes. She apparently asked him for change because he reached inside of his jacket, pulled out his billfold and handed her a bill. She said something more. He pulled out the billfold again and gave her another bill. With that, she disappeared deeper into her blanket.

As she did so, the bus pulled up. The bus pulled away leaving behind only a red blanket, on the green bench, out the top of which a tuft of white hair was blowing in the wind. Arthur settled back into his chair. He reflected that he had yet to be paid a penny for consenting to house the man. Not that he'd asked for rent. He much preferred that K save up for his own place. How he would manage to find a place, with all the background checks landlords undertook these days, Arthur did not begin to know. But then he had no idea how K had managed to get a job. Somehow things just seemed to work out for him.

Each morning, during a glorious week, the day began in precisely the same fashion. Only the headlines changed. Though he never would admit it to himself, Arthur was pleased to have just a bit of company as K departed for work and a bit more around supper hour. It suited them both and became their routine. The gentle clatter in the kitchenette as K prepared his supper was somehow a comfort so long as it required no more of Arthur's attention than he felt he could be pleased to give. He even appeared each evening in the doorway, his presence inviting his guest to a brief exchange should he wish. Answering K's daily questions, about the people and objects that populated his work days, presented an interesting challenge. The shorter the explanation the more it was appreciated by both. Sometimes Arthur was surprised at his own observations. There were many questions even he did not ask himself, of course, and now they came to his attention, or, more precisely, to K's attention.

Far more often, however, Arthur was relieved to have hours completely to himself once again. For all the years had equipped him for periods of time in which he might have to go without such hours his reserves of patience were not endless. By Saturday those reserves were sufficiently recharged that he felt like he could deal with company again. After his guest had finished his morning exercises, Arthur quietly knocked on his door to suggest a bicycle ride. K had not wheeled his bike out of his room all week. When a reply did not come, he slowly opened the door in order to provide an opportunity for protest. Instead he found his guest laughing quietly at a YouTube video.

"There are Czech videos on YouTube," he announced. "The Czechs have always had an excellent sense of humor (though my father would never agree)." He made a face when he mentioned his father. "Some of these are quite funny."

Arthur beckoned to be allowed to use the mouse. K removed his own hand and waited. His host typed 'Guillaume Apollinaire' into the YouTube search box, scrolled down the results and clicked a video. Momentarily, a scratchy audio began, and, following it, a distant voice that sounded like the past. K's eyebrows rose with surprise. "A recording of Apollinaire? Reading 'Zone'?" He received an affirmative nod by way of reply. The two sat listening attentively. "History does exist even here in this Richmond. However little one would suspect." K looked as satisfied as Arthur had ever seen him.

Next Arthur clicked the poem 'Marie' and Apollinaire began to recite it. "He must have liked this poem particularly. There is another recording of him singing it."

K listened to the world in which he belonged, Arthur wondering what it must be like. Even if he only imagined that he was Kafka he lived the role as if he were the real man. He thoroughly believed he was Franz Kafka. Hearing the scratchy recordings must be disconcerting. "I own a copy of Apollinaire's *Alcools* that I ordered from Paris, after the war. The French poets were ahead of their time."

The recording over, Arthur pointed to the number of search 'results' that had been found under the name 'Guillaume Apollinaire'. There were over 10,000. Next he pointed, on the video they had been watching, to the heading labeled 'Views'. There had been some 1300 views over two years. K could not hide his pleasure at discovering as much.

Arthur then typed 'kitten' into the search box. The 'results' were well over two million. One at a time he pointed the cursor at the 'Views' for several successive videos. Each announced millions of views. Most had been up for a few months or less.

"There are hundreds of millions of people on the Internet each day, most with access to YouTube. History interests a few thousand at best, I'm afraid. A tiny percentage. And only a much smaller number of the Guillaume Apollinaire listings actually relate to the poet. All but a few are spurious."

K grasped the mouse, taking control of the moment. He replayed the few dozen lines of 'Zone'. "The poem sounded so new, so full of dissonance and promise. It is strange to hear it sound ancient now. I remember the excitement of traveling to see the airshow at Brescia. Everywhere, except for the Empire, the world seemed to be exploding with modernity."

"Edison visited Prague. So did Einstein. If I'm not mistaken, you met Einstein."

"At Berta Fanta's flat. He might have combed his hair."

"Many people even today would envy you. Did he play the violin?"

"We are not entirely left behind. It is as if the future itself might walk into a café, in which you are sitting, and order a coffee. Even in Prague. But such events are rare. We have motorcars and electric lights but life remains otherwise the same: a round of workers' insurance claims, government forms, bureaus, headaches, insomnia. I longed to get away… and now I long to return."

With a click they listened to the eternally young poet sing a swatch from 'Le Pont Mirabeau'. In the next recording — featuring a cover photo in which his head was swathed in bandages and his smile wan — he recited at only slightly greater length from the same poem. "He is the creation of your Walt Whitman. They all were, more or less."

"All?"

"Verhaeren, Kostka. There were others. Perhaps they are no longer remembered."

"Not likely. Not here. I barely know Verhaeren myself. Kostka not at all. I'm sure they can be found on the search engines, though."

"How, if they are not remembered, do they appear in the search engines?" He did not wait for an answer. "Preserved like rare seeds in a botanical institute, it would seem."

"Something like that. The memory trace is growing dim."

"And the kittens? Is there such a market for them?"

"They help people forget. We've learned that forgetting is an important function in any brain. Every bit as important as remembering."

"So then people need to forget us?"

Arthur could not help but smile to hear K include himself among the others. "You are only just getting over the surprise of having been remembered. Will you already feel the loss of being forgotten?"

K stared at the bandaged head of Apollinaire. The world was such a strange and violent place.

"Do you see Whitman in Rimbaud?"

"No. Whitman was not a poet of sickness. I try not to read such things." K's voice lowered almost to a whisper. "My soul already is sufficiently maimed."

"But you have read Trakl, if I'm not mistaken."

"Who can resist? At least he had the excuse of having experienced the carnage of the war. Rimbaud simply preferred to comport himself in the most shocking possible way. Still, I speak of neither in the presence of impressionable young writers." Each sentence was followed by a long pause, his long fingers spread before him on the table then raised in the attitude of prayer the tips brushing his lips. "I try not to encourage the depravity that has followed the war." Again he brought his fingertips to his lips and stared vacantly ahead. "I made Max promise to destroy all of my papers after I died."

"He said that he refused to promise."

"Perhaps he did." K's look was impossible to interpret. "Apollinaire wrote his poems before the war. For all the war destroyed him, as well, after he wrote them." The subject was an uncomfortable one. "Brescia, too, was before the war. It was such a wonder to see the aeroplanes leap into the air, engines sputtering, and circle the field. Anyway all of it would appear to be a dream the world is in the process of forgetting. Who can want to remember bi-planes in an age of flying hotels? Or character in an age without sin?"

"Yet there is no sense of wonder in your stories."

"I thought there might be in *The Man Who Disappeared* at different stages. But somehow it did not come out that way. There is something about me that won't allow it. Paris, Brescia: they were exciting but they were only vacations. I was soon back in Prague and the suffocating embrace of the Empire, writing endless reports, citing endless rules."

"The suffocating embrace of your father."

"You and your Doctor Freud... There were no embraces."

"Of course, he is not *our* Doctor Freud. He was Austrian, after all."

"There you have it. The wonders of the Empire: the filthy, maimed soul, trapped in endless official paperwork... *and the opera*. An excursion to Paris or Brescia is only the briefest respite. Then it is back to the Empire." K's face took on the strangest of expressions. "Kittens. Freedom, in the end, has come to endless videos of kittens. Who could have imagined?"

Arthur laughed more openly than was generally the case. It signaled an unguarded moment. "Who could have imagined?" he repeated. Suddenly they both were laughing.

"Are there recordings of the voice of Dostoevsky?"

"He died before most people knew such a thing was possible. Your soul is maimed?"

"Oh, irretrievably. But at least it was not a *product*. Is he still read?"

"Dostoevsky? His words, yes. Does it matter do you think?"

"Only his words?"

"You've spent most of the morning browsing the Internet. A month ago you could not resist any chance to watch the..." Arthur hesitated for emphasis. "magic screen."

"That is because I have so much to learn and too little time."

"You will be leaving us soon, then?"

K's fingers were once again spread before him on the impromptu computer desk. "I can only hope so."

"Is it really a matter of time? Before movies even included sound you regularly warned that they were destructive — that they took people's wills from them. The magic screen has already convinced you that you control *it*, rather than the other way around, and it did not exist in your world until two months ago. Can you imagine never having lived in a world in which it didn't exist?"

"So then, tomatoes still exist but they have no taste. Seafood is..."

"...available now even if one lives hundreds of miles from the sea."

"For which reason the seas are depleted to the point that it is imitation seafood. People still exist but the soul is a product. Dostoevsky's words are read but nothing more is left than the words somehow because of the magic screen."

"There is more left *here*." Arthur made a sweeping gesture with his hand.

"In a tiny apartment which you leave as little as possible." With that K rose and stood looking out the window into the parking lot of the next building.

"You of all people should know that it is vastly bigger than it seems."

K relented. "Not so many people read Dostoevsky in Prague, either."

Arthur rose abruptly and with an exaggerated vigor. "I came to ask if you wanted to go out for a bike ride."

K had wanted for some time to see the capitol area, he informed Arthur. If his host wished to come along he was most welcome. There was a glint in his eyes as he enjoyed turning the tables. He had gained confidence from having fended for himself for an entire week. He had a sense of where he was and how he fit in — a sense, Arthur reflected, that could only prove to be an illusion in the end.

"I am surprised," said K, as the two rolled their bikes out of the apartment door. "I would not have thought that this Richmond would be warm enough at this time of year to allow for riding. I must somehow have gotten the wrong impression."

"There's an 'El Niño' this year. The strongest one ever recorded."

The two began walking their bikes. "An 'El Niño'?"

"A special weather pattern over the Pacific Ocean. It's made more powerful by climate change."

"I must be even more confused than I think. Aren't we half way around the world from the Pacific Ocean?"

"All the weather patterns around the world are interconnected. It's so complex that even our computers cannot yet fully understand it."

"And climate change... I notice it everywhere in the news. It seems it is caused by something called the 'greenhouse gas'."

"Mostly CO_2 . It is the exhaust gas that comes out of a car or a smokestack."

"We have motorcar and smokestack exhaust but I am unaware that we have El Niños or climate change."

"The effect is cumulative. You hadn't yet put enough into the atmosphere to cause warming. At least not noticeable warming."

The elderly woman from the bus stop placed herself in K's path. "Not today, I'm afraid," he said, walking around her as he did. "So then it is unusually warm here because of this El Niño?" As he asked the question, he found the woman in front of him again. "She possesses the virtue of persistence," K announced to his companion as he walked around her again.

With that she was beside him: "I can get a sandwich at the store for three dollars," she observed. Receiving no reply, she went on to explain that she had not eaten since the day before. She seemed to feel that any pause in her explanations would defeat her purpose. She knew her craft, as it were. K stopped, drew out a five dollar bill and handed it to her. "For another dollar," she immediately added, "I can get a soda to drink with it." K picked up his pace so noticeably that she gave in to the fact that she would not be able to wheedle more from him and turned and walked back the way they had come.

"She walks continually up and down the street every day," said Arthur, his eyes straight ahead. "Begins three blocks back and walks to the intersection here and turns around and walks back."

"Will she actually spend it on food?"

"I don't know. Her clothes are always freshly laundered. Her hair is always washed."

"But unkempt."

"I've never seen her drinking on a bus bench like the others."

K looked confused yet again. Arthur waited for a question as they continued on their way. When the question did not come, he interpreted K's silence to have asked it. "She has an apartment around here somewhere. Probably receives a small government check to pay for it. The check also helps pay for food."

"Why, then, does she beg?"

"The government payment is probably quite small. She probably doesn't like to stay inside the tiny apartment she can afford with it. She has learned that people find it difficult to refuse the pleas of an elderly woman in ill-fitting, disheveled clothing. Apparently they do not notice that it is freshly laundered."

K could not help but laugh. "How can you know this?"

"The same way I can know that an El Niño is causing the weather to be unusually warm."

"When will the normal weather return?"

"The El Niños are getting worse. It could be years."

"Will it be warm all winter?"

"If the pattern holds, unusually *cold* weather will arrive late in the season."

"How does this make sense?"

"Weather is complex. Air pressures will drop. The winds will swoop down from the Artic." Arthur mounted his bike as he spoke and K followed suit. Soon they were passing Monroe Park and through the VCU campus. Next they passed the Jefferson Hotel and the Public Library. At last they were at the edge of the capitol area. Arthur cut across to Broad Street.

As they turned toward the capitol the buildings grew more modern with each successive block. The Broad Street of small and vacant shops, with gaudy, peeling paint, through which K had traveled each day of the past week to Mr. Mendelssohn's office, was left behind. The brindled sidewalks bustling with a mix of street people and adventurous students, winding their way through nodding, vague-eyed figures disabled in mind and body, were now spotless and empty of pedestrians.

At first the buildings were of the same vintage but better maintained. They featured small sandwich shops and eateries mostly. Next came a mix of white granite government buildings interspersed between newer, taller office buildings. The vacant storefronts were much bigger and better maintained. These were followed by even taller, even newer buildings.

K called for Arthur to stop. He did so as he straddled his bike in front of a clothing store. Unsure how much longer he might be in Richmond, he wished to see what might be available by way of fine dark suits. His experience had been that such attire was rare in this Richmond. As best he could tell, tailor shops did not exist at all. The manikins in the display window suggested he may have stumbled across a resource.

Arthur peered up at the name of the store and into the storefront windows. He was vaguely familiar with the chain of stores, though not because of its fine suits. An idea came to him. "There is something I would like to show you here."

"You are familiar with the wares, then."

"Not particularly. I've read about the chain, though. They must only recently have opened a store here."

Arthur locked their bicycles to a tall street sign. He opened the door and ushered K inside. "Where will we need to go in order to see this item that you wish me to see?"

"We won't have to go anywhere. Let's walk slowly across the foyer, here." Some ten meters to their left, two middle aged women were walking side by side as they consulted their Smartphones. Arthur nodded in their direction. They seemed somehow to be the 'thing' that his guide wished him to see.

"How could you possibly know that these two women would be here?"

"Watch the lights overhead."

The lights brightened above the aisle ahead of the women, much as the freezer lights had done at the market, but this occurred before they were close enough for a similar sensor to detect their approach. At the same time, the overhead lights had brightened above the third cross-aisle ahead of them. K's eyebrows rose together with his curiosity.

"They have received text messages. The store has sent them electronic coupons customized to their purchasing history."

"How is that possible?"

"The computer has checked their previous purchasing histories and is subtly raising the lights to attract them to the items they are most likely to purchase. They probably don't even notice what is happening."

"What computer?"

"Actually, it is a network of computers."

"How can this be? How can the computer possibly know who they are?"

Arthur nodded toward the far wall opposite the glass doors by which they had entered. "There's a camera there that takes your picture when you pass the doors and passes the image along to a computer. The image is matched against pictures in a database in the network the computer is connected to, in order to identify you, and, once identified, your purchasing history is accessed.

Depending upon your Smartphone settings, the phone may update the computer with still more recent purchasing information. The store computer passes customized coupons to your phone based upon the purchasing habits revealed in your information. There are cameras strategically positioned high along each wall. Each takes your picture and correlates it to your location as detected by your phone so it knows where you are."

"The computer knows everyone who shops here?"

"The computer knows no one. It just does what it is programmed to do: match photos, load up information, purchasing history, and so on."

"But what if one has no purchasing history or picture in the... 'database'?"

"That is what I brought you in here to see. We have been in the store for several minutes, now. The computer has found no data on us. It has checked the criminal databases and the records of disruptive persons throughout the network of stores that subscribe to the service. It hasn't found us listed in those either."

"What will it do?"

"It will notify the management that there are two unknown persons in the store. That young woman coming from the back corner, as we speak, will prove to be the assistant manager. A largish young man will momentarily begin browsing the clothing on a rack nearby, trying not to look directly at us. He will be a security guard."

"But all the racks in this area would seem to be women's..." K stopped short. Two racks over to their left was just such a largish young man. He was considering a floral cocktail dress.

"Surprisingly overstated for a place like this," Arthur observed at a whisper. "I begin to lose my respect."

As he said it a slender young woman approached. Her hair was gathered in a bun at the back of her head. She wore a dark blue skirt-suit of high quality material, modestly cut just below the knee. "Is there anything I can help you with?" She asked. The man to the left tried to size the two men up without them noticing. He moved slightly closer under the pretense of browsing the racks. Beyond him, K noticed, a finely dressed middle-aged woman was in the process of somehow paying with a Smartphone for her purchase.

"Not today," Arthur replied. "My friend," he went on, nodding toward K, "is in town for business. He's from Prague." The assistant manager seemed a bit at a loss, probably because she was unaware that their database did not include persons from Prague. "I wanted to introduce him to your store. He will be looking for a suit, something painfully understated. Is everything here off-the-rack?"

"No, of course not," she replied, shooting Arthur a sharp look. "The tailoring section is in back." She hesitated as she said it. The computer, after all, did not know them, and anyone could say they were from Prague. But the fabric K was wearing was of a quality she seldom saw even in their store. It was all a little disconcerting.

"I think he has seen enough," said Arthur with a sly smile. "We'll be going."

"May I ask the gentleman's name?" asked the Assistant Manager.

Arthur was stunned to hear K begin to reply. "Mr...".

He quickly talked over his companion. "My friend is very private. We may be back." With that, he ushered K back out of the glass doors and onto the sidewalk. Looking over his shoulder, he noticed the Assistant Manager had followed as far as the glass doors and was watching from the other side.

"I wasn't going to say 'Mr. Kafka'," said K, slightly piqued. "I had settled on 'Mr. Gracchus'."

"Damn." Arthur's brows shot up to imagine it. It would have been perfect. "If I'd known I would have let you go on. Whatever name you gave her would go into the incident report she wrote for the computer."

"Incident?"

"Yes, we were an incident. She will need to report it in order to bring the computer as much up to date as possible. The name you gave would have been entered in the report and forever attached to your face."

"My face?"

"The computer has seen you now and it will never forget that you have been here on this date, at this time, and enquired after tailored suits. If we had been able to walk through the store, it would remember precisely the path we took and what items we turned our gaze toward."

When the bikes were unchained again, K made no attempt to ride his. Instead he walked it along deep in thought. "Is another network recording our itinerary as we travel across this Richmond and attaching it to our pictures?"

"Not yet but it is only a matter of time. If we travelled in a car (like normal people), the newer models would continually transmit our position, our speed and other parameters, though."

After walking the bike for a long, thoughtful block, K slowly shook his head. "As the days pass I think of writing. It is not so much what I do as who I am. There can be no Franz Kafka without writing. But then I receive another of your lessons and I realize that my characters could not exist here. I cannot exist here either."

Arthur mounted his bike again. There would be enough time for brooding when they returned home. K mechanically did the same. They were soon amongst much taller buildings: office buildings and hotels. All were cement grey or occasionally the grey of unpolished granite. The sidewalks were once again composed of red brick laid out in a herring bone pattern.

On a sunny day the effect was really quite uplifting. So much so that K found himself enjoying the ride the clothing store and all it implied notwithstanding. There was a tall pedestal atop which a statue portrayed a majestic George Washington astride a charger. Behind it was a shining white complex that Arthur confirmed was the capitol itself. He was surprised to discover that it was smaller than he had imagined the capitol of an American state must be. Many of the signs indicated that most of the state's business took place in the monumental granite buildings with herringbone sidewalks past which they had already pedaled. He struggled to distinguish between business and government offices. A sense of trepidation crept back in as he wondered why he was so sure that there was less difference than he might approve. For a moment he returned to thoughts of how so little in this 2015 turned out to be what it presented itself to be, how much was imitation.

As his spirits lagged momentarily K noticed that Arthur was steadily pedaling a full block away. There was nothing to do but to follow him. The two left the capitol behind and were soon approaching the train station with its comforting clock tower. The Farmer's Market was open and K took the opportunity to select a few vegetables to buy now that he had pocket money. As Arthur pointed out several items he too would appreciate having, he explained that the market would soon be no more. It was going to be removed in favor of more lucrative development. K despaired of ever being unequivocally pleased with even the simplest experience.

Once the purchases were safely in Arthur's backpack K walked slowly along the old vacant storefronts alongside the market. He had only explored them the once with Jeremiah but the memory had stayed with him. It was almost as if he were closer to home. Each shop had its own personality even with its windows empty. Each was built from a different batch of red brick therefore slightly different in color. The shop windows were comparatively small, each of the doors humble. The trim of each was formed of wood and painted a different peeling color still. One by one he caressed them like aging friends. They had impressed him as the most alive of all the buildings he had seen in the city. Now they appeared ghostly. This was the one place in Richmond in which he felt somewhat at home and it soon would be gone. He was determined to be gone before it.

The sun was getting low and they had a long way to go before they were back home. Arthur called out. "We'll need to stop at the market for a bag of candy."

"Will we?"

"Yes, it's Halloween. We'll need it in case some kids come to the door."

"Do you think they will come?"

"This will be the first year if they do. But I always have some candy on hand just in case."

Chapter 12

Receiving a paycheck changed K. Soon he had gained so much confidence that he began returning to the apartment in a taxi sometimes as late as 10 or 11 at night. After he kept the schedule for three days in a row Arthur became concerned. K was far too steady for alarm or suspicion but there was reason to wonder whether he was being *over* confident. He was 132 years old, so to speak. At that age one needs one's sleep. It had only been a few weeks before that he feared to cross a busy intersection and blanched at the approach of a city bus. He had only just stopped calling the town '*this* Richmond'.

Asked, upon returning on the third night, where he had been, he was vague. For at least part of the time he may have worked late at Mr. Mendelssohn's home. Various evasions were employed to avoid saying just where else he might have been. It only made matters worse that Arthur himself could not begin to afford taxi fare. He was still not being paid a penny for taking in his guest. The decision that he would rather K keep his paychecks toward renting his own place seemed a bit naïve given the circumstances. He realized that, more than a little offended in these ways, he was once again in danger of being accusatory and let the matter drop. He could not, however, bring himself to forego asking small leading questions on those occasions when they passed in the kitchenette, K for a late supper and Arthur for a beer.

In the meantime, an invitation for Thanksgiving dinner had arrived from Jeremiah and Lori. K and Lori had become in the habit of taking more frequent excursions. Arthur suspected that this was a sign that his guest found his answers to various questions during their own excursions unsettling. On one or another of their days out Lori purchased a disposable cell phone for him. She felt that he would need it in order to have any kind of prospects in today's world. K having, as the result, become far and away the socialite of the apartment, it was he who received the invitation while talking on the telephone with Lori between late nights taking dictation at Mr.

Mendelssohn's home.   He accepted with alacrity, and, having forgotten to mention it, informed Arthur several days later.

Arthur was scrolling through the morning funny pages when he learned of the invitation. He was laughing aloud at a particularly funny Dilbert cartoon when K thought to inform him of it, offhandedly, as he headed out the door toward the bus stop. Arthur continued to scroll, distracted, barely noticing the cartoons. Here he was, host to Franz Kafka, or some psychotic variation thereon, and slowly realizing that nothing about his relationships was the least changed. The patterns of a lifetime continued even in this the most unimaginable of unions. His landline telephone sat quietly beside him, precisely as he preferred,... and the world could not agree more. It would call if its computer needed work and none of the more socially relevant candidates had proven able to accomplish it. His roommate was none too slowly becoming all of his roommates: natural, unreflective, subscribing to whatever opinion was popular at the moment, bending toward whatever direction the sun shone. He had a cell phone now — he who dismissed the *homo telephonicus*. It was a sign shared with all the world. Consequently, modest amounts of money and ever larger amounts of belonging flowed toward him. He received the invitations to Thanksgiving dinner.

K was Kafka because everyone found him and the name entertaining.   (But only so long as he was staying at Arthur's apartment.) Arthur was Arthur, on the other hand, because the name was on his birth certificate and the family and he had reconnected from time to time over the years to find the name unchanged. It had been a name associated with confusing signals and discomfort as often as not, until at last he learned and it became a name associated with reticence.

This indulgence of K made perfect sense, of course, as those family members themselves periodically went by other names: fresh nicknames, sometimes new married names, sometimes the name the electrical bill went under in order to receive services in spite of outstanding payments due, sometimes Facebook aliases. There was less adjustment to meeting someone who called himself "Franz Kafka" than one might expect. K was Franz Kafka because he had managed to engage people's interest by being Franz Kafka. Nothing else had been necessary, in the final analysis, and nothing else would do. He had a regular job, he had a cell phone, he went out to do shopping and be treated to lunch. He shopped, as well, for his preferred way of looking at the world, a way preferred because it was shared with others who just wanted to be happy together for a few hours now and again.

In the final analysis, however, even Arthur had to admit, now as always, that the emotional calculus resolved itself as the equations demanded. It always did. It was all perfectly predictable — and nothing so much as the unpredictability of it — if one invested the time to do the math. But for all it had become second nature to him, after so many years of effort, it would never be *first* nature. He could not lose himself in the collective project of becoming oneself. That would always be something he observed from the outside. In important ways, K was more a denizen of 2015 than he could ever be.

Arthur emerged from his reveries with difficulty. A lifetime of experience made clear that he would float in and out of them all day. But for now he had regained a bit of focus. It took him a half-hour to make his way through the remaining funnies. The news tickers reported a preliminary hearing for two local members of the Aryan Brotherhood who had been caught planning to bankroll racist attacks by means of a crime spree. The Republican primary candidates were in Florida announcing their plans to repeal national health insurance, increase fossil fuel consumption and lower taxes on the wealthy. The Republican Congress was threatening to vote down any climate change treaty that might result from the upcoming Climate Summit in Paris. Nothing much had changed except that momentarily there were no reports of new wildfires or flooding.

After another half-hour of distractedly 'Liking' Facebook baby pictures and posting birthday wishes, he stared into the screen seeking answers. While he could not live them, working with the equations of the calculus was impossibly addictive. Facebook was stop-action database of emotional call-and-response. What did social media come down to: the cascade of tabloid news stories, the identity-politics support networks, the quotes from the Dalai Lama and cartoon characters, the memes, the cyber-gangs, the perfectly assured screeds?

A Psychology Today article on the behavioral effects of constant 'screen time' on children next caught his attention. The magazine being a bit of a throwback, the issues and studies were presented in about 1000 words (astonishingly discursive for the Internet Age). The warnings it contained were understated.

All the babies in the pictures he had 'Liked' had been born into a world in which those 1000 words were already becoming oppressive, in which they were more generally 300 words if a venue hoped to survive. The children whose pictures he had Liked yesterday were being diagnosed with attention deficit and emotional regulation disorders at deeply saddening rates. They had to be medicated in order to function in a structured environment such as a classroom. Other 1000 word articles, in other magazines, quietly declining under prevailing economic realities, followed them into college and beyond, finding that the medications have lifelong aftereffects which would likely require further medications. The children whose pictures he'd Liked the day before yesterday were demanding college courses tailored to their preferred realities, much like the 300 words of tailored clickbait that had convinced them that such demands were feasible.

Too soon the parents who took those pictures with such love and hope would be gone. Those children would have endless 300 word articles, designed to be popular enough to generate advertising clicks, with which to deal with rising sea-levels, erratic, frequently extreme weather, crumbling infrastructure and bankrupt safety net programs that those parents would leave behind them.

Stare at the screen as he might, Arthur could not see a way out. It was not the first time and it would not be the last. The next he looked up, the sun was late afternoon pale.

As his thoughts returned yet again to the world at large he was intrigued by a news story that appeared at the top of his French newsfeed. There had been a shooting at a small restaurant, in Paris, called *La Petit Cambodge*. The word '*fusillade*' had been used, suggesting sustained firing. All that seemed to be known was that there had been a shooting. Still, there was something not quite right. He looked for English language stories but there were none yet. Why had someone shot up a Cambodian restaurant? Was there a

Cambodian underworld in Paris of which he was not aware? It seemed unlikely.

While he pondered what the matter might be, older model cars began to pull into the parking lot outside his window their drivers back home from a day's work. The maintenance man who had been doing repairs to a vacant apartment two doors down was patiently rolling up his hoses and extension cords and stowing them in the various compartments of his dilapidated green pickup truck. He was an older man trying to keep his prices from being driven down by younger men more adept at salesmanship than performance. Their trucks were new. His 401k was much too small. The effort and disappointment showed at the end of his day.

As Arthur looked out the window new stories began to flow in. Now there there were reports of "*plusieurs fusillades*," several shootings. He opened the France24 television site in a new browser window. Now there were reports of hostages at a music hall called '*Le Bataclan*'. There might be as many as 50 hostages. There had been explosions reported but the announcers were not sure quite where. Live reports began to transmit from opposite *La Petit Cambodge*. Large picture windows had been shot out, leaving jagged peninsulas of glass. The English language media was beginning to post stories with information badly misreported for being a mere ten or fifteen minutes out of date.

The French announcers began to lose their composure about half an hour in. Only slightly but enough to make clear that something was very seriously wrong. Numerous explosions began to be mentioned. The exact locations could not be determined. The number of hostages at *Le Bataclan* began to grow. Now there could be as many as 160.

The explosions, it was soon reported, had occurred outside of the soccer stadium. There had been more than one. No details were available. Film crews began to get closer footage of *La Petit Cambodge*, across yellow crime scene tape. Two other restaurants had been attacked nearby. Bodies lay motionless on the sidewalk, blood flowing away, generally, from their heads. They cut away to *Le Bataclan*, where another film crew stood back as little as they could manage, live cameras rolling, as the police and the assailants could be seen exchanging automatic-rifle fire around corners.

Momentarily, the end of the hostage situation was announced. Stunningly, it was said that over a hundred might have died. With that, the world was waiting to learn if the attack was over or whether this was just the beginning.

Then it happened: video of the attacks began to be posted on the various amateur video sites. The images often shook and went off-kilter as gunfire erupted and the people filming retreated to film from safer spots. Some were taken from hiding places or the window ledges of apartments on upper floors.

Men in black masks simply stepped out of cars, with Kalashnikovs, and began spraying people with bullets. Some fell to the ground, others tried to hide only to be discovered and shot point blank as they begged to be spared. Some escaped in the confusion. At *Le Bataclan*, members of the audience and staff ran out of the exits, many clearly wounded and desperate to escape, some carried along by their friends. Bursts of gun fire periodically followed another group out, one or two falling prone on the sidewalk, no longer moving. The moaning of the wounded was mixed with the weeping of some who were huddled in doorways. A pregnant woman hung from a second story ledge calling for help. As each video loaded, small advertisements appeared across the bottom declaring that Arthur's computer security had been breached and directing him to click a download button in order to correct an urgent problem that had been detected. He quickly clicked them out, intent to investigate each horrific detail of the massacre. U.S. news outlets, citing wire reports only minutes old, were reporting that at least two people had died at the music hall.

France24 began to interview people who had survived the restaurant attacks. They were shaken and thankful to have escaped harm. They described the experience in rapid fire detail, frequently pausing to catch their breath. These interviews began to be interspersed with interviews of city officials who carefully tried to preempt the accusations they expected would come in the days ahead. A panel of terrorism experts began to gather in the studio: retired police officials, academics who specialized in the phenomena and authors of popular books on the subject. Just over an hour and a half after the first attack had occurred, President Holland was on the air to calm Paris and the world with an announcement that the

French police had the situation under control, the military had been summoned and France would be revenged. People should shelter in their homes unless ordered by authorities to do otherwise. Soon after, the U. S. president held a brief news conference to offer his nation's condolences and support.

In two hours the entire world had changed. It felt like two years had passed. Attention deficit disorders would have to wait. The children would have to wait. The thanksgiving invitation had been given to whoever it had been given to.

News outlets from around the world were now reporting on little else but the Paris attacks and increased security measures being instituted in their own countries. Soon Facebook posts began to appear, some offering "prayers," others declaring that France's restrictive firearms laws had been the cause of the carnage. An armed populace, they crowed, with a sense of victory, could have fought back. The terrorists would have been killed with otherwise little loss of life. Others excoriated President Obama for failing to crush the upsurge of terrorists in the world thus preventing such incidents. Diplomacy and 'leading from behind' had been a terrible failure. He was a disaster as a president. We needed someone as president who would take the battle to terrorists with overwhelming force.

It was as if the entire world were a single great body, its police units white blood cells rushing to the site in order to combat the infection, its ambulances red blood cells clearing away the dead and the wounded matter around the gaping wound. In concert with first-responder cells, scaling off the traumatized tissue, the nervous system was sending cascades of raw data, momentarily overwhelming the brain with shock and chaos and surges of adrenalin to aid in the body's primal defense. The body's eyes rapidly scanned faces, license plates, the routes that each took. The digitized images traveled to the brain's visual processing centers to be matched against stored memory, some patterns being flagged to be passed along for evaluation in the higher processing centers. Emergency procedures must take control until the danger was sure to have passed. Reflection would have to wait. As of yet it was impossible and even dangerous.

Yet the wound was not life threatening. It was the possibility of repeated such wounds that constituted the existential threat that the individual cells acutely sensed (but *only sensed*). Once matters had calmed somewhat, the brain would begin to assess what needed to be done and allocate the necessary resources, disperse the necessary funds. The excess levels of adrenalin accompanying the wound — but, more especially, the potentially destructive ambient levels — was an ongoing concern and would receive its own evaluation once the body had been secured.

Arthur had watched incident after incident ever more certain that this was what he was seeing. It was wondrous and terrifying at once. Only the body realized its existence. The individual components knew only their personal roles. Like so many undifferentiated tissue cells, Facebookers sent their signals of anger and fear, popped their supper into so many microwaves and returned to comment some more. The nervous system quickly dispatched comforting signals. Like individual neurons, government bureaucrats each followed their procedures based upon the inputs they received. Like the frontal lobe's executive process, presidents made rapid decisions based upon nearly numberless inputs from afferent bureaucrats no one of which they were aware existed, and no one of which knew them. They dispatched those decisions via nearly numberless outputs from efferent bureaucrats no one of which they were aware existed and no one of which knew them. Should any component show so much individuality as to go off script, even in the slightest, the entire body stood in grave danger of stumbling over its own two feet in the middle of a dangerous situation.

Arthur quickly grabbed a frozen dinner from the freezer, checked the directions and popped it into the microwave. It was well past supper time. Some five minutes later, he broke away from the screen again to bring the meal to his workstation. A last few straggling cars entered the parking lot, their drivers vague figures in the dingy yellow light of the two security lights that remained working. The English language media were finding their footing by then. Most of it was a rehash of the events now that the attacks seemed to have ended. The France24 panel of experts had little to add. The night was winding down. The sudden release of tension that follows such incidents left him thinking about a BBC evening concert, or perhaps a Debussy CD, and sampling from a few good books. The key to sleep would be dipping into one quiet pleasure after another until the events of the day floated away.

Arthur was listening to Debussy's *Claire de Lune* and reading from the diaries of Virginia Woolf when the telephone rang. It wasn't until that moment that it came to him: K had yet to return from work. Jeremiah was on the line. There was a situation. He would pick Arthur up. He was five minutes away from the apartment as he spoke.

He arrived in the new car. The dashboard lights looked like an airplane control panel. "I only know what a few buttons do. I figure I'll get used to it eventually."

Arthur found the LED glow kind of festive at the same time its implications were mildly distressing. "What's the matter with Franz?"

"Liegh called. She says he is at a bar downtown."

"Liegh...?"

"A friend of Lori's. Her daughter, Heather, is a student at VCU. She sees him at the downtown bars. She says he is pretty popular with the VCU girls. She has been keeping an eye out in case trouble finds him."

"Liegh...?" Again, the pattern. How long had the others known? Why had they seen fit to keep K's new lifestyle choice their secret? "There's no right on red here." The car jerked to a halt, the distraction of the dashboard momentarily overcome in favor of watching the road.

"No. Liegh's daughter." Jeremiah's tone was angry at having been caught out. "Don't start picking apart everything I say."

"And has trouble found him?"

"Some of the guys feel like he's interfering."

"Intruding in their territory. That is worrisome, I admit, by why couldn't it wait until the morning?"

"One of them decided to solve the problem by calling the police and reporting him as a suspicious person."

Arthur lapsed into silence reflecting upon the implications of what he had heard. "And we're going to try to talk the police into releasing him to us? Jeezus, he'd better not give the apartment as his home address. He'll probably give the apartment as his home address."

"The girls have invited him to go with them to another bar nearby. A place called 'Shinies' or something. With a little luck we'll be able to pick him up there before anyone else knows what has happened."

"Jeezus. You don't even know where the place is?"

"I know about where it is." Jeremiah was alternately watching the road and looking down at a blinking light on the dashboard. "If there's any problem, Liegh will call her daughter and she'll direct us to the exact address." He tried a switch and the mysterious light continued to blink. He returned the switch to the original position and still the blinking did not stop. "I'm gonna have to read the owner's manual for this thing."

Jeezus. Planning was not Jeremiah's long suit. Most times it was just frustrating but this time it could have very unfortunate consequences. Arthur knew better than to bring it up. Somehow things always seemed to work out for his brother.

It turned out that finding Siné's Irish Pub was easy enough but finding parking was a much bigger problem. Jeremiah's phone rang. "At Siné's? Uh-huh. Alright, we're almost there." As he hung up a parking spot swam into the headlight beams. "C'mon, we better be quick."

"Why the call? What's up?"

"The guys tracked him down at Siné's. The girls are trying to talk them out of calling the police and reporting his new location."

"Jeezus."

The pub was not large — a fact that did not in the least deter vast numbers of VCU students from packing in. The interior was trimmed all in pine. Large flat-screen televisions flickered behind the bar. A band loud enough to cause hearing loss was playing on a small stage. Young men, many in red suspenders that seemed to be the uniform of the place, shifted from one foot to the other by way of dancing. In their general vicinity, young coeds swayed with their arms in the air. It was not clear how they would find K. They both scanned the bar and the dance floor for tell-tale signs.

In the end, it was Jeremiah and Arthur who were found. They stood out enough that Heather found *them*. She led them through the maze of dancing bodies to a far corner. Before them was K, in suit and bowler, stiffly holding a beer mug and surrounded by a giggling phalanx of young women. They somehow made themselves understood in spite of the music as the man around who they were gathered smiled and mouthed replies like a taller Charlie Chaplin in a silent movie. He was clearly used to being the center of the attention. Arthur could not help but laugh (not that it could be heard above the music). He walked up to his roommate who was visibly surprised to see him.

K protested at being followed around. He could not have imagined that such a thing might happen but then he never could have imagined anything to do with 'partying'. It was enormously loud. His ears would ring for hours afterwards. And the young women... The young women danced with such graceful abandon. His protest was measured. For all he knew, this also was some kind of inexplicable custom.

With the arrival of Jeremiah and Arthur, the circle of girls around him opened slightly. Two gently urged him towards what were apparently going to be his wardens. He objected.

Arthur leaned next to his ear. "The police have been called."

With this revelation K's face went wide with panic. He was frozen in place for a moment by confusion and then realized the purpose of his escort. The three men followed Heather back through the crowd, K handing off his nearly full mug like a football to a young man in red suspenders who recovered quickly from his surprise, shrugged his shoulders toward his companions and quaffed off the beer at a single gulp. The sea of bodies closed behind them as if they had never existed.

Arthur and K were quickly out the door and headed towards the car. Jeremiah lingered behind a moment to consult with Heather on any loose ends there might be and to thank her for her vigilance. As he turned to leave, two police officers entered and stood along the wall just inside the door peering as best they could through the crowd. He stepped aside to let them by and casually exited. He took a circuitous route to the car in case the offended young men might identify him as having spirited away the culprit.

As K and Arthur stood in the shadows back from the car wondering what Jeremiah's delay might portend, a beep sounded and the welcome click of door locks opening. Or at least the sounds were welcome to Arthur. K, instead, wobbled slightly with confusion and followed his guide with all the dispatch of a prisoner escaping the gallows.

"What's with the bowler?" Arthur asked. For the moment, it was the only comment that came to mind.

"It makes me look younger."

Chapter 13

The temperature was already approaching the 60s as Jeremiah arrived, on Thanksgiving morning, to drive the roommates to Mechanicsville. While he had been waiting, Arthur could not help but notice the weather was also unseasonably warm along the California coast. The high tides had flooded most of the coast making streams of roads, shallow lakes of parking lots and leaving beach houses soggy and stranded. Much of the Midwest was on alert for flash floods due to torrential rains but it was the deserts of the Middle East that were precipitously under water for having received a year's worth of rain in a single day. Amusing photos of thawb-and-kufiyah-clad Arabs in tiny dinghies in what used to be expanses of desert sand were everywhere in the news from the area. Still stronger storms were expected at any moment.

While there had not been recent flooding anywhere in Canada, its government insurance company announced that it had struck an outside contract for expert risk-analysis for the years ahead. They needed to know what was their level of risk, given the upcoming effects of climate change, in order to develop realistic budget numbers and coverage. Its in-house actuarial methods were no longer valid. The same was true of the long experience of their personnel. They needed to learn how to assess the additional cost of a world and climate that was rapidly changing.

Nevertheless Laburnum Avenue somehow seemed never to change. Somehow that, too, was part of the Thanksgiving tradition — a particularly satisfying part even. As they turned onto Laburnum, Jeremiah mentioned that he and Lori had been watching the Macy's Thanksgiving Day Parade. Had Arthur been watching it? No, he hadn't but there was quite a bit on the news wires about the massive police presence in the wake of the Paris attacks. Already occasional pictures of police in combat gear, featuring M-4 automatic rifles, had become a staple of the season. This year the pictures were more frequent and the officers less self-effacing. They posed, with stern but not too stern expressions, crowds of civilians looking on from behind metal barriers.

But it would have been tiresome to bring that up. Arthur merely said, "No. I can't remember the last time I watched one. Probably when mom and dad were alive."

As they passed the grandstands of the Richmond International Raceway, Jeremiah suggested that his Dallas Cowboys had a "pretty good shot" against the Panthers on the 4:30 game. Romo was back from injury to play quarterback.

The rest of the way the brothers talked about football games while K looked aimlessly out the window. It was surprising to him how familiar this landscape, with its dingy strip-malls and fast food restaurants, had become in so short a time. It was easy to imagine having traveled the route for years, oneself just another nondescript part of the experience.

Somehow he was changing. What else could be the case? When he returned to Bohemia — for he was certain that it could only be a matter of time — he would be a different person. He had learned a new perspective. He would see himself less through his father's eyes. For all that it had nearly cost him, he could not help but notice that this world without sin moved with an attractive ease of the sort he had always sought. He had learned that he was guilty of much less than those eyes constantly implied. But if the Empire and its inscrutable bureaucracies felt oppressive before they would feel impossibly so after these months away. If Prague felt claustrophobic before, its limits would feel even closer now.

Still, outside of the apartment everything was traveling at the most fearful speeds to get nowhere in particular that he could tell. The minutes passed like the numbers on the odometers of the cars that so dominated life and enhanced those speeds. The tenths of a minute quickly added up but without means of measuring toward what they had gone. As for that there was no accounting. Nowhere among the vast numbers of people with their blinking odometers did he have the least prospect of an audience. He had to return.

But what of the insomnia and the headaches? Would they return together with his return to his proper life? What of his tuberculosis? It had come as a gift as much as an illness. Would he be discovered to have recovered and have to return once again to giving the Insurance Institute his most precious hours?

Upon his return to his audience (an audience so small he was almost embarrassed to call it one), he would need every available moment to put toward his writing. It was the one thing about which he felt absolutely certain though he hadn't the slightest idea, even in Prague, what gave him the confidence. He couldn't imagine where he would begin. Would he become another H. G. Wells, writing robust scientific romances about speculative futures (in his case perhaps not so speculative)? It seemed unlikely but far less likely things had somehow come to pass without so much as a 'by your leave'. The feeling that he had the least control over his own life was tenuous now in ways that would stay with him so long as he recalled this unlikely trip to Richmond and 2015.

His return was beyond his control. Each day he remained left him changed from the person he had been the day before. In a week's time this day's questions might prove to have entirely changed. There simply was no longer any way to know.

The talk of football games continued in the front seats until the car turned into the driveway. Of course the conversation spoke of more than the games. Thanksgiving spoke of more than a meal.

As they walked toward the door, Arthur looked down the length of the spacious backyard he had surrendered in his own life. The family dog came running up and rolled on its back solicitously to have its stomach scratched and was obliged. Although he had not realized it for many years, he had long ago surrendered all of this. As difficult as it was in many ways, there had been, by every calculation, no other choice.

Inside the door hugs and Happy Thanksgivings awaited. The smell of slowly roasting turkey was all through the kitchen. Darlene was at a friend's house for the day, glorying at being old enough to make her own decisions on such matters now. Shawn was at his father's house, the visitation agreement allowing alternate holidays to each parent. The adults would have the house to themselves and a comfortably slow tempo to go with it.

There was little that was new to report. The lives of all that belonged in 2015 went on much as usual these days and Lori had already been brought up to speed by K, during a recent phone call, on the details of his bar-hopping adventure. Arthur and Jeremiah were soon in their accustomed chairs in front of the big screen television watching the first football game of the day. Lori was on the front porch smoking a cigarette (her electronic cigarette beside her like a promise to do better next time) and talking away with her best friend on her cellphone.

Jeremiah wondered if Arthur might have a moment to look at something. The 4:30 game being hours away, the two ascended to his hobby room where Jeremiah opened his laptop, clicked on the small reading lamp on the desk and opened an email. While his brother read as well as cheap, misprescribed glasses and aging eyes would allow at the distance, Jeremiah explained that it was the most recent of several exchanges about a necklace he had ordered as a Christmas present for Lori.

He had received a confirmation email from the company but it was a particularly busy week at work that week and he didn't notice the email until the week after. The email showed an order for three necklaces. The company understood him somehow to have ordered three.

He had only ordered one. He was quite sure of it. But the order had failed to appear on the electronic voucher so he had tried again. Actually, that might have been something else he ordered on another site. He wasn't totally certain. But he was almost certain that he had not tried to order anything three times, necklace or otherwise.

Anyway, he sent an email to the company and they said the quantity was probably a misprint.

"The email specifically said 'a misprint'?" Arthur asked.

"Something like that. Either way, the order was placed over ten days ago so it couldn't be cancelled." Maybe he could send the extra necklace back for a refund once he received it. Had the company rep told him that? No, he was just thinking that he could do that. And maybe the quantity three was just a misprint, anyway.

"Do you have a copy of the email?"

"Actually, it was an online chat. That's all you can do with their customer service. Well, maybe you can send email but I didn't see how."

"It's possible that there's still a record of the chat on your customer account page."

Jeremiah navigated to the sign in page and entered his email name and password. The sign-in failed. "I must not be remembering the password right."

"You mistyped your email address."

"Oh yeah." He reentered the information with the email error corrected. The sign in failed again. "I must not be remembering the password right."

Had he used his credit card for the purchase? Yes, he had. Then he could check his credit card transactions to see if he had been charged for three necklaces. But he wouldn't be receiving his statement for weeks yet. Or he thought so, anyway. He'd have to ask Lori to be sure.

He could check it online within a day or two of a transaction. Had he checked there? He wasn't sure they had an online account. Anyway, if they did, he didn't remember the password. Maybe Lori had it. He was thinking that he might give Donna one of the extra necklaces if he couldn't return them. That way they would have matching mother-daughter necklaces. They'd probably think that was pretty cool. He wasn't sure what he would do with the other. Maybe he could return it for a credit. He wasn't sure what he might want to buy with a credit, though. What did Arthur think was best?

K remained in the kitchen, at the desk where Lori kept her laptop, surfing the Internet like an old hand. The recent incident at the bar had been an even greater shock than any of Arthur's narrated tours. Since then, he spent most of his free time on the computer. With just a little care, the possibility of catching viruses was minimal. Even if he did pick one up, Arthur would be able to remove it the next time he had a few hours free. He very kindly tended to make the time. The virus he'd picked up back when he was exploring porn sites had been removed by the next day.

He did still feel the need to dip into the books on Arthur's shelves, as well, from time to time. Books, of course, had always held a central place in his life. But they were part of a greater whole that remained back in his Prague, together with Max and Werfel. The thought of all of that now took him back to attending the Yiddish performances at Baum's with Lowy and failing again and again before he finally learned the ease that would allow him to walk spontaneously up to an actress and start a conversation which she would not escape at the first possible moment. Somehow that was all part of a whole. Reading in Richmond was the reading of an exile the length of whose deportation was not known. At times he found himself reading as if he would never return and set the book aside barely having remembered a word.

As for Arthur, K had come to understand that he too was somehow an exile. The fact could have made up for some part of the losses he felt, being so abruptly torn from his context. If the two had been acquaintances from Prague who had rediscovered each other in their foreign captivity, there might have formed a special bond but his host was exiled from a place every bit as foreign to K as Richmond — perhaps more so. He resembled nothing so much as Dostoevsky's 'Underground Man' — thankfully, without the self-defeating bitterness that comes from secretly having despaired of ever belonging. He simply accepted his fate. On the occasional birthday or holiday, he moved easily but somewhat distantly in the world into which he had been born — in which he had long ago become a visitor. It was a talent K wished he could share.

The Internet, on the other hand, was like living in a continuous dream. When he had predicted the 'frictionless thinking machine' he could not have begun to imagine all it would entail. The world it had created was unimaginable. It had no context — *could* have no context at all.

How could he have conceived that the most shocking aspect would be not its accomplishments but its grand ironies? On the computer screen all was huge, inviting movie star smiles and nearly naked bodies, such as even the most pridefully decadent cafes of Berlin could not possibly have imagined. To give the bodies substance — to venture out into the world it purports to portray — even to buy a simple mug of beer — or what is *called* 'beer' here — and to strike up a café conversation, at the edge of a wreathing mass of bodies, is a deafening, overwhelming experience, designed to strip the personality as well to its most primitive elements. Then in an instant the jungle could become deadly without one sensing the slightest hint that anything had gone awry, as if a Bengal tiger had leapt out seemingly from thin air to snatch one in its jaws and carry one away.

Not only that, but those beaming pictures smile out from the margins of news articles rife with typographical errors announcing every disaster and the inexcusable maltreatment of seemingly every person. If K had awoken in the country called Syria, incendiary devices to beggar all description would be raining down on his head. Young men without access to such devices would be strapping bombs on their bodies and detonating them in the midst of crowds, wondrous ambulances, lights whirring and klaxons sounding, arriving behind them to collect the desperately wounded and the scattered limbs of the dead. Here, in Richmond, movies of it all, taken at the moment of the events, would instantaneously be available with the click of a mouse.

And what of the world one traveled through between stops at the café? What of the scowling, frumpy people harried from place to place trying to stay a step ahead of the beggars that call out to them as they pass?

This being a holiday, the President and his family could be seen in all the news outlets smiling broadly and spooning out food at a food pantry near their white house, an example of his country's compassion, directly beside stories excoriating him for having misgoverned in every imaginable way. His daughters were modestly dressed, by the standards of this world, and their smiles perhaps just a little less broad than forbearing. As always, the borders of the stories were decorated with pictures of products K was sure he had never seen in Richmond, interspersed with close cropped pictures of nearly naked women with the most incredibly voracious expressions on their faces. Everything associated with the nearly naked women promised to be 'jaw-dropping' if one clicked on the advertisement to experience the revelations uncropped.

K had already learned that stories about the Kardashians were everywhere and had no interest for him whatsoever. Even the hint of a naked 'selfie' was (according to Arthur) nothing more than a 'clickbait ploy'. Elsewhere he was informed about a woman who practiced the 'Pastafarian' religion and wore a colander on her head for her driver's license photo, about exercises that would give him 'fabulous abs,' sexual activities guaranteed to cause women endless orgasms, and 'superbugs' that could no longer be treated by some things called 'antibiotics' that were vitally important not to overuse. He received expert advice on how to take off the 10 pounds that he would gain as an average celebrant of the holiday season.

On the other side of the house, the crowds in the Colosseum erupted in cheers, on the television, as if a lion had run a Christian to ground, after which Arthur and Jeremiah followed with animated conversation, one eventually asking the other whether he wanted anything from the kitchen while he was going in that direction. Whichever it was paused momentarily in the doorway to look toward K's back where he sat at the computer then continued to the refrigerator to remove two carcinogenic (if one were to believe the endless articles on the matter) sugar-free beverages and quickly returned to the living room hoping not to have missed a 'play'.

All of this still constantly shocked and astounded K but there were only so many times one could stand frozen in place, unaware which direction to flee, before even disorientation itself became just one of the familiar experiences of life. Kept safely at a distance by the magic screen, that familiar disorientation proved to be part of the irresistible attraction. As dust motes lazily traversed the beams of pale sunlight that entered in at the window beside him, somebody chained at the neck, called 'Mad Max,' was engaged in frenzied combat on the screen. Had K been in the place depicted in the 'trailer,' he would most certainly have been killed in the most painful imaginable way. Instead he watched wide-eyed with excitement.

It was only when he learned that Thanksgiving Day was followed the very next day (actually earlier: this very afternoon) by something called Black Friday, that apparently involved much the same experience and played out in the real world, unmediated by script or screen, that he was once again stunned by the possibility that he might find himself facing unimaginable terror. Surely he was mistaken. He called up the news clips only to discover not impossibly muscular actors but much more humanly proportioned combatants flailing away, with homicidal fury, in aisles of what appeared to be retail establishments. The victors were rewarded with the most popular electronic goods and children's toys. Ambulances arrived to gather the wounded. The news announcers assured the watcher that this would soon be going on everywhere in America.

Surely this was just one more thing that he was misunderstanding. He even had the self-control to wait until his roommate and trusted source of information walked through the door in search of the next round of beverages. It was the first occasion, since they had arrived, that K turned around to meet his gaze. The look on his face made clear to Arthur a near panicked level of distress and he stepped closer confused as to what might be the danger. In a supreme act of self-control, K regained his composure and enquired after the tradition of holiday combat called 'Black Friday'.

Arthur turned toward the refrigerator and opened the door in order to regain his own composure. As he turned back, he replied, "Jeremiah and I are going to take you along with us to a Black Friday mall after the Cowboys game."

"We will be going together to participate in mortal combat for electronics goods after the football game?"

"The 4:30 game. Jeremiah wants to see his Cowboys get slaughtered one more time just in case he doesn't come back."

K was at a loss for what to say. He sat as dazed as if he had already been whacked over the head with a Gameboy console.

"It will give us some time to digest. You don't want to participate in hand-to-hand combat on a full stomach. It slows you down. Some of those guys are well over 200 pounds and they have incredible reflexes into the bargain." With that, Arthur returned to the living room and the game.

"How could this be true?" K asked himself. But then how many things about this Richmond were utterly unbelievable? The naked women, the young men with 'seriously ripped abs,' the wreathing bodies and thunderous music, the enormously popular professional combats in great Colosseums... What in all of that would suggest that an annual melee could not possibly be part of the holiday traditions?

When Lori stepped back into the kitchen to check on the turkey, she found K staring off into space. The look of panic that he could only attempt without success to conceal made her look around the room for a source of danger. Uneasy seeing none, she asked what was wrong.

"Will you be going to Black Friday malls after dinner?"

"No. It just seems too commercial to go on Thanksgiving Day. I plan on going tomorrow. I'm sure there will still be enough going on to make it worthwhile."

K added a look of utter astonishment to his panic. Try as he might, he could not imagine Lori engaging in mortal combat for sale items or anything for that matter. There was still a great deal he did not know about this Richmond. Nonetheless, her answer provided hope. "Will you be able to drive me home after the meal?"

"Jeremiah will be happy to drive you back."

"But he and Arthur will be going to Black Friday."

"Jeremiah and Arthur?"

"So Arthur informs me. They will digest their food while watching the 4:30 game, after which we will go together to a Black Friday mall to engage in mortal combat for sale items."

Lori had neither the time not the inclination to explain Black Friday. "Don't worry. Jeremiah will be taking you straight home."

With that she immediately marched into the living room. Peals of laughter followed, so loud that K could only make out the scolding tone of Lori's voice. The content of what was said could not make its way back to the kitchen. As she returned to finally check her turkey another round of laughter came behind her. That she herself could not suppress a broad smile made the sting of having fallen for the ruse even sharper.

It turned out that the dinner on this Thanksgiving Day was served in the early afternoon. The next time Lori returned, she placed the side dishes on the burners and set out the dinnerware to lay the table. K softly closed the laptop and stood at the ready to help in the kitchen. Lori was already too aware that his help would have to be supervised step by step and accepted only so much as would make K feel that he had done his part. When she suggested that he return to his work on the laptop he did so without objection.

He was reading an article labelled 'sponsored content' about how to get 'killer abs' when Lori called everyone to the table. The plan called for only minimal physical exercise. The secret was a regimen of 'supplements' available only from the company that had sponsored the content. Recommendations by numbers of men and women with remarkably developed musculature declared that it all was true. If anything, the product was actually better than the literature promised.

Following a brief 'grace,' dish after dish was handed around the table and Arthur explained that dinner always used to be served around noon when America was an agricultural country because farmers worked hard and needed to replenish calories for the afternoon of hard work that lay ahead. Lori had already told K about the pilgrims and Indians during their most recent telephone call. They were a bit like Passover stories and he could not help but feel solemn at first until he realized that he was alone in the sentiment. The resulting confusion was short lived. A moment's reflection reminded him that the day had thus far been more about watching videos of enormous parade balloons uploaded onto YouTube and football games on the big screen television. He asked for the green bean casserole which had passed by without him noticing. Never having eaten turkey before, he allowed himself a small sample only half of which he ate.

A feast without sons and daughters did not feel altogether strange to K. Once she managed to marry her way out of the flat his sister Elli would be absent from the family gatherings more often than Darlene. When her husband Karl was drafted into the army, she was positively defeated to have to return to the family Seder celebrations. But Valli would not think to miss one. She is so attentive to the few traditions that have taken root in the household's single feast that Ottla and he are little more than spectators any longer. Father would make it clear, in his arsenal of ways, that he would be quite satisfied if there had been no feasts or traditions at all, so of course the Seder revolved entirely around him exactly as he intended.

Still, as tortuous as those holidays are — or droll when he and Ottla manage to exchange a furtive wink and struggle to hold back their laughter — they are momentous compared to this Thanksgiving Day in which people were intent upon keeping it simple and informal. Father reading the traditional texts, the rest of the family silently attending, marked the day as special in a way this day's brief and rote grace could not possibly do. Once again, the freedom of this 2015 came at a cost he was not sure he could choose to pay. For all he found his own family perverse he could only wish that he were with them. It was not a realization that this day had brought about in him but he felt confident that the last of his struggle with it was ended.

Most of the conversation consisted of calls from Lori's family, each offering auxiliary greetings that she dutifully passed along to all of the guests at the table. Jeremiah was 'on call' for the members of one of his many Alcoholics Anonymous groups and his ring tone sounded about fifteen minutes into the meal. Such conversations being private, he excused himself and retired to his hobby room.

As everyone gathered back at the table and the meal came to its end Lori called for a picture to commemorate the day. Arthur and Jeremiah gathered around K where he sat and all tried to guess when the picture was being snapped so they would be smiling. When a picture had been taken the Smartphone was handed around for each to approve the image in the tiny window. Next, Jeremiah struggled with the phone to get a picture with Lori in it which made everyone laugh and several fine pictures at once.

The 4:30 game proved to be a blowout before halftime. Arthur, seeing no reason to put his brother through accompanying commentary, suggested that a good time had come to return to the apartment. Jeremiah would be able to settle in for the night without the prospect of driving halfway across town. More hugs and pictures followed. Compliments for a fine meal reminded Lori that she had yet to gather together leftovers for her two guests to take home and everyone lingered in the kitchen exchanging a few last words as she snapped plastic covers onto bowls. K reminded her how much he had enjoyed the pumpkin pie, which he had never before eaten, and the entire remains of the pie were quickly wrapped and added to the food he was to take home with him.

Jeremiah and Arthur talked quietly in the front seats on the way back to the apartment. In the back, K watched the world play out its tiny dramas before the lighted facades of the various small stores they passed along the way. Old men sat, heads down, and listened as young men told stories and everyone laughed. Women no longer quite young carried out small bags of groceries, fueled their motorcars and called out greetings.

Jeremiah and Arthur talked about the football game. Suddenly Jeremiah cried out in frustration. Arthur asked him what was the matter. "We left the battleaxes at the house. We're going to have to go back." They laughed so heartily that Arthur finished with a coughing fit.

Chapter 14

The end of Thanksgiving left K with three days before he must return to work. He found it too little. Something had given way in him. The Internet had become the world in which he lived. He remained in his room except to venture out as quickly as possible to the kitchen to microwave a meal. The end of each day found him exhausted from his travels throughout the world.

Dirty dishes no longer seemed of the least concern to him. Countertops were mottled with bits of food. Arthur suspected that the change must have been underway before the holiday. As best he could tell, the toilet had not been disinfected for over a week. There was no longer the shuffling sound of morning exercises. Instead, there was the clatter of plastic keys. While this amounted to a not entirely unwelcome return to the pre-Kafka normal he could not help but be concerned. Concerned in the odd moment, that is, as he also could not help but feel more at home. It helped that the key-clatter was not evident in the morning without straining to hear if his guest was up and about.

Thankfully, K was able to forestall one habit he was learning from Arthur. No bouts of cursing occurred, as, one after the other, the pages on the screen shook with advertisements hidden like so many landmines. As they exploded in the middle of the columns of text abruptly sending the paragraph he had been reading out of sight down the page he steeled his jaw. When they disappeared just as quickly sending the text he'd momentarily managed to get back into view out of sight up the page his shoulders sagged under the weight of his effort. Even as ambush ads leapt out obscuring the text altogether, he remained silent. It took enormous self-control. But the moment his host was up and about and at his own computer K cried out his frustration. He would not have thought himself capable of such outbursts — muffled versions of which reached Arthur at the other end of the apartment — but now they were just one more inevitable aspect of the 2015 experience. There was something about its Internet that made one swear like a sailor.

After this manner, he wrestled with articles explaining that the Turks had downed a Russian fighter plane. K repeatedly watched an unimaginably sleek and powerful fighter jet streak through the air in the distance and then catch fire and plummet toward the earth. Tensions, some of the articles explained, had already been high. World leaders cautioned against further hostility. Still more daunting weapon systems were said to exist and Russia announced it was in the process of moving them to the battle theater.

Strangely, a number of articles referred to fears that the incident would result in 'World War III'. Never having heard of a 'World War,' K searched for it on Google and let go with his first bout of cursing for the day. A message appeared informing him that he was not authorized to view the search page. There could be no slowing his pace, however. When a proper moment arrived, he would have to ask Arthur what such an error message meant.

In the midst of the stories, mention was also made that Russia had invaded the Crimea in another recent conflict for which they were 'under sanctions'. He could only wonder why the giant had invaded its own territory. K turned his search effort in that direction next and encountered no similar error messages. In a matter of seconds, Google had directed him to the information that Russia had transferred the Crimea to the Ukraine in 1954. A great many acronyms confused the matter to the point that he could not entirely understand what had occurred before he felt compelled to break off his search in favor of more engaging subjects. The upshot was that the Soviets had been dismantled (after a short and disastrous experiment, he assumed, that having been his expectation from the first) and the Ukraine was now a nation under attack once again from its historical oppressor. It was all as chaotic and perfectly impossible to follow as it had been in 1920. Some things Internets did not change.

Elsewhere floodwaters were sweeping away motorcars in the Midwest. African-American protestors had been shot in a city the name of which he had never before heard. Something called the 'Walking Dead' had just had its 'midseason finale'. Bodies covered in rotting flesh, their heads wistfully tilted to the side, were everywhere. The 'fans' were generally quite satisfied with the 'episode' as evidenced by some feature called 'Comments' which he had begun to notice. The leaders of the world were attending something called a 'climate summit,' trying much too hard to exude confidence that they would 'hammer out a deal'. The political faction called 'Republicans' controlled the U. S. Congress. They were vociferously warning that they would vote no funds to support any agreement. These Republicans, it seemed, found every action of the American President profoundly un-American. The details, they asserted, did not matter. The Congress, he learned, 'wielded the power of the purse,' but much to its consternation the President proceeded without concern for its powers. Wherever there were Comments, the President was excoriated in the most insulting terms imaginable by people identified by names such as 'Patriot716' and 'NObama'.

After reading several dozens of these K escaped to read about the plight of Texas. The state was particularly hard hit by the flooding. The cost of recovery would be high. Some people were demanding that a declaration of emergency by the governor not be honored by the national government because the state's Congressional Representatives had voted against funding similar declarations by other states. By Sunday, the state and its neighbors were hit by devastating ice storms and a young woman named 'Miley Cyrus' was 'on tour,' a thing which, by all appearances, involved sticking her tongue out a great deal. In pictures from something called the 'MTV Awards' she stuck out a great deal more. K caught himself lingering, and panicked, turning his browser elsewhere, fearful that he might have to face Arthur again having introduced another virus onto his machine.

It was as if K suddenly had found himself possessed of the multi-faceted eyes of a fly. The faster he moved from page to page the more the experience was disconcerting and exhilarating at once. He had to know more. Once one achieved a certain speed, even understanding was an unnecessary impediment.

At night, however, he was paying the price. His insomnia returned. What little sleep he managed was shot through with strange dreams filled with the war wreckage and dead bodies and ghoulish faces and motor cars flowing away in torrents of water that he had found gripping when awake. In them he found himself in crumbling buildings unsure which way to go. A strange rustling followed him. When he tried to make it out, he seemed to hear the muffled breathing of some kind of lurking beast. He inevitably woke with a start, so sweat drenched he could only wonder whether his tuberculosis had managed to find him in Richmond. But once he started the computer in the morning all such concerns disappeared.

As Arthur checked the news tickers, on Monday morning, a different K emerged into the kitchen. He had risen late, hair vaguely brushed, and ate his breakfast as he set out his clothing for the day. Arthur could not help but be concerned. K's suit was disheveled, a thing he would have considered impossible. K quickly brushed and polished all as best he could with the few minutes he had before he must walk to the bus stop. It was clear that he was very much at loose ends. In unguarded moments, his expression implied a sense of shame.

Back home from work, he once again went directly to his room. As he passed, he mumbled something that must have been a greeting. Arthur saw him again for a moment as he microwaved a late meal and returned from whence he had come. He had not lingered long enough to share a few words about his day or to ask any questions that might have arisen.

If the emerging pattern was beginning to worry Arthur the fact that K did not arrive home after work on Wednesday worried him far more. Most of the day, however, he had obsessively been following news of a terrorist attack in San Bernardino, California. K and the rest of the world barely existed. As is common in the Internet Age, television reporters were talking with persons on cellphones sheltering in place inside the buildings, waiting to be rescued by the police. Two persons had been seen in black fatigues and ski-masks, perhaps three. They were not heard to speak. The attack was on a single conference room. Dozens of dead and wounded lay on the floor there. There may have been an office Christmas party underway.

Coming so soon after the Paris attacks, his determination to understand what could be deduced about people who committed such acts was even more than usually intense. It was frustrating to have his time taken from him again so soon. It was as if, unable to assimilate him with its endless bag of cheap tricks, the world was determined to have him through his desire to analyze its collapse.

Why had the terrorists chosen the location? He had the Google Maps Street View feature up in one window. It was a small office complex engaged in no activity which might be noticed, much less offend. What did their escape in a waiting SUV suggest? They would hardly come from outside of the area to spray automatic rifle fire at a group of social workers in a conference room. A rental vehicle would only guarantee that they could quickly be identified. The vehicle must be their own or perhaps stolen locally.

The Satellite View revealed that the office complex was in a sparsely populated area. There were few routes of escape. A railroad crossing nearby left open the possibility that they had turned off onto the service roads alongside the tracks. But that would imply an even more intimate knowledge of the lay of the land. By public or by service road, they must have had a personally meaningful destination in mind rather than a plan chosen to maximize ease of escape. There were no populated areas nearby, no wooded areas along the railroad tracks in which to hide. They must not have chosen the conference room on the basis that it was the most likely target to leave them free to fight another day. A longish drive left too many opportunities for detection.

They were driven by emotion not executing a rational plan. But, still, it is all but impossible that a person with a momentary emotional gripe has stockpiled automatic weapons and explosive devices. The military precision of the attack also suggested considerable planning. Part of the evidence suggested emotion, the other rational planning over a period of months at least. Pieces of the puzzle remained unsolved.

It wasn't until daylight waned outside Arthur's window and he began to feel a need to eat his first meal of the day (as the terrorists were going down among a hail of bullets, having been discovered by various California police departments) that Arthur realized that K had yet to return from work. While the last time his guest was out late was the day of the most recent terrorist attack, there was no particular reason to suspect trouble. Still, he did not take coincidences particularly well. He could not help but feel ill at ease.

Had he known that K was being treated by Mr. Mendelssohn to dinner at Max's, a small restaurant near the import-export office, he would only have altered his reasons for feeling uncomfortable. K, too, was aware that his appearance had suffered of late and suspected that the invitation might relate to the fact.

While his boss recommended the braised short ribs, which he ordered with a side of *moules*, K selected a small salad from his large plasticized menu and a glass of ice-water. Encouraged to order something more, he demurred. In the course of the evening, his host explained that he ate most of his meals at various small establishments. Having eaten most of his own meals out of Tupperware bowls for months now, K could hardly imagine such a habit. It had been his observation that the custom was much too expensive at 2015 prices and had gone out of practice. Even had he been so forward as to order more, being a vegetarian he could not have followed his employer's recommendation.

Mr. Mendelssohn must have guessed his guest's thoughts as he stressed that he was very modest in his expenditures. The old bachelor custom of eating his meals at restaurants was the lone exception. He was a busy man. He did not have servants. It was the one pleasure he allowed himself.

He noticed that his time travelling secretary 'Fletcherized' his food, chewing each mouthful fifty times before swallowing, and laughed good naturedly at what he deemed a ridiculous affectation. The practice, he averred, was ages out of date and had been foolishness when it wasn't. With all the confidence of a successful man his host strongly advised giving up the habit. K tried to eat as little as possible without seeming unappreciative.

The waiter must have been a favorite as Mr. Mendelssohn addressed him by his Christian name. The young man showed the attentiveness that comes with the expectation of a handsome tip. He stopped back regularly to ask if everything was 'alright' while his best customer steered the conversation, at the table, toward K's recent changes in demeanor. Had he recently been feeling unwell, perhaps?

It was less a matter of asking after K's health than a gentle warning that his performance must not falter. Delivering the message over an invitation to dinner — during which German was spoken, as always between them, and respect dictated that he not condescend to address K in the informal '*du*' — was meant to express just how much it would displease him to have to let K go. His skills were irreplaceable but there was a principle at stake.

It was clear from K's demeanor that something was the matter and he chose not to take his employer into his confidence as much from courtesy as evasion. The message having been received Mendelssohn turned to K's remarkable claim to be Franz Kafka, Hermann Kafka's son. So long as K did his work well, it hardly mattered, but surely K had to admit that the claim encouraged any number of questions.

"I do not understand, myself how it is possible for which reason I can answer few if any such questions."

"You simply napped off in a second class carriage on the way to Matliary and woke up here in Richmond?"

"Yes."

"Well, your German and Czech are certainly out of date for all you speak them beautifully. And you are the spitting image of Franz Kafka."

"My Czech is a poor attempt, I am afraid."

"Not at all. You underestimate yourself, as always. It is excellent. It seems to me that you would have to be a genius of some sort in order to manage not only to speak the languages but to speak the dialects one would expect and to use phrases with ease that have been all but forgotten for 100 years. Some of them I would not know if I hadn't grown up in my grandfather's house in Prague."

"I believe I have met him."

"I hope you will forgive that I have checked your hand-writing against the documents generally available."

"My roommate has, as well."

"I am not an expert but I must admit that I can see no difference. Of course, I could never have succeeded in business if I allowed myself to believe such tales."

K nodded with an expression of resignation. Having been perfectly disciplined in his selection of entrée, he felt at liberty to choose a large fruit pastry from the dessert cart. He also took the liberty of changing the topic of conversation to 'Israel'. He was experiencing difficulties, at times, finding information on it. Was Mr. Mendelssohn a Zionist?

His host answered with an inscrutable expression. "I do not use computers. That I leave up to my clerks. My best understanding is that there is no lack of information on Israel."

"There seems to be a great conflict there."

"I have paid for the meal. The waiter has called you a cab. It will arrive any minute. Thank you, Herr Kafka, for the delightful company. Please do arrive tomorrow kempt and normally precise." Mendelssohn rose and stepped into a taxi of his own and was gone.

K passed through the front door of the apartment with an apology if he might have worried Arthur. His host barely realized he had arrived before he was in his room brushing his suit and setting out the items for his morning routine. Lori called and he let the call go through to voice mail. An hour later he was in bed with a copy of Kierkegaard's *Either/Or*. He felt as comfortable as he had in weeks and more deprived. Several times he considered turning on the computer and gathered up the discipline to resist the temptation.

In the morning Arthur was surprised to see him lint free and going through his normal routine. He carefully cleaned the bathroom before consenting to use it and mumbled something about attending to the kitchen after work. Something must have happened the night before but he could not guess what. Whatever it was, his guest did not seem particularly pleased to meet the new day.

That evening he arrived back at the apartment directly after work. When he did not clean the kitchen before microwaving his supper Arthur peeked around his door to see him sitting in front of the computer oblivious to the world around him. He had intended to spend just a few minutes. Those few minutes grew to hours. Arthur had fallen asleep before the light went off in his guest's room.

Still K was up bright and early intent to keep up his appearance. He intended to have more self-control during the evenings. For this one morning he would overcome his malaise and arrive at the office precisely groomed and attentive to his duties. It would only be one day.

Only too predictably that one day became another… and another. The pattern continued the rest of the week. Late nights were followed by mornings of agitated preparation.

The computer beckoned to him every waking hour. To K's amazement, he discovered that the president of Germany was a woman. The mayor of Prague was now someone named Adriana Krnačová, also a woman. He laughed to think of Ottla becoming a mayor. He felt he had at last begun to understand why 2015 was such a crazy time. Women were running it. Undoubtedly they all had coffee mugs reading 'Sexy and I Know It'.

In America the presidential candidate named Donald Trump was reported to be 'sucking all of the oxygen out of the room'. By report, he was something called a 'Birther': that he had challenged the African-American President Obama to produce a birth-certificate to prove that he was not born in some country in Africa of which K had never heard. As he waved a fleshy hand at the public the words 'We're Not Gonna Take It' were repeated again and again to a thrumming downbeat. It was a song that something called 'Twisted Sister' had given him permission to use. Entire news stories covered the issue.

A Google search brought up yet another astonishing picture, this one of large manlike creatures (he was sure they must be American Indians) in war paint, grimacing, their state of partial undress a sort of bizarre cross between the 'Walking Dead' and the nearly naked women to be seen everywhere on the Internet. When he moved the cursor onto something labelled 'Official Video,' and clicked, an even more bizarre opera began in which an unkindly father chastised his sons and they instantaneously turned into the large Indian warriors singing

> "Your life is trite and jaded
> Boring and confiscated"

while repeatedly throwing him out of windows on the upper floor of a two-story house. From time to time the camera turned to a sea of young bodies swaying with ecstasy to the rhythm of the music. K could not help but laugh at the father's comical expressions. It was even funnier than his favorite Katzenjammer Kids comic strips.

The video ended and the show had only begun. After a commercial message, another mini-opera followed. Then another and another. All of them were foremost energetic, all of the music as deafening as that on the dance floor he had just barely escaped. But there was no need to fear here in the apartment. With a little distance it was... What was it, actually? It was nothing if it was not obvious but still no words came to mind.

After a half-hour, K finally realized that the music was thunderously loud. He quickly turned the volume down. This greatly reduced the effect. Without the thunderous volume there was much less to recommend it. Suddenly the 50-ish next door neighbor's so called music made a bit more sense.

Something in K resisted returning from the thunderous mini-operas, with their grimacing long haired men and grimacing bald headed women, to the news coverage that seemed so wondrous only an hour before. The flooding this time was in England. The news was accompanied by the usual pictures of the tops of motorcars peeking out of the water and residents being rescued in skiffs. It was the worst in more than a hundred years — a phrase that was common, he observed, to all flooding and wildfire stories from wherever they originated. Elsewhere, protestors in Paris were dispersed by something called 'tear gas'. Photos showed them tearfully clutching wadded clothing over their mouths and noses.

But somehow it all felt much too tame, now. Even clicking the 'sponsored stories' promising 'jaw-dropping' revelations or pictures of 'epic plastic surgery fails' was a tedious experience. K returned to the music videos, picking them out like chocolates from a candy box until he was gorged to a nauseous ecstasy... and then he watched some more.

When he could manage to break away, his attention began more often to be drawn to pictures of feet with toenail fungus promising to inform him how to recognize the signs of impending heart attacks and tired faces promising to reveal the secret of removing dark circles from under eyes. He read about wardrobe malfunctions and nip slips and sex robots and the reasons they should and should not be created and why they were inevitable anyway and about how to know if one's boss was a psychopath or boyfriend a narcissist. He watched flash mobs and military fathers surprising their children and every imaginable heart-warming way of proposing marriage.

Having escaped the mini-operas again, K was reading with astonishment about motorcars that drove themselves when the mouse became erratic and he found it difficult to direct the cursor. He had learned from Arthur's past examples, piercing the silence of the apartment, that one curses at the quality control department at the manufactory at such moments and the lesson was not lost upon him. When the entire computer function froze up he dutifully cursed the 'company CEO,' whatever precisely that was (he made a mental note to do a Google search in order to find out), and the Caribbean vacations the CEO could so readily afford because he made shameless amounts of money selling 'crap'. These incantations seemed to work surprisingly well as function returned shortly thereafter.

Arthur could not help but be concerned. On Friday Lori called on the landline. She had been leaving voice messages on K's cell phone for days without receiving a reply. Had something terrible happened? Was he okay? The next morning, Arthur knocked on his guest's door. When no answer came, he eased it open. The bed was not made. Various articles, once neatly laid out, were scattered about in a haphazard manner. K was peering into the screen as if he hadn't noticed that Arthur had entered.

"The weather is still nice. I was wondering if you would like to come along for a walk."

"Will we be walking to a retail establishment to engage in mortal combat?" K continued to type as he asked the question.

It was the first K had mentioned it. Arthur was at a loss what to reply. He was terrible at this kind of conversation, was stricken by the memory of how many times it used to be he who was the butt of the joke. His throat constricted. It had been meant as a harmless prank.

K was surprised to sense the effect of his comment. So much so that he looked up. He would have expected a glib, deflecting reply. Instead their roles had been gratifyingly reversed. Arthur was the personification of guilt. "Do you think it wise to spend all of your time in front of the computer?" he asked, after a long silence which K did not choose to break.

"No one has called the police to have me clapped in a jail cell yet. That would seem to argue that my decision is better than most I have made."

The change of subject noticeably lightened Arthur's expression. K could not choose to let him off the hook so easily. "No one likes to be made a fool of, even if they come from 1920."

"I'm sorry. I didn't stop to think," he replied with a grimace.

"Does Siné's Irish Pub have eyes, too?"

"Security cameras? Yes, probably. Why?"

"So the great database now knows me as a strange unaccountable man who asks questions at fine clothing establishments and hovers around young women?"

"*Stalks* young women."

"*Stalks?*" The word came out as a cry of pain.

"Pretty much all of that kind of thing falls under the category 'stalking' now."

It would have been impossible to imagine K looking any more dejected.

"It's unlikely that Siné's is on the same network. Or any network. Its cameras are on a loop. In a week your image was permanently erased — recorded-over with new images, actually."

"My images only existed for a week?"

"The one's from bars and restaurants probably. Yes. Such places don't do data. At least not yet."

"The images of my... *stalking*... were recorded over in a week?"

Arthur hesitated. "Unless the police requested a copy, yes. But they have neither the time nor the money to record security footage every time some young guy gets jealous."

"Your demeanor these past days suggests that you feel guilty for what you did. How can that be?"

It was Arthur's turn to look confused.

"In a place where there is no sin there can be no guilt. I have seen no expression of either in the entire time I have been in this 2015. Except, that is, for Jeremiah and Lori's dog."

"I'm a throwback."

"A throwback?"

"I was born before there was any Internet. Not that sin wasn't already being challenged. It's bad for business. But changing entire societies is much slower when it's done the Jehovah's Witness way."

"The *what* way?"

"A metaphor. Everything is accelerated by the Internet. Sin was already scheduled to be discontinued."

"It died with your Dr. Freud."

"A metaphor…"

"Are you to decide for me?"

"Apparently, yes. Anyway, his was the last among many blows: the mortal one. But sin was taking a long time dying before the advent of the Internet. Still, a sense of guilt is said to be possible for having trespassed the social norms of the group."

"And you believe this?"

"Of course not. Only fear. But sin has taken a long time dying, regardless. In *The Trial*, Joseph K…"

"He would never have thought of it as sin. He could not have chosen to call it sin."

"He did not call it anything. He did not know the nature of his crime or that he was his own accuser. Did I miss the point? That is why it had such power over him."

"And from this you gather that sin was dying?"

"No. Joseph K did not convince me. You did. You convinced me that the irrational God of sin and guilt had been thoroughly coopted by an inextricable justice system. What remained the same was the desire to hold at bay an internalized sense of guilt."

"But there might have been an actual crime."

"Precisely."

"Must this world be the only possible outcome, do you think?" K spoke the words at just above a whisper. It was obvious that this had not been the first time the question had come to him. "Is your 'System' the necessary outcome of perceiving the nature of sin and guilt?"

"Of freedom from internalized authority? Perhaps. Anyway, history can only have one outcome. There is limited benefit to asking what other outcomes might have been possible."

"So all the world must suffer because Joseph K could not understand that it was he who accused himself?"

"Without the Internet, would you feel that it was suffering? Has suffering increased or has your awareness of it?"

"That is not what I meant. There is endless stimulation, endless advertisements, endless buying and selling, and no longer any meaning."

"There are *endless* meanings."

"Which is to say the same thing, or maybe even worse. I can't imagine why I write if matters can only come to that. What reason could there be for all my nights of struggle? I could have told the whole tale in an evening at a café table and slept well for at least one night."

"There was nothing you could have done."

"My work is merely the obsession of a sick man, a dangerous failure. I told Max to destroy my papers."

Arthur had entered the room with a book in his hand. He turned the cover toward K. It was called *The Pickwick Papers*. "My friend thought that the idea for *The Trial* had come to you from reading about Mr. Pickwick's trial."

"Perhaps. It hardly matters, I should think. You said you never read Dickens."

"It's my first."

The change of subject revived K's spirits just a bit. "It is an excellent book. Anything by Dickens always is. Perhaps we will find some time to talk about it as you progress."

"They all had happy endings," Arthur said, with an eye-roll suggesting skepticism.

"Yes. Well, that can be refreshing from time to time. Will *this* story have a happy ending?"

Arthur smiled to have his guest so deftly steer the conversation. The smile was brief. "I hope so. But I can't see how."

K returned to peering into the monitor. "Neither could I," he replied, typing and clicking as he did. "I told Max to destroy my papers."

Chapter 15

The dread moment was approaching. Arthur helplessly watched it draw closer. Even K had managed to break away from his computer monitor twice in order to spend time... Christmas shopping. He had begun checking his voice mail again, once or twice a day, between online articles on the secrets of the world's most creative geniuses, how to get that first sentence written and video tours of 'Kafka's Prague'. Lori and her girlfriends were thrilled at the prospect of teaching him the pleasures of the chase and the locations of the prettiest vegetarian lunch spots. While these safaris took nearly as long as a work day, K returned with numerous small gifts, new hygiene items to be tried and considerably more energy than when he left.

The entire crew arrived outside the apartment door, on the first occasion, as if a flock of starlings had descended, chirping excitedly. K, who apparently had received a call as they approached, passed Arthur in his chair, playfully tipping his hat as he did, and swept out the door. As he emerged he joined the flock. Scores of dashboard lights were blinking like a Christmas tree as the door closed behind him and various beeps and warning voices added to the general twittering.

Hours later, the flock once again descended. Goodbyes were added to the chatter and K entered with an armful of gifts, most for himself. He had succeeded so admirably in complaining that they should not buy him 'things,' with an air of being overwhelmed with their kindness, that of course they bought still more. To these, Arthur had every confidence, more would be added under the Christmas tree. To add to the effect of his arms full of gifts, K struggled, upon entering, to once again tip his hat. After settling his 'things' on shelves in the bathroom and bedroom, came the clatter of plastic keys. There was no time to be lost.

Before the second excursion, K made the mistake of stepping out of the front door without waiting for the call. He was greeted, as he did so, by Rhonda, who had been trawling the parking lot for her

Christmas quota of converts to her evangelical church. "Where had he been?" she wondered. She hadn't seen him in weeks. He stuttered out something about being very busy.

For all K tried to head her off at the pass, Rhonda, being the stronger of the two, launched into her standard sales pitch. She had lived the life of the street for many years. She was broke and sodden for the umpteenth time, taken advantage of by false friends, at a loss for how she was going to pay rent, before her own evangel finally convinced her to cross the transom of the church. She never looked back.

The last time their paths crossed, he and Arthur had been returning from the bicycle ride to the VCU campus. They had stopped on the way back to pick up an inexpensive bag of candy, in case children might knock on the door for Halloween that evening, and were greeted with how much she 'sincerely hoped' that they were not participating in 'that demonic holiday'. Somehow she managed to sound as friendly as ever while she did so. She was every bit as cheery and engaging for the next twenty minutes as she did the very best she could to dissuade her neighbors from their sinful course. Her love for her fellow beings was as sincere as is possible only without reflection. Her cheerfulness remained undented regardless that Arthur finally yelled out that she was a wonderful neighbor, and that the building was much the better for her presence, as he grabbed K's arm and the two leapt into the apartment.

Since that day K had been in the habit of cracking open the door before egress in order to check that the coast was clear. On this day, however, he let his sense that all in the world was well overcome his caution. "You promised that you would come to church with me one day," Rhonda cried out as she crossed the parking lot like an eagle descending upon a hare that had momentarily forgotten itself. Aware that the case was hopeless the hare stood frozen in place.

K had promised no such thing but could not find the courage to contradict her or the celerity to escape within his lair regardless that it might offend her. She was, after all, the friendliest lodger in the apartment complex and it bordered on a criminal act to hurt her feelings. The best he could do for himself was to attempt a gambit. He confessed that he was Jewish. Much to his chagrin, she replied, at considerable length, that all people were welcome in her church, 'even Episcopalians' (which was apparently evidence of insuperable powers of forgiveness should the sinner be repentant). There was something of the sermon in her tone to give him a preview of what lay in store should he fail to accomplish a graceful escape. He was sorry, he said, but friends were coming at any minute to take him away and he must brush his hat. Reaching back as he said it, he grasped the door handle and firmly turned it only to discover that it had been locked. With more desperate speed he extracted his key from his pocket, unlocked the door and stepped through, with the best appearance of calm that he could manage, gently shutting it behind him.

Inside the door he found Arthur, in his customary chair beside the window, doubled over for trying to laugh as softly as he might manage. His laughter grew more raucous, in proportion to the growing distance as Rhonda rushed away to engage another neighbor who had emerged into the open. K could not help but laugh for all he was equal part furiously angry at his host's prank.

His cellphone rang, as he stood there, and the matter was at an end. In a moment the starlings arrived once again. K waved to Rhonda as he stepped into the motorcar to be greeted with a satisfying enthusiasm. On the way to the mall, he told the tale of his adventure considerably altered to impress upon the group how especially unkind Arthur had proven. By tailoring his account to highlight his suffering at least he might receive a few extra 'things' for his trouble.

While Arthur would not think of admitting it, the flock brought the spirit of Christmas to those days on which it descended. Until, that is to say, it brought to mind the fact that he, too, must give in and go shopping for the few remaining people on his Christmas list that he could not in good conscience send only a Christmas card. As the number of available shopping days had dwindled his desperation to think of some other subject had grown less and less effective. When his thoughts were once again hijacked to the matter, it was too much to bear. Determined to struggle no longer, he powered up the gimpy HP printer, its ink more expensive than liquid platinum, and printed out three more Christmas cards. As he folded them he popped twenty dollars into each, then, as he was about to seal them into envelopes, took each out once more to put in another five dollars. That done, he sealed the envelopes with a sigh of relief. The gifts would be on the way on Monday morning.

K returned, once again bearing gifts the flock had bought him for being so sensitive and to comfort him in his extraordinary circumstances. Arthur's earlier prank seemed to have been forgiven as K returned and stood waiting while his host glumly read an online article about the collapse of the market in e-books. At last he looked up.

"Amy's wallet has been frozen," K announced with a look of horror.

"Amy?"

"Lori's friend. You have met her I am informed. Everyone is quite distraught."

"Her wallet?"

"It seems that wallets can now be… *virtues?* Whatever that might mean."

"Virtual: it means they are no longer physical. Almost all money nowadays consists of ones and zeros. Soon there will be no physical currency."

"It is part of the transition?"

"Yes. She'll have to use her regular credit cards until the matter is straightened out."

"She no longer keeps credit cards. Her wife told her that they were better off to switch to the wallet."

"Her wife?"

K's 'things' were becoming a bit much to cradle while talking. "It seems that there can now be marriages between two wives," he called out over his shoulder as he set them down on the already cluttered all-purpose laundry-folding, troubleshooting and soldering table. "I hoped you might be able to explain."

As K turned from the table to continue his query, a small electrical meter teetered on the edge. Arthur leapt to his feet and pushed past K to grab it before it could fall. As he swept the meter up to place it upon an even more cluttered upper shelf, nearby, one of the dangling test leads knocked a small bottle of cologne to the floor.

K was relieved to see that it hadn't broken. "This is manufactured in a small village outside of Prague," he said as he placed it back on the table. "I travel there often for the Insurance Institute."

"Yes. Wonderful. I'd prefer that you not put things on the table. I cannot afford to replace equipment." In his agitation Arthur knocked over a tall pile of folded tee-shirts and cursed as he returned with a dismissive wave of his hand to his chair.

K collected his 'things' and placed them on various shelves in his room and the bathroom. As he walked into the bathroom, he noticed two new shelves had been installed while he had been out and a strict apartheid instituted between their toiletries.

"She is no longer able to pay her suppliers."

"Her suppliers?"

"She owns a small shop. A linen shop. We stopped there today. It was then we learned of the wallet. It is really quite nice. The shop, I mean."

"The matter will be cleared up when she contacts her bank. Until then she'll have to write checks."

"She reports that her other accounts are locked, as well."

"Then she'll need to go to the closest brick-and-mortar location." Arthur scrolled through news stories as he spoke. "She'll have to call ahead to set up an appointment with one of the account managers."

"Lori says she has read 'horror stories' in which persons locked out of their accounts were not able to get them open again."

"She said that to Amy?"

"No. She would not choose to distress her by saying such a thing. She said it later when we were having lunch at a tiny vegan restaurant called Ipanema. The most remarkable thing: it occupied the basement of a tattoo parlor. It was warm enough to eat on the tiny patio. I was reminded of Paris. Is there nothing more that can be done? Lori suggests that you might know."

"About the tattoo parlor?"

K stood, head lowered, to await the moment when Arthur would return to being serious.

"I couldn't say without looking at Amy's account activity before they were locked. Even then it would be likely I could only advise her to go to the brick-and-mortar location. That and pray."

"But the money is hers."

"Not any longer it isn't. Actually, it never was. It wasn't in your day either. If I'm not mistaken, the picture of the Emperor is on your bank notes. Those notes are not yours, they are yours to use at his pleasure."

"But the Emperor would never think of suspending my notes."

"Should your bank see fit to refuse you access to your secret account, as representative of the Emperor, you would be in much the same position."

"People know about the secret account?" K could not help but stamp his feet. His face was red with anger. "The bank holds that in the strictest confidence."

"For us it was over ninety years ago. You've long since emptied the account. Your father never learned of it. I wouldn't worry about it overly much."

"But neither the bank nor the Emperor would think to refuse me my own funds."

"The Emperor's funds."

"A mere technicality."

"Actually not. Your money is perfectly safe because the Emperor and his bureaucracies don't know you from Adam. For that reason you can't have upset them enough that they would suspend your privilege. They have no reason to take back *their* notes from you."

"Are you saying that Amy is personally known by the President and *his* bureaucracies?"

"Whose picture is on the zeros and ones that are now most money?"

K hesitated, trying to picture what an answer might be. "No one."

"Exactly."

"Exactly?"

"No one's. They are just zeros and ones."

"So they belong to Amy alone."

"Then let her give them to her suppliers."

"To whom, then, do they belong?"

"The System."

"And The System knows her?"

"The System knows everyone and no one."

"Why is it offended with her?"

"She will have to set up an appointment at the nearest brick-and-mortar branch of her bank and try to find out."

"They will resolve the matter?"

"Probably not. Not until after a good many subsequent appointments, reams of paperwork and even then only by the grace of God."

"The System. But she has done nothing wrong."

"How do you know that?"

K sensed the weakness of his answer but could not resist. "She says she has not."

"Does she know all of the things that she might do wrong?"

"There was some mention of a thirty page agreement and a great many rules."

"A 'User's Agreement'."

"I do believe so, yes. Her wife says they should sue them."

"Them?"

K stood at a loss for what exactly to say. There was still a great deal he did not understand about the conversations around him.

"The 'User's Agreement' she signed says that she waives the right to sue 'them' for any matter related to the service."

"You have read it?"

"All of them say it now. By signing it, she agreed to engage a mediator if she has any unresolvable complaints. She has also agreed to limit the company's settlement, should it lose, to simple recovery of direct damages." Arthur hesitated in order to get his interlocutor's attention fully back. "Anything more is friction."

Being a lawyer, K was aware of the general nature of what had just been said. "What if she can't get access to her money in time?"

"God works in mysterious ways. It would not be inappropriate to call her 'Josephine K'."

The words struck K as an accusation. "There are differences!" he fairly cried out. In an instant he realized that the only person who had accused him was himself. The realization left him silent and confused. He would not have expected his own answer.

"Yes. There are differences," Arthur replied as he shifted his attention back yet again to his computer monitor.

Amy's crisis had not passed by Christmas. At first the starling telephone-tree anguished over her loss. All possible contacts were contacted. They were pleased to try to be of help though they seemed to have been none. Amy herself proved quite adept at fending off creditors with promises. The members of the flock made extra Christmas purchases and in cash. Her linen shop actually experienced a brief uptick in sales.

For all K knew there was little he could do, he spent time each day for nearly a week looking very closely at such arcane subjects as 'User's Agreements,' 'credit ratings,' and 'virtual wallets'. Subsequent queries to Arthur were uniformly disappointing. He could not help but reflect that for all this 2015 was a wonder in so many ways and so free of the oppression of the Empire it had its own oppression, perhaps worse. Imitation food, people roughly jostling one another out of the way, motorcars careening, paper-thin walls, noise at all hours, 'User's Agreements,' the invisible hand of a God who had somehow become very real and who offered no covenant of love or justice to its people, only stimulation.

But mostly he watched mini-operas and 'jaw-dropping' videos with breast nipples obscured and shocked expressions. He could not help but be thankful that he had been found unfit for military duty, during the Great War, every time he watched Syrians explode with the impact of bombs and other enormously powerful armaments. He clicked on the adverts at the bottoms of the videos, at first, to see what 'video games' with names like Mortal Combat were about. There he found still more violent footage that 'gamers' were invited to enter and enjoy as a form of entertainment.

Soon K found himself suffering from insomnia once again. It was a disappointment but he'd spent most of his adult life struggling to sleep. He was perfectly confident that he would survive, even thrive. He was up early in the morning, doing his exercises, regardless how little he had slept, brushing his clothing, preening his hair until it was perfect and microwaving his breakfast. If anything, he was even more obsessive about cleaning the bathroom and kitchen each day before he left for work.

By the time the family had gathered at Jeremiah and Lori's house for Christmas dinner, there was a peace of mind, among the members of the calling-tree, for having done all that could be done for Amy. The matter was no longer in the air. K sensed that the day was especially happy. Both Donna and Shawn were free of other plans and opened their gifts with abandon. Lori placed surprising emphasis on the fact that it was K's first Christmas, after a fashion, while Arthur and Jeremiah rolled their eyes each time she mentioned it and continued watching a game on the television in which men bounced a round ball on the floor to roars of approval from the spectators. Photographs of everyone, in various combinations, doing various holiday things, were the order of the day.

But even with the shopping safari's and calling-tree and the excited voices that went with them K could not help feeling that something was out of place. Actually, more than one thing. He missed Ottla. When his thoughts weren't about her, they were about the Internet. Somehow it had taken from him the ability just to be present. Every gift now seemed to arise out of an unaccountable swirl of ones and zeros to cries of joy. The little gifts that Ottla once so appreciated were impossible to imagine now. The advice he too officiously gave her was now Medieval. Perhaps she would be the mayor of Prague now. In the matter of a few weeks, one hundred years had grown into an impassible chasm.

He explained it to himself as a growing homesickness. Yet there could be no denying it was related to what he saw each day on his computer monitor. It was a magic screen. There could be no denying it. But the moment he found himself asking what it all might mean the implications left him apprehensive. Amy's wallet had gotten him in the habit of asking Arthur for explanations again regardless that they tended to be disturbing. The questions did not end there. His host's cynical answers did not seem so cynical anymore.

The Internet was a window into a world in which everything that did not affect The System was becoming equally right and equally wrong, to hear it from him. There was no opinion (K could only confirm) that was more supported than another. Each had its virulent supporters and its virulent opponents.

Or the only ideas that were uniformly rejected out of hand were those associated with the centuries of history over which K debated with his friends in the cafes of Prague, laying claim to the youthful prerogative of change. In place of reason, epithets were the stuff of argument. That history was dismissed as an insidious tool of oppression. It throve only as a charming affectation, a travel destination. To offer it in debate was to unleash a firestorm of alternative histories each considered somehow 'a right'. The Dadaists had won but by means even they could not have begun to imagine. The miraculous world one saw in one's monitor made all of reason not associated with more effective consumption of products appear useless or worse.

According to Arthur, it was all becoming just so many ones and zeros. Every content being equal was the same as there being no content at all. The System could only be pleased that history was dying. It hummed like a healthy body hummed, each cell in its place. Infectious bodies slowly being removed. Each cell becoming resigned to its role.

"But such horrifying deaths are displayed every day. Are they all some sort of infection?"

"Were there no innocents in the Great War? If their deaths were filmed and played each day for you would you think it less horrifying than now? In fact, you would become inured. The System depends upon it. Actually Life has always depended upon it. Hasn't it? The System is only using the tools immediately at hand."

"Is this not just your narrative?"

"Undoubtedly."

It was maddening, all a matter of one's product preferences. The fervor of the omnipresent Comment threads was nothing more than an instinctive behavior — an algorithm — amounting to a collective thought they did not even know they had formed. Like those neurons, of which Arthur was so fond, that fired without knowing anything about the final thought in which they have participated. It all was meant to arrive at nothing now and nothing in particular that would cause friction in The System. The gifts that were opened that day were given with love but his little gifts to Ottla — mean in comparison — were not available any longer for even the greatest sum. He saw that nothing was left of the world in which they could once be purchased for mere *pfennigs*. He never loved that world more.

After a pleasant and uneventful Christmas, filled with turkey and pictures, K returned to his long evenings with a determination that had not gone before. He may only vaguely have understood its source. "How can it be that you are the only person not fading away to ones and zeros?" he asked Arthur, at one point. He was sleeping less even than usual and it was having its effects. "How is it that the Great Arthur is the only person impervious to the effects?"

Arthur was saddened to hear 'the Great Arthur'. It was not the first time he'd heard the like. He might have hoped he would be spared it. But each day before the magic screen K was more desperate to believe there were other answers. He could only choose to believe that his host's commentaries were what was insidious. What played out before his eyes could not be what it seemed to be.

Regardless where or when K came from, he had developed no immunities. Each shock was a fresh insult. To explain to him the fate of those who managed to the least extent to live within the system without living within The System could only increase his distress. Or perhaps that had been the source of the distress that turned him into Kafka in the first place. Perhaps it had all already proven too much for him to bear and he had escaped in the way he could. He became Franz Kafka.

"How can this God be so unconcerned for the creatures it rules? How can people live like this?"

"The System is without emotion. It does have a distant understanding that people have emotions, though, and that those emotions must be added to the equation or matters fall apart rather spectacularly."

"Your infamous 'algorithms' are not the same thing as understanding emotions."

"They are 'understanding' enough. There will still be quaint little vegan restaurants. More people will have the chance to dine in them than was the case in Prague. There will still be jobs and paychecks, marriages, births, funerals. In another generation, no one will even notice what is lost. They won't even know it ever existed."

Each answer felt more devastating than the last. K stared out the window at the parking lot next door.

Arthur quietly continued. "You need to stop spending time on the Internet." He knew that the suggestion would not be well received but it had to be said. "In a few days you will begin to feel like yourself again. It's not your world, anyway."

"Isn't it?"

"There are plenty more volumes of Kierkegaard. If you are tired of him there are Dostoevsky, Dickens, Flaubert, Poe: all of your favorites are here. Lieutenant Musil wrote a novel called *A Man without Qualities*. I hadn't thought to mention it yet. It's really quite remarkable."

"Musil is a gentleman," K replied, comforted to feel for just a moment like he was back in his element. It only lasted a moment. "Who can read any of them now? How can they bear any relationship to this world?"

"There are 7 billion people in the world, Franz. It only matters what a tiny number of them read, if it even matters then. Just read them because it pleases you to do so."

K looked at him as if he were a tragic figure. "Is that what you do?"

His reply, however, betrayed no sense of tragedy. "I write a little something now and again. Their names come up on the off chance that it might amount to something. Regardless, they're behind the words. Can't help but be. No one reads my stuff, though. It's probably just something to do."

"You write for no one?"

"Probably. Almost no one, anyway."

"What use is there to it, then?"

"We all delude ourselves when we must, Franz." Before he knew it, he confided more than was his habit. "My life would be grim without purpose even if the purpose were only an illusion."

The doorbell rang as Arthur said the words. It was the widower up the walk. He had cooked more chicken than he could eat. Had they had supper yet? He had two paper plates wrapped in aluminum foil in his hands. There was also potato in each, he informed them, and a hot biscuit. The two thanked him without inviting him inside. There was nothing but books inside. It was no place to entertain normal guests. K being a vegetarian, the second plate was settled in the refrigerator for Arthur to heat up the next day. K microwaved a meal for himself and returned to his room and the computer.

As K had become more obsessed, Arthur had realized that it was only a matter of time before far worse came to pass. He had taken what precautions he could: blocked the most direct keyword searches, stayed away from certain conversations. Still, when K stood shaking in the hallway from the kitchenette, pale as he had ever seen him, and struggling to speak, there was no doubt what was the problem.

"The search pages that I have not been able to see...," he cried out, his eyes wide with the terror of what he had seen. His anger came back to him. "The ones that said I did not have permission to access them... *you* were doing that."

"I was only trying to spare you pain."

Distraught as he was, his thoughts were scattered. "It cannot be true. It cannot be true." None of the endless shocks that he had received in this world could possibly prepare him for this.

Arthur made no reply. What could possibly be said?

"I am in a coma and the dream has become a horrifying nightmare, true, but it is only a dream nonetheless." K looked around as if seeking a way out of a hostile place. "They hate us but even they could not do such a thing."

Arthur was not sure just how much K knew. Perhaps he did not know the worst. It was best to remain silent: to listen and to say nothing.

"You are here from the depths of my mind to torture me. You are the punishment of my father." K stood straight and defiant, eyes flashing. "I do not believe it." Then he slouched with utter defeat. "This is inconceivably cruel." Next came a look of horrified realization. "That is why I saw no fear in Prague on your Google Maps. There are no Jews there anymore. They're all gone. A more human world than you could possibly imagine. All of them are gone. Only the synagogues remain and your tourists flock to them as just one more source of stimulation offered by your bloodless God of zeros and ones."

"There is nothing I could say to comfort you."

K took his head in his hands. "Oh, you have *said* quite enough!" His words were formed by a terrible distress. "You and this horrifying world of bloodless zeros and ones."

"It happened in a world that was far more yours than ours, Franz."

"You and your explanations! Always it was the *same* then. Always the *same* there. Don't tell me that it was the same! I was there. They hated us, yes. I warned people, yes. But it was not the same." Suddenly an answer came to him: a way out. "This is just words. The videos are just another ugly series of videos. None of it is real. It is you. It is all in your cruel imagination. How did you bring me here?"

"Now who is being cruel? I have imagined nothing. If it is any comfort to think that you are imagining it, please take what comfort you can.... What could I possibly say?"

"Can they really all be dead? Ottla? All of them?"

So then, he did know. "She is said to have been remarkably brave."

"Is there nothing more known of the others except that they died in... *extermination camps*? We are Jews. We are not vermin." With the word 'vermin' K's face went wide with recognition. He cried out. "I told Max to destroy my manuscripts." His thoughts were coming almost randomly. "My parents?"

"They died natural deaths years before. They knew nothing of it.... It had nothing to do with your stories."

"I must go back. I must make Max destroy my papers."

"It would change nothing. There is nothing you could possibly do."

"How can you know that?" It came out as a cry of desperation. "You cannot know that.... I must do *something*. There must be *something* I can do. I could warn them. Convince them to flee."

"Perhaps. I couldn't say."

"I must go back."

"How? By clicking the heels of your ruby slippers?"

K had only half been listening. "What?"

"Not important. How will you get back?"

"I will find a way," he said, as he turned and walked back toward his room. "I *must* find a way."

Chapter 16

Arthur woke late. K had made little if any attempt to sleep during the night. There had been distracted mumbling until the early hours. His host could not bring himself to complain. What could he possibly say? One thing he did decide, as sporadic noise from his distraught guest repeatedly woke him, was that K must go. It (whatever *it* might be) had already gone much too far. He would address the problem in the morning.

When he did rise, all was silent. He soon had a warmed-up coffee in hand and the news wires on screen. The first snowstorm of the season was about to strike. He had loaded extra groceries into his large Alice Pack, the day before, and pedaled up the hill from the market. It was a treat to be able to get out during the winter. The exercise was good for him. Nothing more was necessary. He kept his needs few.

Lori and friends had stopped by over the weekend with extra meals and fresh laundry for K. He was repeatedly asked if there was anything else he might need before the snow would begin to fall. Did he have enough hair gel (for he was sensitive about such things)? Had he brought any boots from Prague? He had packed for snow at Matery (or whatever exactly the name of the place was), right? Were his cellphone batteries charging properly? Why didn't he check quickly while they were there? It would put their minds at ease. He was to give a call if any problems arose. Somehow Jeremiah would find a way to help. He was used to driving in snow, quite expert at it. Come to think of it, K was to give an occasional call even if there had been no problem. They would worry if they didn't hear from him.

News video about the storm had been streaming since the day before. Every official advisory and pre-advisory had been dutifully reported and reported again, every alternative storm track analyzed. Every flake that had fallen as the storm traveled north seemed to have received individual coverage. They were as ready as they would ever be. The last thing Arthur wanted to watch was another online primer on how to prepare for the storm. For him it was just another day. When it arrived, he would look out the window from time to time to watch the snow float to the ground outside the window. If the power stayed on he would be safe and warm as he did so.

The rest of the world went unaffected on its own way. Local governments struggled with their own issues. The tides were now regularly bringing water up over the raised seaside walkways of San Francisco. Elsewhere it gently lapped at the doors of shops. On the near coast it was much the same in New Jersey and the various inlets nearby. A Massachusetts group had just released a political ad photo-shopped to show the presidential candidates of each party standing in waist-deep water behind their debate podiums.

A gnarled, middle aged black man pushed a shopping cart into the parking lot as Arthur read about Northern California's worsening tidal flooding. He was a familiar figure on his way to the dumpster to scavenge for aluminum cans. Someone must have challenged him the last time he came through for he was not in the habit of showing up at first light. He usually appeared around 11:00, his cart already brimming with black plastic bags full of cans. After his stop he would crush cans on the sidewalk beside the church in order to make room for more from subsequent stops.

The Union of Concerned Scientists had released a study that showed many times the historical rate of tidal flooding along coastal areas already. Swatches of video showed children making their way to school by balancing on fence lines, above shin-deep water, and pulling themselves along hand over hand. It did not mention the plummeting property values in those areas or the inability to get flood insurance. Already, many of the houses could not be sold at all. The owners were trapped. Their investment was entirely lost. The old man pushed his cart out of the parking lot toward the main road. Beyond him, on the other side of the low hillock, a flashing blue beacon suggested that a morning commuter had been pulled over.

A mosquito born disease, called 'Zika,' had been wreaking havoc in Brazil for months. The first cases were beginning to be diagnosed in the U. S. It was associated with a condition called 'microcephaly,' in which newborns were being born with undersized brains and heads. Already, one researcher was pointing out that global warming trends meant the mosquito — and therefore the cases of the disease — would travel father north into the temperate latitudes of the states. It was an effect that wouldn't end with Zika and would become more pronounced as the planet grew warmer. There would be other tropical diseases. They would spread ever father into the ever warmer north.

A jogger passed alongside the road, checking his Smartwatch (for vital signs or step-count probably), as Arthur read that Republican presidential candidate Donald Trump had received the endorsement of Sarah Palin. The temperature had turned chilly but the jogger wore only red running togs, nonetheless. The clips from the late night comedy shows were going to be pretty amusing for a while. Arthur looked forward to the prospect of Tina Fey returning to do a takeoff on the bizarre speech in which Palin announced her support. Of course, President Obama was strenuously blamed for every ill including the recent arrest of Palin's son for domestic violence.

The socialist Democrat Bernie Sanders was much more in the news of recent days. His platform was surprisingly popular with young voters. They had yet to accept that revolutions, for all their attraction, almost always failed. In the wake of the failure, even incremental progress was sunk.

They had their own media, of course. The headlines were as exaggerated as those of their opponents. Often they went beyond exaggeration to falsehood. The Comment sections were as raw and aggressive as those from the extreme media on the political right. The slightest deviation from the party line was met with a fury of pat answers and ridicule that soon drove moderation away. In those instances in which the opposition had violated their sacred space with a dismissive comment the enemy was engaged often resulting in days of the worst kinds of insults.

In Richmond there had been an Open Carry Rally on the lawn of the capitol building. A number of persons in the crowd were proud to announce that they were 'packing' right there at the state capitol. No one, however, appeared to have been foolish enough to attend carrying an automatic rifle.   The dress code had been 'handguns only, modest display'. The cameras did not show any of the protestors strutting and theatrically displaying their arms. Several conservative officials up for reelection briefly offered statements of unconditional support. Some called for the ouster of the state's Attorney General for having ordered an end to honoring out of state permits.

In Texas stores that had posted signs forbidding firearms on the premises were being excoriated by advocates of the state's newly instituted open carry law. Anyone who could pass the background checks for an open carry permit, they averred, was a customer with whom proprietors should especially wish to do business, a model citizen. It was those who didn't have a permit whose character was in question. Just how owners would ascertain that a gun-toting customer had a valid permit was not mentioned.

The city of New Orleans had voted to remove its confederate statues as inappropriate in the wake of the shooting at the Emanuel A.M.E. Church and the subsequent confederate symbol controversy. A contractor had been hired to remove Confederate statues from the city. His Lamborghini had been torched overnight. In the wake of a Richmond man's arrest for making a pipe bomb and threatening to kill the members of a local mosque the city council had passed a resolution against anti-Islamic hate crimes.

Arthur had had his fill of the news wires when he switched to Facebook. There he found calls to buy girl scout cookies and to share Jesus if he was a real Christian. One of his gay friends was on a roll and a good many pictures of shirtless beefcake with bowties were the order of the day. Family and friends made their own stands on various issues. Clergymen and women were thanking him ahead of time for his kind donations for Stewardship Sunday. It didn't really matter which Sunday one was being thanked for, they all were special fundraising Sundays now.

But there was something else that drew him there. Pictures of the children with their mothers, aunts and grandmas, were sure to pop up on a regular basis. (Fathers and grandfathers appeared in their share, as well.) He lingered just a brief moment more over these. It was impossible not to be buoyed by their smiles and crayons. For a few minutes he liked to forget about the world impending around them and to share their simple, happy, innocent moments. On some mornings he felt it was important for him to remember that lives were made up more of moments than of years and decades.

He would die soon enough and they would live on. Theirs would be a different world not in the sense that previous generations had always been different than their parents' generation but in a way that their smiling parents hardly imagined. Those parents were not prepared and if Arthur tried to help them they would quietly 'unfriend' him taking their children's smiles with them.

Perhaps voting for a Bernie Sanders would bring about revolutionary change. Perhaps certain matters were so unjust or otherwise so intractable that it merited the kind of risk that accompanied wagering all on a single throw of the dice. Perhaps aggression could only be defeated with aggression and what seemed like a hopeless mêlée was somehow a hopeful sign. Or perhaps losing the wager would assure that voices of more moderate change, more likely to be accomplished, would lose as well and the worst come to pass unmitigated.

As the light grew stronger the sound of the neighborhood children shouting at the corner in front of the church, waiting for the school bus, grew louder. Arthur cleared a path to the spare plastic shelf in the corner where it had been pressed into service as a temporary staging area. He moved the computer parts he'd found for pennies on the dollar at various thrift shops and swap meets to the laundry table. Opening the window in the backroom he set the shelf outside and tested it for stability. That done, he brought out the extra blankets and sweatshirts. The apartment being in a more impoverished neighborhood the power grid was forever old. As often as not it went out during even minor storms. During the winter months the shelf served as a backup refrigerator on such occasions. A diet of bread and cold cuts made the oven unnecessary. The library would replace the computer — so well, in fact, that he would be in no rush to return to civilization.

There was a new detail that had not been properly attended to, though. It was unlikely that K was prepared to do without the amenities of heat and electricity for a few days. It was this thought that reminded Arthur that his guest was still asleep. He hadn't heard a sound from the room all morning. If K slept any later it was unlikely that he would sleep that night. As much as Arthur wished to be understanding, he had no intention of suffering another night of restless sleep while his guest moaned and bitterly chastised himself. He knocked gently at the door. It had to be done. No answer coming, he knocked harder. There was still no answer. There was no choice but to enter and to shake the man awake.

When Jeremiah saw K's caller ID he let the call go through to voice mail. He had another truck to load before lunch. The shipping schedule had been moved up in expectation of the snowstorm. His boss wasn't going to be pleased to see him wasting time on the phone. Once he found himself waiting for the next pallet to be stacked with boxes and rolled out to the loading dock, he checked the message. Surprisingly, it was not K but Arthur. When he redialed the number, it was Arthur again who picked up.

"Why are *you* calling on Franz's phone?"

"He's gone."

"Franz? Franz is gone? What do you mean?"

"He hasn't been in the apartment since sometime last night."

"You didn't call Lori, did you? Where's he gone? Did he say anything?"

"He's just gone."

"Lori's going to have a fit." For a moment Jeremiah could only think of the discomfort to come. He pushed back against fate. "But I don't care. I'm not driving around to find him. He's a big boy. He can take care of himself. He was probably invited to an afterhours party or something. He'll be back."

Arthur was speaking from inside the bedroom. "All his stuff is gone."

"What? What do you mean?"

"His hair brush, clothes brush, everything."

"Did you yell at him or something? Maybe he went to the church woman's apartment."

"His travel trunk is gone. Everything. Nothing of his is left at all."

"He left his phone. You're calling from it."

"Everything that arrived with him is gone. Everything else is still here: his colognes, his bike, the cellphone. He couldn't have carried his travel trunk away alone. I would have heard him if he had tried. It is too big to go out the window, even if he had help."

Jeremiah stood at a loss for what to say. "Another pallet's coming out. I have to get back to work. He'll be alright."

"He couldn't have carried his travel trunk away."

"He's crazy. Crazy people can do all kinds of things that seem impossible. After work we can go look for him. He can't be far."

"You're not hearing me. He couldn't have carried his travel trunk away... just like he couldn't have carried it to the Roach Motel. I know it's crazy but it has always been crazy. I think he may have gone back to wherever he came from."

"He knows a snowstorm is coming. You'd think he'd wait a few days. It would only be a couple of weeks, at most. Lori's going to have a fit."

"I know it's impossible, but I think he has gone back wherever he came from... to be with his sister. I think he's gone back to warn Ottla."

"To warn *who?* About *what?* Look, I've gotta go. If the boss catches me on the phone I'm gonna hear about it. You still planning to watch the Super Bowl at my place?"

"You've got the best pizza in town. I wouldn't miss it."

"Gotta go."

Jeremiah hung up. Arthur looked around as he sat on the bed in K's room. He checked the dresser drawers a second time. They were empty. He checked the refrigerator. It was piled with plastic containers of food. There was nothing left that had arrived with K, nothing gone that hadn't.

The computer was on. Arthur woke the monitor. What he saw left him frozen in place. The screen was filled with the picture of Franz and Ottla Kafka in front of the Oppelt House where the family occupied a flat. He had loaded it up as the wallpaper for his desktop. K looked as happy as Arthur had ever seen him. Ottla was smiling also but with her head slightly down in a demure pose that must have been habitual with her. They resembled each other so much in the picture that one would have thought they were twins.

K must have flailed around a bit trying to figure out how to load the picture up. Arthur wasn't even aware that he knew the feature existed. In the process, he must have inadvertently reset the browser clock to Wednesday. Yet the date somehow remained January 21st. Curious how such a thing could happen, Arthur looked closer. The full timestamp read: '8:32 AM, 1/21/20'.

Franz Kafka lurched awake as the train came to a halt at the Matliary station. He hadn't meant to nap for long but it felt as if he had slept for a very long time. The other passengers in his car were busily collecting their luggage from the overhead racks as he slowly returned to consciousness. It seemed vitally important to him for some reason that he not forget the dream he'd had. He blearily searched his pockets for a pen and paper. Not finding paper, he could only struggle to recall as much as he could as he woke.

A hand gently grasped his shoulder and shook it. "You are Doctor Kafka, yes?"

"I am."

"There may be an unfortunate problem. Could you come with me please?"

Still not fully awake, Kafka rose and followed. "Were we delayed in route?"

"No, sir. We have arrived on time."

The answer confused him slightly. How did he have such a sense of having napped a very long time? Puzzling over the question brought him fully awake.

He thought to check his pocket watch at last. It was indeed almost exactly midnight. The porter escorted him to the side of a car at the back of the train. Large doors stood open revealing compartments now partially loaded with larger items of luggage. As they stood there, before the compartments, several people laid claim to their items. It was below zero and porters briskly carried the items away. The owners followed, the men in overcoats and the women bundled in heavy seasonal dresses and hand-muffs. Kafka stood close to the cloud released periodically from the steam brakes in order to keep warm but not so close as to get his frock coat damp. He found himself in the way of a woman from one of the parties, stepped aside and doffed his fedora. She lowered her eyes by way of acknowledgement and continued demurely on her way.

"Your driver tells us that he is expected to load a travel trunk of yours onto your conveyance." Kafka turned to see what must be the man waiting in the distance. This seemed confirmed by the fact that he waved and pointed toward his sleigh. It was difficult to tell, however. His mind was still not entirely awake. A heavy, wet snow was falling and nothing was properly visible beyond a few feet. "Did you change your plans at all in this regard?"

"I did not," he replied.

"Do you by any chance see your trunk here among the remaining items?"

"No. It is definitely not here. Is there no other baggage car?"

"Very unfortunately this happens from time to time, Herr Doctor. We will immediately contact the stations through which this train has passed. Our own drayman will deliver the trunk to you, at Matliary, tomorrow. We are very sorry for the inconvenience."

Kafka had not thought it necessary to carry an extra change of clothing in his valise. This, added to the indignities *en route*, merited a strenuous complaint. But then what indignities had there been exactly? Somehow he felt like he had suffered a great deal. In fact, he was perfectly sure of it. But from where the feeling came, he could not imagine. It was late and the driver was waiting. The matter would have to wait a better time. He merely scowled and turned away. This gave the porter a most welcome opportunity to escape.

The bed of the sleigh repaid him for much of his trouble. The surface was covered with a remarkably soft bear skin. He pulled a heavy blanket over him and they were on their way. The landscape was magical in the falling snow. Open fields gave way to a mysterious, looming forest as they climbed the side of the mountain. There was no other sound than the crunch of the horse and sleigh as they took their familiar way. He felt a peace that came over him like a long awaited embrace.

Kafka was rested from his nap, wide awake to all that lay about him. At one point, well along their route, it came to him that he had not written down the dream that seemed so important when he woke. His dreams had been so strange since he had caught the tuberculosis: as if he entered other worlds unimaginably beautiful and tragic. There would be others, he assured himself, every bit as compelling. Still, he had the strangest feeling.

In the morning he must remember to write Ottla in order to assure her that he had arrived safely. If he waited longer she might think he had forgotten her.

www.ingramcontent.com/pod-product-compliance
Lightning Source LLC
Chambersburg PA
CBHW070449260626
47161CB00004B/1254